Graveyard Gods

Joseph Daniels, Bryon Arneson, Steve Higgs

Text Copyright © 2022 Steve Higgs, Joseph Daniel, & Bryon Arneson

Publisher: Greenfield Press Ltd

The rights of Steve Higgs, Joseph Daniel, and Bryon Arneson to be identified as authors of the Work has been asserted in accordance with the Copyright, Designs and Patents Act 1988

All rights reserved.

The book is copyright material and must not be copied, reproduced, transferred, distributed, leased, licensed or publicly performed or used in any way except as specifically permitted in writing by the publishers, as allowed under the terms and conditions under which it was purchased or as strictly permitted by applicable copyright law. Any unauthorised distribution or use of this text may be a direct infringement of the author's and publisher's rights and those responsible may be liable in law accordingly.

'Graveyard Gods' is a work of fiction. Names, characters, businesses, organisations, places, events, and incidents either are the product of the author's imagination or are used fictitiously. Any resemblance to actual persons, living or dead, and events or locations is entirely coincidental.

For Mary,

Whose encouragement has been my light in dark places, when all other lights go out.

Also, for Josh W.

a man who knows how to dream and scheme, and took a hefty chance in supporting the books.

Contents

1. Chapter 1 — 1
2. Chapter 2 — 11
3. Chapter 3 — 19
4. Chapter 4 — 31
5. Chapter 5 — 46
6. Chapter 6 — 55
7. Chapter 7 — 59
8. Chapter 8 — 82
9. Chapter 9 — 86
10. Chapter 10 — 106
11. Chapter 11 — 110
12. Chapter 12 — 124
13. Chapter 13 — 135
14. Chapter 14 — 154

15.	Chapter 15	160
16.	Chapter 16	171
17.	Chapter 17	190
18.	Chapter 18	193
19.	Chapter 19	200
20.	Chapter 20	210
21.	Chapter 21	221
22.	Chapter 22	234
23.	Chapter 23	240
24.	Chapter 24	252
25.	Chapter 25	266
26.	Chapter 26	270
27.	Chapter 27	288
28.	Chapter 28	303
29.	Chapter 29	318
30.	Chapter 30	325
31.	Ready for the next adventure?	336
32.	Want to know more?	338

Chapter 1

IN THE SHIPPING LANES of the Gilded Isles, the winds blow where they will, the currents sweep east, and the dead float south. The corpses in the mist whisper deathly tales, a quiet keening of coarse cloth scraping fragile skin, and the swishing of grey waters murmur taunts to stopped ears; those who witness the tide's lament are left wondering, *where do the bodies go?*

There was plenty of wonder to be distributed among the shaking bones of the sailors patrolling the forbidden waters—a desolate stretch of the Western Sea, south of the great city of Carabas. The second night of their patrol followed the coolest midsummer on record. From where he stood, hands gripping the lacquered taffrail of his new charge, His Imperial Majesty's Ship *Intrepid*, Lord Captain Augustin Mora was the first to spot the body.

"Abaft twenty degrees!" he shouted, his commanding voice cutting through the mist. "Body in the water!"

A few of the sailors peered over the railing. The lookout called down, "Just a bleedin' floater, captain! Not one of ours—poor blighter."

Augustin turned towards the main deck, his hand moving to the hilt of his rapier. Augustin's frame was trim and agile, a fencer's body, with well-muscled forearms that strained against the sleeves of his uniform. He had tanned skin and black hair tied back into a short tail. His dark eyes were shrewd and piercing beneath a curved brow, like the gaze of a falcon. His thin nose hunched neatly over a trimmed mustache, and a closely cut beard of bearskin black framed his face, marred only by two gray hairs that hid like ghosts on the right side of his square jaw. He gripped a tricorn hat with one hand against the wind as a breeze tugged at the golden tassel indicative of his station.

Augustin strained to see in the mist, then settled to face the direction where he knew the first mate would be keeping eye. "Cristobal," he called. "Eyes on, if you please!"

He heard the muted sound of creaking wood beneath firm footsteps, a low murmur of conferring voices below, then Cristobal called across the ship, his heavy Dumasian accent rolling like thunder. "Hard to tell, Lord Captain! Looks like pirate work, though. Missing his fingers."

Augustin gave a curt nod. The pirate clans had been raiding the southern island of Dumas all winter. With the seasons change it made sense that they'd follow the mist North. Many of the clans relied on the heavy fog of the Western Seas to ambush the merchants who sailed between the domains of the Gilded Isles, but Augustin couldn't believe even pirates would be so foolish as to cross forbidden waters. *Then again,* Commodore Severelle recalled the other patrol ships, he thought. If the *Intrepid* was caught out of position by a pirate clan moving in force, well, even for an Imperial Frigate that wouldn't be as much a fight as it would be a massacre.

"Nay—that's the Signerde, that is," came the growl of another voice. "The drowners delight in makin' their prey suffer 'afore they gut 'em. Filthy blighters—a pox on the lot of 'em." This, Augustin recognized, as the voice of crewmaster Agreo—the man had been in line to be first mate before Augustin was given the command. He had not taken Cristobal's appointment gracefully.

Augustin lost track of the body in the curling mist and hurried down the stairs to the main deck. He spotted crewmen leaning over the railing and peering into the sea. Cristobal loomed over the edge like an enormous gargoyle—the man stood nearly seven feet tall with arms as strong as the foremast. A knight, his former commanders had told Cristobal he was an 'intimidating presence' in a skirmish. Which, Cristobal had confided, served as another way to say, "target." The gigantic Dumasian had been shot and stabbed more than any man Augustin had met. Even through the mist, Augustin could spot the first mate's ear—or, rather, more appropriately, the place where an ear *would* have gone, had it not been claimed by the wild swipe of a Kurkek pirate's toothed cutlass. Cristobal's left arm hung slightly lower than his right—his range of motion compromised by a stray musket ball to the collar bone in the battle of Borgo Tortrugha. By Augustin's count, Cristobal had been shot six times that day. Even with the aid of their Lord's alchemists, the first mate had never healed completely.

In comparison, Agreo was as useful as a buoy made of sour pebbles. Where Cristobal was tall, muscled, and strong jawed,

Agreo was short, round, and snaggle-toothed. Where Cristobal was blunt and affable, Agreo was disagreeable and fractious. To an extent, Augustin could understand the crewmaster's foul temper. Agreo's brother, some well-known Baron who traded in seal silks, had been the first choice to receive the captaincy when the Commodore had given it to Augustin instead, and judging by the evil eye he gave his new captain, Agreo seemed unlikely to forget.

The Crewmaster's grudges notwithstanding, it was small wonder the crew had gathered around so quickly. There wasn't much to do in this damned mist. It had not taken long for the newly minted Lord Captain to learn that 'patrolling the forbidden waters' largely amounted to sailing in circles while fending off bouts of boredom. Augustin had asked Commodore Severelle why these waters were forbidden, but the wiry older man had evaded any clear explanation, and Augustin Mora remained uncertain. However, the Admirals weren't ones to send ships, especially not frigates like the *Intrepid*, on frivolous ventures, and the Commodore had at least been clear that this order did come from the Admiral. Whatever crypt, shipwreck, or creature lurked beneath the seas South of Gamor, it was deemed worthy of the attention of a 44-gun frigate and its 150 crew.

By now, the sailors who weren't below deck enjoying their time with dice and bitter drink had stopped their rotations around the ship to peer into the murk.

The body drifted lazily on the water, facedown, hair floating on the current like gossamer strands of spider lace.

"Gives me the chills," said Cristobal, shaking his bald, one-eared head. "How come they do that?"

GRAVEYARD GODS

"Do what?" said Agreo. "Float?"

Cristobal shook his head. In answer, he tore a large splinter from beneath the railing and tossed it into the water.

The captain, the first mate, and the crewmaster all watched as the wood drifted away on the westward currents, crossing paths with the corpse as it continued South.

"*That*," said Cristobal, teeth clenched. "Isn't natural for a body to float against the current."

"Bodies float South. Everyone knows that. Been that way for fifty years." Agreo snorted. "Haven't been at sea long then, have ye?"

This, of course, was true. Augustin had walked the deck of the *HIMS Intrepid* for only two weeks, trading his horse and spurs for a captain's hat. His rise through the ranks had been swift, but not unpredictable, and despite her efforts to hide it, he saw his mother's hand in the appointment. Augustin disapproved of his mother's political games, but he had taken the commission, nonetheless. Augustin's lips tightened as he remembered the snide look on Commodore Severelle's face while the man dubbed him 'Lord Captain' Mora, and Augustin hoped his mother's games and bartered affections wouldn't end with his head on a pike.

Still, though Augustin was only in his twenty-ninth season, and Cristobal was near enough to the same, and though they had spent a month training together under the same captains, Cristobal and Augustin were still struggling to put nearly three decades of land-living and warm nights aside.

It will be worth it, Augustin thought, watching the mist swallow the bloated body as he suppressed the feeling of shame within him. *It will be worth it for Isobella.* The first time he'd seen her was a formal dinner nearly six years before. She had made eyes at him, parting her lips and blowing on her soup in a way that straddled the line between playful and indecent, and the memory of it still warmed him. He had feigned shock at the revelation that she was a hellcatcher, a demon hunter, a slayer, but inwardly he smiled. He, a freelance knight with nothing but time and the open road, and her a demon hunter on patrol, had spent weeks on the road together, sharing a fire and a bed. The memory of her departure smeared and blurred in his mind. He would not think of it. Not here. Not now. Instead his mind stepped forward another year to when he saw her again, at a gala tournament hosted by the Admiral of Gamor. Palatial gardens and sweeping ballrooms larger than his family's entire estate, and a pier overlooking the titanic ships of war that commanded the seas of the great isle. An estate fit for royalty. Her father's estate. Despite their wants, it was clear that she understood duty just as he did. As things were, they could never be together. For Augustin to even have a *chance* at Isobella's hand, he'd have to impress her father, the Admiral Fernand de Morecraft. He'd have to be nobility.

Am I mad? Augustin thought, not for the first time. The Admirals stood second only to the Emperor himself. Each ruled one of the Gilded Isles. Their daughters, even scandalous hellcatchers, were fit partners for powerful Commodores and to secure alliances with the continental powers, not landless Lord Captains with only a single frigate to their names. Even the *Intrepid* wasn't really his—not until he paid either five years worth of wages, or was gifted it by the Commodore for distinguishing himself in his command, and it was rare to win a ship that way, especially a 44-gunner. Unless, of course, you had a plan.

Almost by instinct, Augustin touched the breast of his officer's coat. Folded letters crinkled within its inner pocket. Each had been sealed in white wax and stamped with the symbol of a lily. Five letters from five knights. His brothers in arms. *The Order.* It wasn't that Augustin didn't trust Agreo or the rest of the sailors—they were all Emperor's men, after all, but in Gamor, as well as the rest of the islands, one could never be too careful. One thousand swords in one's charge could be offset by a single blade at one's back.

"Captain!" called the lookout, his voice caught somewhere between hoarse whisper and alarmed cry. "Eyes to starboard, sir!"

"What you shoutin' at the captain for!" Agreo called back. "Give your directives to the crewmaster first you gutted trout! I'll decide if it's important enough for captain's ears."

Despite this, Augustin joined Agreo in a brisk walk to the opposite rail. He frowned, hand on the pommel of his rapier, watching the mist; at first he spotted nothing. But then...

"A boat," Agreo said, softly. "See it?"

Augustin leaned forward, one hand still on his rapier as the other gripped the rail. The knuckles on both hands whitened. For the faintest moment, a gusting breeze swept the mist into a dance, lifting its skirt and allowing Augustin a peek.

He spotted the silhouette of a tiny fishing boat drifting in the water. It looked like one of the fat bottomed vessels the village fishermen called a 'dogger.' Three figures huddled together on the dogger's deck, whispering among themselves and gesturing wildly towards the ship.

"Ahoy there!" called Cristobal. "Declare yourselves!"

The gesticulating of the figures intensified.

"Crewmaster Agreo, have we found the source of our body?" said Augustin, turning his head slightly towards the sailor, but keeping his eyes fixed firmly on the trespassers, lest he lose them in the mist.

"Villagers in these parts don't fish this late a'night. Leastwise in forbidden waters," said Agreo. "They're up to something. Should I sink 'hem or grapple 'hem?"

The old sea dog was eyeing the deck cannon with a hungry look, but Augustin shifted his gaze to the coiled grapples at Agreo's feet. "Bring her in," he said.

Cristobal shouted at the barge again. "Name yourselves!" he bellowed. "These are forbidden waters—you're trespassing!"

Another silent pause hung in the air, almost as if the three huddled forms pretended not to hear. Then, a nasaly voice called out, "Whose authority?"

Augustin frowned. The only frigates in the Gilded Isles were all under the Emperor's authority. Pirates preferred smaller, nimbler ships, and forays from the naval forces of the continental powers had all but ceased with the Glutted Accords, nearly fifty years ago.

"We're Emperor's men!" Cristobal called back, an edge to his voice. "Who are you?"

GRAVEYARD GODS

"Your emperor can suck a briny fist!" a voice shouted in return.

The crewmaster, the Lord Captain, and the first mate all bristled at this. Despite their differences, and various interpretations of the word "duty," they were men with honor staked in the good name of Emperor Baltasar II.

"The gun?" asked Agreo, raising an eyebrow. A couple of the men busy untangling the grappling hooks from the rope stopped their efforts and looked up, hopeful.

Augustin weighed the request. The insult caught in his throat, but his duelist heart knew baiting words when he heard them. No, something wasn't right here. "They'll answer for the insult, but we'll not sink a trio for the foolhardy words of one," said Augustin. "Mercusi would frown on such an overstep."

Cristobal nodded quickly, curling his fingers as if he were grabbing something near his heart and tossing the air away from him in a gesture to ward off evil. For Cristobal, invoking Mercusi, the god of justice and duty, would be enough. The big Dumasian indicated the men should continue readying the grapplers.

"Didn't see the other two in any hurry to contradict him," muttered Agreo, spitting into the sea.

Cristobal called, "What business do you have here?" The mist fell around the dogger and the three men seemed to be whispering again.

One of the men gripped the arm of another, trying to tug him back. Just then, though, a shrill voice called out from the mist, "Our only business is that of flint and steel. Death to the Emperor!"

A flurry of motion rose from the dogger's deck. Then, a thunderous flash as a pistol fired.

Chapter 2

EDMOND MONDEGO WAS BUSY trying to calm Felex and didn't think to worry about the pearl diver's twin sister. That is, until the gunshot resounded in his ear.

The grave robber whirled around, hissing sharply. He had a face that would have blended in with any number of the coastal villages—tanned skin, hooked nose, grey eyes. Even his scowl, which was now levied on the diver, was notable only in how ordinary it was. Edmond slapped the pistol out of Fiora's hand, his back prickling against the scrutiny of the frigate's watchmen. Goosebumps attended to the ocean breeze pawing down his spine as the mist hugged the three figures in the dogger, swaddling them like a mother tending her innocent young. But Edmond was no child, and innocence was the currency of the naive and the devout.

There were many gods in the Gilded Isles, and most mortals found an altar before which to bend a knee. Edmond preferred to fray his trousers in other ventures, however, rather than the altars of the gods, Edmond was more interested in the locations of their tombs.

He was so close. His eyes flicked from the rolling sea to the ghostly shape of the imperial frigate as the mist coiled between them. They couldn't run. Not when they were so close. The mausoleum of a god lurked, dark and brooding, beneath these waves. He was sure of it. Given the scope of the score, Edmond had expected opposition and guardians, but a bloody frigate?

He cursed softly as the mist moved to reclaim them and soft cries carried across the waves, accompanied by muted voices and hurried footsteps against creaking wood. Edmond's dark clothing fit his thin, athletic form. Beside the alchemical satchel on his hip, his ensemble would allow him to slide into tight, claustrophobic spaces. Even as the boat rocked and the divers glared at him, moving to secure their purchase on the hull, Edmond stood steady, his balance perfect in the precarious dogger. There had been those who suggested Edmond moved like one of the Signerde, and if they had known half his history, likely they would have doubled down on such a proclamation. History aside, Edmond was all too focused on the present, inclining an ear towards the same strong, booming voice from before. It called out, skimming the waves that hedged the frigate, "You've attacked a Lord Captain!"

"Belay those grappling hooks," hissed a second voice, quieter than the first, but no less fervent. "Man the gun!"

"Shite," said Edmond, casting frantically about.

"You knocked my pistol into the drink," said Fiora, jabbing a finger into his chest.

GRAVEYARD GODS

"Better there than in the hands of an imbecile," snapped Edmond, eyes flitting about the floor of the dogger for the latch. He knew he should have painted it or tied off a colored rag—of course, this time it had been a rush job, and he had not anticipated the frigate. Behind the frantic movements of his eyes, his mind calmly cataloged the thought. It would never happen again— if he made it out alive, that is. It had cost him near everything to get the map in Carabas, and the journey here had left him broke as a bare-armed bravo. He'd been lucky to have funds enough to hire the twin divers and buy this rotting boat.

He could hear the groan of a cannon moving into position, metal protesting its bed of rust with ominous scraping sounds.

"See them?" came a distant voice.

"Aye, there!"

Felex puffed his chest as if preparing to shout something back, but Edmond reached out and clapped a hand over the pearl diver's mouth. He was having serious doubts about the help he'd hired. The pearl divers of Sile were renowned for their ability to hold their breath up to five minutes, some of them boasting as long as ten, even on the deepest dives. There were whispers of alchemical help or that the divers had Signerde blood in their ancestry, but Edmond, who had a significant amount of experience with the magic of The Brewers, had yet to see any such signs.

Regardless, their breath holding capabilities would soon be put to the test.

Edmond's fingers found the latch. He gripped it tight with his left hand, inhaled a couple of times for good measure, then pulled.

Immediately, water starting rushing into the bottom of the dogger in a cold, churning spray.

"What are you doing!" Felex and Fiora shouted in protest. In turn, sighting in on the sounds in the mist, the deck gun fired, and a small cannonball whistled overhead, crashing into the dark waters somewhere out of sight with a tremendous splash.

"Too high. All I heard was water," called the booming voice from the direction of the frigate.

"Blue fire and black fish!" came an irritated reply. "Can't see for all this blasted fog—hurry up with that shot."

Edmond felt a sharp pain on his wrist. He looked down to see Felex's calloused fist gripping him and squeezing tight. The pearl diver's white eyes peered out from his deeply tanned face like bright shells settled in summer sand. The diver wore no shirt. Even in the mist, Edmond could see his well-muscled figure, and his thoughts whispered mention of the large scaling knife tucked in the back of the diver's pants.

"What are you doing?" Felex repeated, his chest heaving. He loosed his grip on Edmond and started rapidly scooping at the water, trying to shovel it overboard. "You're sinking us!"

"I'm saving us," said Edmond.

"By sinking our boat?"

"It's *my* boat."

"And we're on it," snapped Fiora, also using her hands to bail. "Gut him, Felex—I knew we shouldn't have taken the gold of a tomb raider. Nepir—may her eyes be blessed—has cursed this venture!"

Edmond licked his lips and eyed the knife at Felex's waist. "I'm sure a goddess of the sea has more important distractions than our enterprise."

"What would a godless man know of it," Felex snapped back, his voice more frantic than before. By now, the dark water had reached their knees. The twin pearl divers were still frantically bailing water, but to no avail.

Another shot resounded from the frigate, but this time the cannonball's splash sent a spray of sea water over the dogger's deck. They were getting closer. The week before, Edmond had debated whether he wanted to delay his journey and spend a day painting the dogger black, and preparing the latch—but now, given how things had turned out, he was grateful he had. And for all the twins' complaining, Edmond was feeling downright blessed in all this obscuring mist.

Felex gave up bailing at this point and began to prepare his lungs, inhaling deeply through his nose, then exhaling through the mouth. "I'm telling them *you* fired the shot," said Felex with a growl, between breaths. "There's two of us and one of you. I'll not hang for a godless grave creeper."

"You've angered Nepir," said Fiora, gesturing to the rising water like it confirmed her assertion.

"May her eyes be blessed," added Felex between deep breaths.

"I told you he was all wrong. A man who leads with his left hand is cursed. We should have thrown him overboard."

By this time, there wasn't much board left to be thrown over. The dogger had all but sunk, the water now lifting Edmond off the deck—the cool liquid lapping against his skin. He'd have half a minute, at best, before they were completely treading water.

Now was the time.

"Here," said Edmond, pulling three vials from his pocket. These too had been readied during the day of preparation, and again, he was grateful for his past self's patience—it was not a strong suit of his. But *this* job... This job was the culmination of nearly seven years of effort. He'd be damned if something as stupid as *impatience* cost him his prize. He'd never found a *god's* grave before; in the past his scores had included the resting places of a couple of admirals, a baron, even the grave of a chief of The Children—the Signerde grave he'd left undisturbed.

"What is it?" said Felex, taking two of the vials and handing one to his sister. Fiora didn't respond; she was drawing long slow breaths, preparing for submersion.

"Something I prepared," said Edmond. "Quick, drink." He looked down to the lapping water. Only a few moments until they would be completely sunk.

"Tridents and whips and shark shite—You're a grave robber *and* an alchemist? We're dead."

"I dabble. Now drink." The twins looked to each other, their eyes uncertain. "Or you could swim out to the frigate and take your chances with them."

"Is that right? And where are you going with no boat?"

In answer, Edmond placed one of the vials to his lips, crushed the gel cap with his teeth and sucked the sweet liquid. Instantly, his vision began to darken, his throat seized as it refused to draw more air. With a significant look in the twins' direction, he pointed, directly down.

Felex eyed him, then the vial. "If you're playing us, our cousins saw you when you hired us. They'll remember your face."

"Noted. Drink." Edmond said with the last bit of air in his lungs. He waded to the dogger's keel, leaving the scowling divers to stare at the vials and mutter between themselves.

Their threat had been as veiled as the bosom of a Caraban prostitute. Still, Edmond allowed himself a small smile. It always tickled him when people threatened that they knew his face. Especially since Edmond could barely remember it himself. This was what, his thirtieth in the last seven years? The Signerde called him the Man of Faces. The locals called him the Grave Creeper. The divers called him Godless. Names as interchangeable to him as the faces he wore.

Edmond liked to think he was a bit of all those things. But more important than titles and names, Edmond was relentless. No one, divine or otherwise, dead or living, would stand in his way from seeing this through.

By now, the potion had completely taken over. He could no longer see, and though he could breathe again, the air was thin and he fought to control the spasming choke that rose in his throat. There was nothing left for it; he could only hope the pearl divers were smart enough to follow his instructions. If they did decide to swim to the frigate and turn him in, it would matter very little. By this time tomorrow, he would either be dead, or a man with a new face, a new identity, and a new direction on his mission.

Edmond closed his eyes firmly—this next part would hurt—then he ducked underwater.

Chapter 3

The wooden hull of the dogger groaned as the mast began to tip. Slowly, almost lazily, the fat bottomed fishing boat rolled. The mast struck the water with a tremendous splash.

"Did we hit them?" confused voices murmured and shouted from the shrouded frigate.

Augustin's eyes narrowed as he squinted through the mist. This wasn't right. If they'd scored a hit from this range they would have heard it, but as the mist began to part—

"Lord Captain Mora, she's capsized sir. No sign of 'em in the water."

"Well, I'd say that's a job well done then," said Agreo, patting the smoking cannon with a malicious grin towards the sinking dogger. Even as they watched, churning bubbles rushed from the sides of the inverted hull and the last bit of barnacled wood slipped beneath the waves.

JOSEPH DANIELS, BRYON ARNESON, STEVE HIGGS

The crew gave a terrific cheer and flashed obscene gestures to the sunken vessel.

"Filthy brigands!"

"-what you get when you insult the Empire-"

"-float south with ye!"

Augustin stared into the sea. His hand reflexively squeezed the sword hilt at his side.

"Orders, Lord Captain?" said Cristobal. The man's heavy voice cut through the jeers and celebration like the blast of a horn and the crew fell silent. For a moment, the only sound was the creaking of the frigate's hull in the gentle waves. The wind tugged at the loose ends of the ship's stowed sails, adding the soft burring of fabric in the breeze. Some crew even began to shuffle towards their stations, expecting they'd be on their way.

"Bring up the lights." Augustin called out. The crew stood in silent confusion, but Augustin continued. "Set the sails and tack to circle the vessel."

"But Cap'n," Agreo leaned on the ship's railing and sneered like he was explaining something to a slow child, "what vessel would that be? The one we sunk?"

Cristobal was on the man like an avalanche, and Agreo stumbled back against the railing, his round back rolling around the rail like bread baked in too small a pan.

"You are speaking to the Lord Captain of this frigate." The giant Dumasian's voice rumbled like an oncoming storm.

Agreo fumbled for a reply as Augustin stepped to the bridge of the ship.

With hands folded behind his back, Augustin said, "Crewmaster Agreo, as an experienced seaman in His Imperial Majesty's Navy, you are surely aware that insubordination carries a penalty of up to six lashes before the mast." The doughy crewmaster paled and ceased his feeble attempts at a retort. "Of course," Augustin continued conversationally, "I'm certain that you only meant to clarify the order you were given so you may better carry it out. Correct?"

Agreo licked his lips. He looked from Cristobal's 'intimidating presence' to the onlooking crew, all of them staring at him with the satisfaction of squires seeing the division's bully reprimanded by the swordmaster. His face flushed as his mouth twisted into a scowl. Nodding slowly, he stood and forced out a salute towards Augustin, "Aye, my Lord Captain."

Augustin gave a curt nod. "Cristobal, assist the crewmaster in getting the ship underway. We will circle the vessel with lights. Use the alchemical lanterns." He gestured to a set of convex iron plates, hanging from the mizzenmast. "If there are survivors I want them captured." With the final clip of the command, Agreo and Cristobal began to roar out orders, and the crew scurried to their stations. If anyone was in the water, they'd find them.

Augustin gripped his rapier again, turning to walk the deck. Beside the main mast, he saw the ship's surgeon, a scrawny young woman with thin hands and a shaved head helping a crewman to sit against the base of the mast.

The crewman hissed in pain as he clutched his arm and mumbled, "Just bad luck, getting nicked like that. Random shot. Why me?" The young surgeon inspected the wound on the crewman's arm with a smirk. Neither seemed to have noticed Augustin's approach.

"Bad luck? Think of it this way. You got a lead ball in the arm and it didn't hit any major arteries." The surgeon shook her head in amazement as she drew out a glass bottle of alcohol and a white cloth bandage. "Just clean in and out. No damage to bone either. Who do you pray to?" The young woman poured the alcohol over the wound and the crewman grimaced.

"R-Raurotel. Of the East Wind. Just like my pa," he said through clenched teeth as the sting washed over his arm. The surgeon nodded and grabbed a new bottle. Opening this one, she rubbed a pungent gel over the wound.

"Well, keep praying. Someone is looking out for you."

The crewman smiled, then winced as the young surgeon clapped him on his uninjured shoulder. The sight caused Augustin to pause and brought with it a memory of leaning against a rainy oak tree. Blood was welling from a gash in his shoulder where a spear had caught him. A dark haired woman in brass spectacles packed the wound as best she could, moving his hand and telling him to press the bandage down. Serenia. Behind her, Cristobal had stared into the red of a setting sun, four proud silhouettes beside him. The giant yelled as guns roared, and spun around to stand over Augustin and Serenia as the shock of cannonfire sent a spray of earth over all of them. Augustin cleared his throat, dismissing the memory.

"How is he, Catali?" Augustin asked the surgeon. Catali nodded up to the Lord Captain as she unrolled a thin white cloth.

"He should be easy with his arm for a few weeks and I'll want to change the bandage and keep an eye for a little, but he'll be right as rain soon enough." Augustin nodded as Catali wrapped the crewman's arm. The misting sea air sent a chill and Augustin fought back a shiver. He felt his neck hair stand, like the feeling before a lightning storm, though the sky was clear apart from the low fog.

"Keep your bag at hand," Augustin said, eyeing the murky sea. Catali looked up at him and raised an eyebrow. Augustin replied to her unspoken question. "I have a bad feeling about all of this."

***

As Edmond slipped beneath the ocean's surface, his throat began to twitch. He hated this part. Slamming a balled fist into his stomach, he opened his mouth and inhaled the sea water. The salt prickled and stung as his throat opened. With heavy, thick breaths his lungs pushed the water in and out of his body, drawing life from the brine. Blinking his eyes, they began to focus. The water below him was dark, and all around him the silhouetted shapes of fish swam in ever-changing clouds.

Like a charm. Edmond thought to himself, tucking the empty glass vial of the Depths Draught into a leather pouch at his belt.

JOSEPH DANIELS, BRYON ARNESON, STEVE HIGGS

Two streams of bubbles flared beside him as the pearl divers dove into the water. Edmond swam over as they struggled and spasmed. He grabbed hold of Felex's shoulder, and the man spun on him, eyes wild; he made a grab for Edmond's throat. Twisting, Edmond brought his elbow up into the diver's gut. A large bubble of air escaped Felex's open mouth, and the panic in his eyes settled into confusion as he inhaled water. Once the man had settled, Edmond pointed to the diver's sister and held a fist up to the man's face. With a disgruntled nod, the man swam to his twin.

The dogger had finally capsized, and Edmond kicked his feet, propelling towards it. Another small benefit of the potion was vision in the murk of the night-time sea. As the pearl divers moved to rejoin him, Fiora seemed to be shouting, ripples of water spreading from her mouth. Edmond pointed to his ear and shook his head. Whatever she had to say, it would have to wait. With a self-satisfied nod Edmond grabbed hold of a metal latch on the dogger's keel.

Fat bottomed doggers like this were usually used for fishing. They were meant to haul huge netfuls in their cramped holds, but Edmond wasn't a fisherman, and the prizes he scored were of a less scaly, and more *glinting* variety. Yanking the metal latch, a trap door in the hold swung open, and a metal anchor spun out. Grotty chain trailed behind the anchor head and drifted down into the darkness below. Edmond waved to the twin divers and grabbed hold of the chain, swiftly sinking down out of sight. Moments later, he felt the chain shake and smiled to himself. *Good, they decided to come along.*

They drifted on the sinking anchor for what felt like minutes as the overlong chain fell further and further into the deep. The potion allowed Edmond to see more clearly through the sea water, but it was still a mist filled night and no tears of moon or star wept into these depths. The chain shuddered and stopped. Edmond looked down toward where the anchor had touched the sea floor; they'd have to swim the rest of the way from here.

With an upward glance, Edmond spotted the twins drifting down. They were not swimming, but simply letting the weight of their bodies drag them down along the chain. With their lungs full of water it took very little effort to sink. As they approached, Edmond fished into his pack and pulled out a metal cylinder as long as his forearm and capped with a ceramic seal. He gripped the chain and the cylinder, then smashed the cap against the metal links. Instantly, a light flared to life, sputtering and sparking underwater like a torch. The three of them squinted against the sudden brightness as bubbles churned away from the broken cap. Extending the torch, Edmond surveyed the murk. Dark shapes materialized out of the sea bed: shelves of rock and spindly crags lurked like ruined fortresses, overgrown with the bloom and twisting weeds of the sea. Small fish fled the light, and on the craggy ocean floor, large shapes with no clear form slunk into grottos and hidden clefts. Edmond thought for a moment, then with a flick of his wrist the cylinder spun off into the darkness. The light drifted across rock and sand of the sea bed as it fell lower and lower. Edmond watched, then stiffened.

There it was.

Out of the crags and boulders rose a platform of rock. Even through the algae and monstrous seaweed, the shape was definite—a rectangle of solid stone with squared off corners. At one of the narrow ends, a stone doorway stood closed and flanked by life sized statues of men and women wrapped in mourning shrouds. The cylinder nestled at the line of statues' edge, giving them a haunted look as the light burned in spluttering pulses from the sandy floor. Edmond allowed himself a small, crooked smile. Seven years of searching stared back at him from the murk.

The other tombs he'd visited and borrowed from were scattered on land. The superstitious nature of the Gilded Islands meant many of the wealthier patrons preferred a proper send-off into whatever afterlife they believed for themselves, and so the well-maintained and fortified mausoleums of mortal men had become a familiar sight to Edmond.

An underwater tomb, though? Where water and rust could destroy?

This was no human resting place.

It wasn't long before Edmond and the divers floated before the stone door of the tomb. With scaling knives and Edmond's own hooked blade, they set about clearing barnacles and algae from the door. Once started however, Edmond paused. The sea stirred around them. At the edge of the cylinder's light, large shapes drifted in lazy circles. Grimacing, the tomb robber reached into the satchel about his shoulders and drew out a glass vial. In the cylinder's torch light, a mix of red, green, and orange liquid swirled with a speckling of lightly colored seeds. Edmond held the mixture with one hand and returned to scraping the stone door. Deeply carved runes and pictographs began to reveal themselves under the insistent scratching of the trio's blades.

The water stirred behind them, and Felex looked over his shoulder. Edmond could feel a cold prickle creeping up his spine. Of course, he'd suspected there'd be guardians... But now was not the time to panic. Just a little more... Edmond renewed his scraping with intensity, forcing his hands to move quickly, but calmly.

Felex, for his part, shot a wide eyed look at Edmond, and grabbed the grave robber's elbow, shaking him frantically. Edmond gave a curt shake of his head and gestured for the divers to continue clearing the door. *Not yet.* Edmond thought. Felex and Fiora both shot nervous glances over their shoulders and Fiora began to move her lips rapidly in a prayer that was swallowed by the depths. Edmond urgently tapped the door with his blade, glaring to the divers. *Don't look at it. Scrape the door.* Felex and Fiora nervously turned back to the door, but they clutched their scaling knives close, not raising them to scrape. *Come on. I haven't got another seven years to waste,* Edmond thought as he rolled the vial between his fingers. Another wave of displaced water rolled over their backs.

"*Don't look.*" He mouthed towards the twins. Edmond gestured quickly with his hand for them to cover their eyes. In the same hand, clutched by pinkie and ring finger, he kept the small vial secured, waiting for the opportune moment to—

There was a sudden rush of water from behind them. *Now.* Edmond raised his hand and slammed the glass vial into the stone lintel of the doorway. As the glass broke, he buried his face against the rough door, shielding his eyes. There was the expected force against his cheek as the vial diffused its contents.

He heard a muted cry, like a drowning ghoul; it was the strangled, keening wail of a being with no claim to the breathing world. The angry screech grated at Edmond's ears, but still he pressed his face against the door and guarded his head with his forearm. The nape of his neck prickled, goosebumps reaching out to meet the shattered cries of whatever *thing* had been stalking them.

Edmond didn't consider himself brave, or reckless. Rather, he believed in the five second rule. Something he lived his life by. He only had to last five seconds longer than anyone else. He had to keep his eyes closed five seconds longer; he had to hold his breathe five seconds longer; he had to stay the course five seconds longer.

The thing behind him obviously wasn't a purveyor of any such life motto. Pity for it. The water behind them swirled and thrashed violently for a moment and Edmond felt Felex and Fiora moving beside him. Then the sound drifted further and further away. Edmond stayed, listening as the sounds of the creature's cries and shrieks diminished completely.

Edmond waited, counting slowly in his head to five. When he lifted his eyes, the water was still and the colorful cloud from the vial had dissipated. Fiora and Felex rubbed at their faces and blinked hard as snot drifted from their noses in strings that hung through the sea water. Their faces were twisted in anguish as a red rash took shape around their orifices. *I told them not to look.* Edmond went back to scraping the door.

Over the next half hour, the twins recovered their vision—somewhat. They used their renewed eyesight to shoot bitter and resentful glances in Edmond's direction, interspliced, on occasion, by searching glances back out to sea.

But the thing didn't return.

Edmond stepped back from the cleaned door, which now displayed the expected carvings, and reaching to his satchel withdrew a rolled bit of leather. He could feel the resentment diminishing from his companions' eyes, as they approached and peered over his shoulder. Edmond unfurled the tattooed leather; inked into the resilient skin were symbols. As Edmond glanced between the stone door and the leather scroll, he reached up his hand. With firm strikes he pressed his palm against one glyph then another, tapping out a string of disparate symbols.

The door began to glow with a cold blue light and Fiora held up her hand, wrapping her fingers into a superstitious gesture meant to ward off evil. Felex contented himself to lick his lips nervously, and glance from Edmond to the glowing door.

After a moment, the glow faded, taking the stone with it. Fiora and Felex's eyes widened as the stone door seemed to turn to mist, revealing an antechamber within. The once-doorway framed a room made of smooth walls and benches over a mosaic floor of sparkling stones. Edmond stepped forward, passing through the mist.

His skin tingled and his heart thudded in his chest as water fled his clothing in gouts, puddling on the sparkling floor. Edmond inhaled shakily, but found no relief for his lungs. He grimaced as he rooted through the leather satchel at his side. The potion would pass on its own within the hour, but he didn't have that kind of time. Lifting a thin green bottle to his lips, Edmond took a hurried gulp. He could hear Felex and Fiora stepping cautiously into the chamber behind him as the purgative wrenched his stomach and he vomited the briny contents of his lungs onto the stone floor.

His head swam and cheeks prickled by the time he felt his throat muscles relax once more. His body tingled and his stomach churned, suggesting that the contents of the potion had been pushed from his veins. He gave it another couple of seconds, then, tilting his head, he inhaled deeply through his nose. Air streamed into his lungs. The tomb was breathable.

Shaking out his bedraggled hair, Edmond beckoned for the divers to follow. There was so much more to do.

Chapter 4

Felex patted his sister's back as she vomited up the last of the sea water. The purgative Edmond had passed them would inevitably leave their stomachs feeling like jelly, but gradually their lungs opened to the air around them.

"Nepir dredge you, bones and blood!" Fiora spat the curse at Edmond's back. "First you nearly get us captured, then you try to drown us, *then* you dangle us before some kraken, blind as babes! It is only by the sea goddess' mercy that any of us live. May her eyes be blessed."

"May her eyes be blessed." Felex repeated. His sister lifted her scaling knife, wiping at the rash still burning beneath her eyes.

"Look at me when I speak to you, tomb-robber."

"It wasn't a kraken." Edmond called over his shoulder. He still held the hooked knife in one hand and with the other he carefully traced the seams and stone panels of the walls around them.

"What?" Felex demanded. "I saw the thrashing tentacles, the great gnashing jaw."

"You didn't see anything. Not through that eye-bane I used. If it was a kraken we'd all be dead. It wasn't a kraken. Now shut up; I need to think." His voice was firm and the twins looked to each other, grumbling curses as they sat on one of the white marble benches that lined the chamber.

Edmond continued to feel over the seams of the stone walls. No more glyphs... There had to be a latch somewhere... He reached into his satchel, pulling out a long, flute-like wand of carved wood with holes pockmarking one side. As he waved the flute, it whistled softly. He frowned, focusing on the noise as he swept the item over the stones. As he did, he heard the twins start to move behind him, followed by the soft grunt of Fiora bending over.

"Felex," came Fiora's hushed voice, "There are moonstones set here. And look, pearl-opal too!"

Edmond glanced back as the twin's brother jumped up from his seat and joined her by the floor.

Felex grinned, but the expression turned to a glower at Edmond's glance. "At least we can earn something for following this forsaken vagrant." Felex held Edmond's gaze for a moment longer, then glanced down again; he dropped to a crouch and placed the point of his scaling knife to the floor, feeling for a crease to pry up one of the stones.

GRAVEYARD GODS

Edmond was on them in an instant like a summer storm. Jabbing the flute back into his satchel, he pointed threateningly at the pearl divers. His dark, bedraggled hair hung in front of his eyes, and he gazed at them with the intensity of a mad man. "Touch nothing. Take nothing," he said, his voice calm in contrast to his appearance. He kept his hooked knife pointing towards the floor, pressed against his thigh, still gripped in his left hand. Normally, being left-dominant gave Edmond an advantage in blade-play. Most people in the Gilded Isles had never met someone left-dominant, no less fought them with steel. In Godshaven, children who 'lead with their left' could expect a firm slap on the wrist, but in the smaller isles it could mean losing a hand.

The twins froze and looked up at him from where they crouched, their own knives glinting in the meager light provided by the moonstones buried in the floor of the antechamber. Felex started to lift his knife, his face twisting in anger, but then he paused, staring at Edmond's chest.

Edmond followed the diver's gaze to where a small potion vial dangled from his neck by a leather thong. It had snuck free of his shirt in the chaos, and the gleam from its smooth, ebony surface almost twinkled in Felex's eyes.

The pearl diver licked his lips. "What's that?" said Felex. "Looks valuable."

Edmond hurriedly stowed the potion back out of sight. "Take nothing. Touch nothing," he repeated. He brushed his sodden hair back and exhaled deeply, deflating the storm as quickly as it had come. "Best to stow that," he pointed to the knife in Felex's hand. "Before you trip and hurt yourself, ey?"

Felex glanced at his sister, communicating silently. He looked back at Edmond, his eyes darting towards the lump pressing against the fabric of his shirt, where the small potion now lay. "Never seen nothin' like that before. Looked old. You know what they say about the oldest potions."

"Forget about the potion," snapped Edmond.

"Are you really an alchemist?" Fiora said from behind her brother.

Edmond glanced at her. "I'm a man who hired two divers to help him on a job. Stow the knife."

Felex didn't glance at his sister this time. He met Edmond's gaze, but seemed to find something there he didn't like. Following a series of muted curses, Felex nearly skinned himself in anger as he jammed the scaling knife into his waistband. "So what's our way out of here? It's not that potion is it?"

"Like I said, forget the potion. Focus on helping me and we'll all get out of this rich."

"And that anklet—I've seen it. Made of gold isn't it?"

Edmond frowned, shifting his weight again and glancing down towards his left ankle. "They're pearls, not that it should matter to you."

"But it glints like gold," Felex continued, testing both his luck and Edmond's patience. "I seen it twice while you dove down here."

"My personal possessions," said Edmond, growling, "Are none of your concern—gold or not."

Felex shrugged and held up his hands in placation. Sour indignity twisted at the twins as they settled back against the walls. Edmond turned, again, to his work, his back itching as he did. Luckily, it only took him a minute to find what he was looking for. There was a loud click and the grinding of stone as Edmond pushed on one of the stone panels in the wall.

A passageway opened before them. Edmond shifted his weight, causing the pearls on his left ankle to shift and press against his skin. The slight pressure brought with it somber thoughts. He was here for more than gold—for more than himself. He was here to rewind history...

Wordlessly, the divers followed him into the dark.

As Edmond crossed the threshold, he paused. He muttered a few words and phrases the twins likely didn't understand, then waited. Nothing happened. He clapped his hands into the darkness using a few distinct rhythms, but only dim echos returned. Rubbing his temple, Edmond groaned.

What was that word? he thought as he stared into the darkness. Then, with a small exclamation, he snapped his fingers and said in a firm voice, "*Aydanlik.*"

All around them, sconces in the wall began to glow with a pale blue light.

The room before them lit up as Fiora whispered, "Sorcery."

"Not sorcery." Edmond stepped into the room and approached one of the glowing sconces. Held in its grasp was a carved crystal. Gnarled grooves showed in its surface as he plucked it from the sconce and held it in front of the twins. "The ancients had forms of alchemy unknown to us now.

They could impress gems and crystals with a voice. Sort of like teaching a dog to listen for certain phrases; 'sit', 'stay', 'speak'. When the stone hears the command word, it releases whatever alchemy was impressed into it." He tossed the stone in his hand, catching it deftly. "Such as light."

Fiora stared at the stone suspiciously and Felex grunted. He did not seem to care for the idea of a stone listening to him, but also didn't seem interested in getting into another argument with the tomb-robber over it. Instead, the twins silently followed as Edmond entered the room.

While the room itself was grandly proportioned and lined with fine white statues, Edmond Mondego ignored all of it. Instead, he headed for the very center where a stone altar lay on a smooth dais. He gripped the pale shining crystal, holding it in front of him, his knife still in his other hand. Gesturing for the others to help, they shoved the altar, revealing a stairwell spiraling into black. Edmond glanced back once more, gave a ghoulish grin—mostly for his own enjoyment—then plunged into that darkness.

Down, down, down—their feet slapped against wet stone as they shakily inhaled moist air. Edmond could hear one of the twins whispering prayers behind him, though he couldn't tell which one. For his part, he could feel his skin tingling with excitement. Seven years was a long time... But even if it had taken seven hundred, it would have been worth the cost. If what he expected to find was down here... *But...* The alchemical lights were also cause for worry. Edmond didn't allow it to show on his face. He resisted the urge to furrow his brow and gnaw on his lip; this would only spook the twins. But, inwardly, he was a mass of trepidation. The alchemy down here was old—very old. The older an alchemical creation, the greater chance *things* could escape. The sorts of things that dwelled on the edges of all forms of magical effort. Alchemy, Edmond knew from his own experience, wasn't so much an evocation as an offering. The ingredients, the combination of magical items or rare components served little function without the touch of the beings that lived in the plane from which magic was drawn. Beings who rarely enjoyed the company of mortals. Beings who would not hesitate to force themselves through the bindings of unwary alchemists. The lower level demons, like imps and incubi, Edmond could deal with, but it would be a close thing. Mid-tier demons like djinn or, their more powerful counterparts, marid, were a threat that could be outrun, but not overcome.

Archfiends though? If one of those showed up, this tomb would serve as the resting place for three new souls.

And if, of all things, a *leviathan* arrived, summoned from that deeper plane... Edmond couldn't help himself. He visibly shuddered, though he tried to pass it off as a reaction to the chilling touch of the stagnant tomb air. A leviathan would spell doom for more than just Edmond and his pearl divers. If they woke one of those... loosed it on the world—

Edmond forced the thought from his mind. It wouldn't do to dwell on such eventualities. In an underwater tomb, who could say what sort of powerful alchemy they would encounter?

The stairwell led to a space that could not have been more different from the chamber above. A damp, moss-covered grotto opened into cavernous, meandering passages interspersed with stalagmites and stalactites. As they stepped down into the space, the water rose nearly to their waists. The pale light from the crystal in Edmond's hand cast glittering shadows about them and the sound of splashing water echoed in strange halting patterns from the darkness.

Suddenly, Felex loosed a cry. "Something in the water!"

Edmond spun towards the diver, hooked knife at the ready. Dingy water splashed, spraying beads of moisture as Felex stumbled back, kicking his legs wildly. Edmond dove forward, towards the divers, but slipped on something slick. As he righted himself, he accidentally dropped the crystal, which *plunked* into the water

"There," Fiora pointed. "See it—right there!"

Frowning, Edmond groped beneath the water. He felt something soft, like sodden wood. He gripped whatever it was, and yanked it up. From the cave water, clasped in Edmond's hand and streaming rivulets of muck, emerged a rotten arm.

The two divers cursed loudly, invoking their gods with wild gestures. Edmond, meanwhile, gripped the wrist of the unpleasant limb, but didn't let go. He pulled with all his might, straining with his back. A body followed the limb. He gripped the corpse by the shoulders, holding it at a distance, but examining the face. It resembled a human face, still, and covered in damp rot.

The light from the crystal wavered and danced from below the water. The corpse was oddly well preserved, its skin pale and seemingly shimmering in the cavorting light. Ridges of pearlescent bone twisted and wrapped about the shrunken limbs like coiling vines. The ears tapered upward into points like the fins of a fish. There was no mistaking it.

GRAVEYARD GODS

"Signerde." Felex spat. "What next on this cursed venture? Death himself?"

Fiora gave a disbelieving shake of her head. "Mischief makers. Storm brewers. Drowners." She spat into the grotto's water. "He got what he deserved."

"She," Edmond said. His voice was soft, and the twins looked to each other, unsure they had heard properly. "It's a woman."

"How can you tell?" Felex said with a mocking sneer. Edmond did not reply, gently lowering the body until he held it just above the water's surface. The sparkling pearl of the exposed bone reflected in his eyes as he stared down at the body.

"Let's take the ears," added Fiora, with an excited tilt in her voice. "It looks fresh enough. When we get back to Sile, we can trade them in for-"

"No," Edmond said, his voice still soft, but traced with venom. "Wait here." Edmond turned to climb the stairway, leaving the confused divers behind. As Edmond hoisted the body back up the stairs, he could hear the twins muttering darkly behind him, making little effort to keep their voices low.

"Did you see the look in his eyes as he held the corpse?" Felex asked.

Fiora spat. "Crazy, godless bastard. Rushes room to room, leaving treasure in our wake. Now he won't let us take the fishlicker's ears. I told you, you cannot trust a man who leads with his left hand."

The twins paused, as if waiting for something. Edmond continued pulling the Signerde's body until he was in the upper chamber. He lay the body on the altar. Edmond paused for a moment, pushing aside the threat of emerging emotion and, quietly, murmured, *"Deniz kardes, annenin kalbi seni aldi."* It was a simple prayer, and the Signerde weren't simple folk, but it was as much as Edmond could spare in the moment.

Then, he heard the voices continue. The fools likely didn't realize, due to the acoustics of the water and the curving stairwell, Edmond could still hear them.

"Can't follow a crazy man," Fiora was saying, her voice barely a whisper. "Maybe... Maybe we should take charge. Maybe we should leave him here, with his fishlicker friend."

There was another pause, then Felex, in an even quieter voice that echoed up the stairwell, said, "I think I know how to get out of here, too. We could take that anklet of his—the one with those gold pearls in it. Or how about—Did you see that potion on his neck?"

"That's our way out of here?"

"I'd bet ten pearls on it."

"Well—maybe we should just ask him to—Shh, here he comes!"

Edmond returned a moment later, stepping back into the water. Without pausing to look at the divers, he stooped down and scooped up the dropped light crystal. He eyed them both. "Sorry," he said. "Did you say something?"

Felex shrugged with his mouth and gave a half shake of his head. Fiora glanced across the room as if she hadn't heard.

"Good then," said Edmond. "Hear that?"

GRAVEYARD GODS

The twins hesitated, but then Felex nodded, slowly. "Splashing?" he said. "What is that?"

"Something only I know about," said Edmond. He gave them a small, disarming smile. "If you want to make it out alive, better listen and follow."

Fiora sputtered. "Why would you think—we weren't—"

"Of course. Just advising you to stay close is all." Edmond smiled sweetly again. The splashing sound in the distance grew louder. "Come along now. We're almost there."

On they walked, Edmond in the lead as he guided the divers through the twisting cavern grotto. The distant splashing sounds repeated. Each time, Edmond changed their path. Sometimes, he held up a hand to call a halt as he listened in the dark. Sometimes, he raised his knife and tapped the stone stalagmites they passed, listening to the metal ringing. The splashing seemed to be coming nearer with each instance until the divers were both clutching their scaling knives.

After nearly ten minutes of this, Fiora started muttering. "We're being hunted, aren't we?" she said, a whimper to her tone.

The most recent splashing sound had been louder than ever.

"We're just going in circles," Felex said, his lips trembling. "You're trying to kill us, aren't you! Those rocks—I've seen them before. We're just going around and around—"

Edmond glared at him, holding a finger to his lips. "They're different rocks. Now hush. We're not going in circles."

"You want it to catch us, don't you!" Fiora said over him though, her voice echoing in the chamber. The splashing drew nearer. "You only have one potion—that one on your neck. There's not enough for all three of us to reach the surface!"

"Quiet!" Edmond snapped. He glanced sharply around a stalactite, and cursed—he broke into a rapid surge forward, plodding through the water in the opposite direction. "The potion is nothing. Now come or you're done for."

Edmond noticed Fiora tighten her grip on her blade, but her protests diminished to whimpers as she followed. Things would have culminated in catastrophe, Edmond surmised, had they not, that very moment, stumbled upon a stone pedestal—not natural, but carved. Its sides knotted and pitted with dark recesses and strange geometry. On it rested a bronze bowl, green with age, and Edmond noted the glint of gold from within. He held up a hand, inspecting the bowl with a careful eye. "No," he said, and with that simple statement, turned to walk away. Another splash could be heard from behind a pile of boulders at the far side of a tunnel.

"No?" Felex said.

Edmond looked back.

The divers were no longer following him.

They stood side by side, knives raised, eyes wide like startled sheep being led to the butcher's block. Felex's face flushed with compounded fear and frustration. "No?" Felex repeated. "To the depths with your 'no'. I did not come down here for the pleasure of your company. We were promised treasure, but every time we see treasure *you* say 'no.'" Felex turned to the bowl and snatched up a handful of coins. Fiora looked between Edmond and her brother, a disdainful twist in her lip. But, her eyes kept darting towards the boulders where the splash had come from. Clearly, she was the smarter of the two.

"Push down on the bowl," Edmond snapped.

The forceful command made both the divers stop, looking over their shoulders to Edmond. The tomb robber held his palm out flat, making a motion as if he were pressing down. "Felex, push down on the bowl, now."

Stuffing the gold coins into the pouch at his side, the pearl diver snarled, "Still giving orders? I don't think so, I think-" A grating of metal on stone shrieked, as a line of spikes erupted from the pedestal. The sound of tearing flesh announced a sluice of blood spurting from several rips in Felex's bare leg. The pearl diver screeched in pain, the sound piercing the cavern.

Fiora screamed too as she stepped to grab her brother. He twisted in her arms, still shouting indeterminably as barbed metal hooks punctured through the meat of his thigh and calf. Desperately, Fiora reached out and pressed down on the bowl.

"Not now!" Edmond raised a hand of warning, but too late. The barbed spikes retracted, pulling Felex's leg against the pillar, they sliced through his flesh like a boning knife, spilling more blood into the water around them.

In the darkness beyond their light, a loud splash echoed.

Edmond was a grave robber, a profession not for the faint of heart. He didn't spook easily and what fear he felt he often managed to suppress until the opportune moment. But now... Now he was afraid. His thoughts about the nature of the alchemy in a place like this and the creatures that lurked beyond came flooding back. His only hope was that whatever was stalking them was of a low enough tier that it didn't spell certain death.

"Leave him," Edmond shouted. Felex bobbed in the water beside the pillar, breathing rapidly. His eyes darted in wild confusion as his mouth gaped like a fish. Fiora blinked back tears and looked to Edmond in rage. She shouted incoherently, pointing at her brother.

"Look at his leg," Edmond said, maintaining at least an appearance of calm. "He's already dead, but we're not. Don't look, just follow me."

"He's my brother!" She screamed, the echo rocketing through the grotto. The splashing drew nearer.

"Shared blood has never prevented death, and isn't about to start now."

Edmond glanced back towards Felex's writhing form. He swallowed, squelching the pity welling up in his chest. Pity wouldn't save the diver now, but it would kill Edmond. The twin would have to decide her own fate.

"Run. Now." With those last words Edmond turned and began a smooth jog into the water, drifting with each push to minimize the ripples. Even so, he couldn't avoid a glance back.

Fiora had turned, peering across her brother's writhing form. A dark bulbous shape, like an enormous octopus, hurtled through the grotto, pulling itself along by grabbing the stalagmites and stalactites around it. Edmond swallowed a scream. *Fuck. A marid. Of course it had to be a gods-damned marid!* In all his alchemical endeavors, Edmond had never been so reckless that he needed to combat one of these mid-tier demons before, and he wasn't about to start now. He put on an extra burst of speed.

With a heart wrenching groan, Fiora released the bowl and ran after Edmond. Behind them, Edmond could hear the grating of metal on stone as the barbed spikes erupted once again. They both ran. The splashing stopped, and they heard the sounds of crunching bone and ripping flesh. This time, neither of them looked back.

Chapter 5

A PIT OF TARANTULAS, a crypt filled with poisonous snakes, and a ravenous tiger, twice the usual size with roped scars up and down its tawny body—these were but a few of the obstacles Edmond had faced on his previous expeditions. Granted, all of those had been above water. Robbing the tomb of a Gamorian noble or an ancient king was one thing...

This, however, was proving to be an entirely separate kettle of rotting fish. Alchemy was a precarious brand of magic—and when it went wrong, it could go *terribly*. The evidence for that sloshed through the blood in their wake. Edmond heard the terror in Fiora's movements as she splashed alongside him, interspliced with the occasional sob. Still, he waited until the sound of churning water and suctioning tentacles were well behind them before pulling her sharply around a stalagmite and gripping her by the shoulder. He held his knife to his mouth like a shushing finger. "I'm sorry," Edmond said in a low voice. His eyes met Fiora's, confronting a swirl of grief and fear. In that moment, her eyes held the same familiar weight that accosted him whenever he glanced in a mirror. He held her gaze for a moment, sharing her pain, but then he looked away.

There was still more to be done.

"He's gone," said Edmond, still quiet. "There's nothing else to be said about it." He felt a momentary twinge of guilt. *This* wasn't entirely true. At least, he suspected it wasn't. If death *were* always, hopelessly a permanent thing—well, Edmond wouldn't have been down here in the first place.

Still, he didn't need to provide what would only be seen as beggar's hope. She wouldn't believe his ambition. Hell, there were times he wasn't sure he believed it himself, and right now, Fiora needed to be consoled.

"At least you're still alive. That's something," he said in what he hoped was a reassuring voice. Fiora shot him a glare.

"I'm—I'm going back," the pearl diver said at last.

Edmond sucked air, wincing. "There's nothing to—"

"I know he's dead!" she spoke in a voice far louder than he was comfortable with, twisting her hands and swishing one leg through the water. "I'm leaving. You go on if you must—but I'm getting out of here. I'll wait for that—that *thing* to pass, then I'll make good my getaway. Nepir save me."

Edmond thought about letting her go, about avoiding an argument. The divers had proven to be of little use to him thus far—incompetent at worst, mutinous at best. He licked his lips and half turned away, but the motion caused the vial on his neck to roll across his chest. The weight so familiar to him at this point that it was like a part of him, a simple, black vial, with neither filigree nor etching, dangling from his throat by its leather thong. Felex had suspected the potion contained within was their ticket out of the cave. This was untrue. The contents of *this* vial—his fingers reached absentmindedly up to readjust the container—were *far* more valuable and important to Edmond than a simple Depths Draught.

It was also a reminder... *River's Gift, keep your heart for me.* The voice of a memory trembled through him, momentarily chilling his bones but warming his chest. Prickles danced across fingertips as he shivered. *River's Gift...* It's what she had called him. He frowned at the thought as a tinge of bitterness crept up from his chest.

"You should come with me," he said, his voice devoid of emotion. "You'll die like your brother otherwise. You have a family—scores of cousins and uncles and aunts. I saw some of them when I hired you. There's more for you to live for."

"Following you *killed* Felex," said Fiora, eyes wide.

"*Ignoring* me killed him," Edmond said as gently as possible given the circumstances. He shot a glance past the pearl diver into the dark. There were no further signs of the monster. Not yet.

"I—I can't go on—I can barely feel my feet."

Edmond cursed softly, but then shook his head. "Fine... Don't come, but stay here. I'll be back for you. Stay hidden behind the rock. That monster hunts by sound, mostly. If it gets near—stay very, very quiet. Understand? Don't move. Don't run. Don't scream. It's your only hope."

GRAVEYARD GODS

"How do I know you'll come back?"

Edmond hesitated; he half thought about giving her the potion around his neck for safekeeping. Surely that would assuage her fears, at least for the moment. It would bestow some amount of comfort, he was sure of it. It's what *she* would have done.

He lowered his hand from his throat and turned away.

He'd never been much like her. *River's Gift* she'd called him... More like a curse. It was a cruel thing to think, but the potion around his neck was worth more to him than the pearl diver's life. If Fiora didn't trust him, that was her decision.

"Look at your brother," he said, coldly. "Or the pieces of him that remain. He didn't listen either—those who don't, end up dead. I've been doing this for nearly a decade; if you want to live, stay hidden behind the rock. Don't make a sound. Understand?" His voice spread across the water, bubbling with an acidic fervor, eating through the tension with corrosive intent.

Fiora's face was a mixture of emotions; a trail of glimmering tears led to a gallows grin. She sucked air through her teeth, both glaring at him and leering in an attempt to save face. "Do what you wish, tomb raider," she said, blinking the tears ferociously from her eyes. "May Nepir curse your winds and sink your soul." With that, she ducked behind the stalagmite, crouching in the water and pressing her back to the rough surface. As she looked away, studying the curve of the alcove's cavern wall, the tears began to stream freely down her cheeks.

Edmond glanced back down the corridor, peering into the black, then he stepped out into the tunnel, wading through the water deeper into the crypt. He didn't look back at Fiora, nor did he allow his mind to spare her another thought. Her curse and her god meant little to him. As far as he was concerned, he was a man cursed by Nameless Death himself—defiance was in his blood. He walked as a mortal in the tomb of an immortal, each of his ragged breaths mockery to the frailty of the divine.

He exhaled louder, breathed deeper, and smiled.

***

The dead end pierced his hopes with needles of doubt, skewering his feet to the sodden floor. Edmond stared at the blank wall, heart in his larynx, breaths coming in shallow groans.

"No," he murmured. "No—this has to be it!" He turned sharply back, glancing over his shoulder into the dark. In the distance, he thought he heard a soft, splashing sound. The sort of sound he imagined emanating from something that was taking great care to move quietly.

A shiver dabbed up his spine, bringing with it all sorts of nasty images of being trapped underground, backed into a corner, flood tides rising, tentacled monster approaching like a spider nearing an ensnared mosquito.

He spun back around to face the blank wall. His hand moved to his pocket and withdrew the tattooed leather, unfurling the rough skin to reveal the symbols and glyphs he'd spotted on the door at the bottom of the sea, but also, sewn into the fabric as a tapestry of black thread, there was a maze. He'd spent the better part of a year memorizing the maze—he thought he'd committed it to heart. But the dead end before him suggested otherwise.

He traced the weathered threads with his eyes, muttering to himself as he did. "...the antechamber...the spiral stairs...the statue...veers off to the—no, yes, here we are. That should be..." He trailed off, glancing back up at the wall. He frowned again, then peered back along the corridor he'd traversed, the floor covered in ankle-deep water. But there were no side-passages or sealed doorways.

He looked back at the map. "Blue fire and black fish," he cursed. "Tridents and whips and shark shite!" This was it. This was where the map led. *This*, supposedly, was where the main tomb was located.

Something splashed behind him; the hairs on the nape of his neck prickled, but in his fury he ignored the urge to look back, and instead looked up, examining the ceiling for any crawlspace or crevice where one might slip a body.

Nothing but sheer granite returned his gaze. He pushed at the ground with his boots. Just muck and stone, and-wait. Edmond paused. He tested the ground, probing it with his heel. *Interesting*, he thought.

The splashing sound at his back drew nearer, softly, though, as if careful not to make a noise. Edmond imagined Fiora tiptoeing through the water, knife raised, sneaking up behind him. He lowered his map, growling, reaching towards the knife at his waist as he turned.

In that moment, his body reacted before his mind could comprehend what he saw. He became stone. His feet froze solid to the ground, his tongue glued to the roof of his mouth. A groan of utmost horror crawled its way from his throat and out the corners of his lips.

Twenty black, lidless eyes, the size of fists peered into the dead-end from a rounded, jelly-fish shaped head. Scores of tentacles spread out, like a web, suctioned to the ceiling, the walls and even the floors. The marid, the demon that had feasted on Felex, hung suspended in the passage, blocking any exit. Though Edmond stared at it, the thing didn't blink and moved slowly through the water, its tentacles shifting and making suctioning sounds as they released purchase and found new grip. It approached like a wall of bubbling tar, roiling with its bulbous eyes. The marid behaved like a predator cornering prey, still moving softly, careful not to alarm its next meal.

For his part, Edmond's brain scrambled to come up with a plan that didn't involve him dying in horrific pain. He took one step back, then another. His hands had gone numb; something in those twenty, globular eyes, which glinted like ink-stained pools of pus under streaks of starlight, had stopped his breathe and numbed his fingers. A particularly large tentacle, the size of a tree trunk shifted through the water like an alligator, moving towards his feet, still slow, still careful. The misty outline of a plan began to form in Edmond's mind. His eyes flitted to the knife in his hand. He shifted his feet, and took a slow breath.

Edmond dropped his knife.

A tentacle darted forward, reaching for his face, ready to suction it. A stench of rot and ancient blubber assailed his nostrils. Edmond gagged as he bent over, reaching sharply for his fallen blade, and the tentacle stuck to the granite wall behind him with a sharp slap.

The creature's eyes blinked once, then a mouth opened, revealing row upon row of soft, fleshy pink mandibles, covered in small thorn-like teeth. The mandibles wriggled and writhed like worms and maggots, stretching blindly for Edmond from fleshless lips.

Edmond slammed his palm into the handle of his dagger. The blade stood upright, with the point stuck into the floor beneath him. He brought down his other hand in a fist and hit the knife, driving it down deeper. The dagger punctured through the floor, as if ripping through membranous cheesecloth.

The tentacled monster froze, going very still all of a sudden. This, however, Edmond knew was *not* a good sign. Like a coiling viper, or a patient leopard, the creature took the posture of a predator preparing to strike with full speed and force. He had mere seconds before he would be ripped limb from limb.

Edmond tried to remain very still above water, meanwhile, bent over, his hand scrambled frantically at the knife. He managed to grip its handle and dragged it back, ripping further into the ground. He twisted the knife and ripped it the other way, then twisted it again.

The monster burped. Edmond straightened up, slowly.

Something jettisoned from the creature's mouth and landed with a splash at Edmond's foot.

It was a dark finger, gnawed off at the second knuckle. A woman's finger. Fiora had joined her brother.

Edmond felt he would be sick, and, as if waiting for such a paralytic reaction, the monster surged forward, tentacles shooting through the air like a score of sinewy snakes. Its mouth opened wide, revealing more of the worm-like mandibles.

Edmond didn't scream. He didn't dodge. He didn't have time to think. Instead, he lifted one leg high and slammed his heel down into the section of floor he'd been sawing at with the knife. His foot slammed through the membranous ground; there was a ripping sound and Edmond fell, tumbling head over heel through a sudden hole gouged in the floor.

His last glimpse of the chamber above was of the tentacled monster sucking on the back wall, appendages flailing wildly, a severed finger swirling in the murk. Then, water was in his mouth, his ears, his eyes. He couldn't see. Something grabbed his ankle and tugged insistently, but he kicked out with his other foot and—after another couple of rapid rabbit kicks—he managed to break free.

He fell down some sort of chute, carried by a stream of water. Something poked him in the eye—his stomach turned as somewhere, in his wild, panicking mind he desperately hoped it wasn't the finger. Then, Edmond jettisoned from the end of a chute, arching through the air. He fell, and continued to fall, terror welling up once more. He was going to break every bone in his—

Chapter 6

Edmond slammed into a hard floor. Something in his wrist snapped. His knees cracked and throbbed with white hot lances of agony. He rolled onto his back, cursing and gasping. Water spilled from his nose and mouth and trickled from his sodden hair. It spilled over his cheeks to pool beneath his head like a murky halo.

After a few moments, as the flaring pain subsided to a dull throb, Edmond dared to open his eyes. At first, all he could see were dark spots. His eyes stung and he blinked rapidly; he reached up with his good wrist and used his hand to wipe at his face. Finally, gasping and wincing, he looked again.

As his vision adjusted and the stinging sensation subsided, Edmond slowly gathered his legs under him. He crouched before an enormous silver statue that stretched from floor to ceiling, nearly thirty feet tall. The statue was immaculately crafted, depicting a beautiful woman made of pure silver—save for the eyes, which boasted two black gems that glinted dully near the ceiling. The woman was, perhaps, the most beautiful creature

Edmond had ever seen. Her high cheekbones settled in a regal face untarnished by weather or age. The pristine silver glinted under alchemical lights placed in a circular pattern in the floor, surrounding the statue. The posture of the silver creation was one of solemnity, with arms crossed and brow furrowed above the multi-faceted gemstone eyes.

Edmond swallowed, and tilted his head back, looking up. He spotted the opening in the ceiling where a small, but steady waterfall fell into a pool behind him. There were no signs of tentacles or mandibles or globular eyes. Without meaning to, his gaze drew back to the gigantic, silver statue, as if it was there to cleanse his palette and offer a striking contrast to the monster in the flooded corridors above. Where the tentacled beast had been horrifically ugly and in constant, wiggling motion, the statue was a thing of pure, glistening beauty, motionless and unyielding.

Edmond winced as he tried to use his injured wrist to take his weight and found it couldn't bear it. He switched hands and got to his feet. As he did, he checked to make sure the potion around his neck was still there. A small sigh of relief escaped his lip as he felt its smooth, comfortable weight brush against his fingers.

Swallowing, Edmond turned away from the statue to examine the walls. There were a few alcoves scattered about. He eyed them, wondering what sort of traps might be in place to prevent any theft. Shambling forward, Edmond spotted the discarded map, soaked against the marble floor a few paces away. He hurried over and scooped up the inked skin, examining it in the dim light from the alchemical stones. As he did, he fell very still. His eyes narrowed and he lowered the map, holding it against one of the lights.

Words he hadn't seen before, which glowed like etched moonlight, appeared across the leather. He frowned, then paused at a sound to his back—a creaking, cracking sound. He whirled around, half expecting the tentacled monster to have found its way into the chamber, but instead, he saw only the statue. He turned back, holding the map up once more and again, he could hear a cracking noise. This time, still keeping the map to the light, he turned.

The alchemical stone was acting as a spotlight, shining through the map. The etched words were being reflected against the silver statue, dancing across the smooth surface of the giant carving. The cracking sound continued, though Edmond could see no change in the statue's appearance.

Strange, Edmond thought. Hesitantly, Edmond lowered the map, leaving it propped against one of the stones, allowing the light to continue to beam through, reflecting against the statue. He wasn't sure what this would accomplish, but he hadn't made it this far in the business by leaving stones unturned. Traps and obstacles usually had a more immediate affect—the slower effects, like quiet cracking noises due to mysterious words in a map, made different promises; the sort of promises that opened long-shut doorways or unlocked secret treasures.

He figured it couldn't hurt, and he refused to leave this place empty-handed.

Edmond left the map propped against the alchemical light, then circled the silver statue. He made a note to himself to double back, eventually, and pluck the gemstone eyes from the figure, but in the meantime, he was certain the alcoves would have *something* of interest to him.

He swallowed, his fingers twitching in anticipation, then he approached the nearest niche.

Chapter 7

Edmond emerged from the third and final alcove with a pile of loot stacked against his chest and cradled in his arms. There were golden discs with intricate carvings, silver jugs with sealed lids. He carried two gem-encrusted swords and a scabbard fit for a king. A bag of glowing blue stones balanced against a dented pewter goblet.

This was the last load—the only remaining items that had yet to be tested.

Edmond glanced in disgust to a portion of the floor near one of the alchemical lights. A small pile of treasure, nearly at knee-height lay discarded there. This was his fifth armload, and, still, he had yet to find what he was looking for. Doubtless, the pearl divers would have sold each other to have gotten their hands on such loot, but Edmond had seen treasure before. As he thought of the divers, an image of Fiora huddled in the knee deep water, tears streaming down her face, flashed in his mind while he listened to her phantom voice scream: 'he's my brother!' With a shake of his head, Edmond snuffed out the image. *No, perhaps you wouldn't have sold each other, but you would absolutely have betrayed me.* Gold and silver had no hold on him at all—it had cost him far too much for him to ever consider it friend again. What he needed would be imbued, something with hidden purpose—something *magical.* Something that he'd hoped and dreamed could be found in the grave of a god.

But now that he was here...

Edmond glowered in disgust at the knee-high pile of treasure. Duds—each and every one. Not a magical item to be found among them. He stalked over to the alchemical lights and dumped his final armload unceremoniously to the ground. He could feel his frustration mounting, but suppressed the emotion.

This had to be it. He couldn't return empty-handed. It wasn't an option. One of these items, *just one* had to have some magical affect.

That won't be enough, said a small, nasty voice in his mind. *Not just* any *magic will do.*

Edmond swallowed, pushing the voice away. Of course, it was true; he needed something special—something that could bring her back. Something miraculous.

Edmond ignored the pile of useless metals and instead turned his attention to the final armload of loot. He pulled the fluted wand from his pocket. Carefully, he began to wave it over the remaining items, just as he had done in the tomb's antechamber, hovering an inch away from their gilded surfaces. A soft hum reverberated in his ears, and his fingers buzzed where they held the wand. He passed across the swords twice, but the wand didn't react. He passed over the pewter goblet and crown, but still no reaction. Reining in his aggravation like an unruly carthorse, he forced his motions to be slow and careful, counting out to five with each pass—he didn't want to miss anything—again he trailed the wand along the golden discs, the blue stones, the sealed silver jugs. He made one pass over the entire pile of loot, then, just to be sure, another.

No reaction. The wand stayed silent. Edmond stared at the fifth and final pile of treasure, breathing in shallow gasps, his cheeks pulsing with a strange heat.

Nothing. Seven years searching. Twenty tombs plundered. Every ounce of treasure traded for this *map*—this God Grave. And still, *nothing* to be found. No magical items, no way to bring her back. His arms trembled and the wand clattered to the stone floor. He'd failed. Square one again.

In that moment the enormity of it all fell on him like a tidal wave. The task of starting over, seven more years of danger and uncertainty, seven more years without her. The thought loomed over him like a dark mountain, casting him in its cold shadow. No, the gods had cursed him. He had dared to hope, and they had robbed him of even that. There would be no going back.

He had lost her for good.

A surge of rage pulsed through him, unbidden, originating in his gut, puffing his lungs and releasing through his throat. "Fuck! Black shite! Cursed pieces of filth and doom on every bastard breath!" He screamed at the ceiling, shaking his fists. He kicked the pile of treasure, sending pieces scattering every which way. He stomped a crown once, twice, and again until it bent against itself and a setting of diamonds popped out and skittered across the floor. He kicked the diamonds to a corner of the room. Arms flailing, he grabbed one of the silver jugs and hurled it into another corner. Then, he lifted one of the swords and set to the remnants of treasure. A couple of times he swiped at the alchemical lights, causing them to spark. The hot rage in his chest boiled over into an inhuman howl that erupted as he set to the pile of loot, slicing and hacking and slashing and gouging. He screamed until his frayed throat collapsed and his cry melted into a whimpering moan. Stinging tears flowed from his eyes, turning the treasure into a golden blur that sparked with each blow he rained down. The sword he held was a ceremonial piece not meant for battle, and its intricately etched blade bent twice before finally snapping. The broken end of the beautiful weapon became a jagged spike, crooked as an accusing finger, and in that moment, Edmond turned the ruined sword on himself, bringing the ragged point towards his own throat.

You promised. The thought came unbidden to his mind, and he might have shoved it aside at once if the voice had been his own.

Edmond swallowed, the knot in his throat scraping past the point of the broken blade. Wide-eyed, gasping with a heaving chest, he stared aimlessly across the chasm, back to the silver statue. He'd made a promise once, years ago; a young man's promise fulfilled by an older man's honor. A promise that couldn't be fulfilled by a dead man. But what good were promises he couldn't keep? Seven years it had been. Seven years of hunting, searching, risking everything—and still, he was no closer to a cure, to a solution, to reversal of regret.

GRAVEYARD GODS

What good were the gods? He'd tried prayer, years ago, but abandoned it. What point was there to mumble one's concerns into the ears of beings that only scoffed in return. The gods of the Gilded Isles were cold, indifferent, monstrous entities. They didn't care about Edmond. They certainly had never cared for his wife. Otherwise, why wouldn't they have intervened? Why wouldn't they have stopped it?

His wife had been devout, though—Edmond hadn't questioned her on it. He'd rarely questioned her on anything. She was a resplendant pearl against a backdrop of grey. Compassion and kindness exuded from her like the aroma of a field of flowers. She had the tenderest gaze. A gaze that could melt steel hearts, and a way with words that often left him woozy. They'd been married for five years and each year had been more beautiful, more intimate than the one before. Of course, he'd known her far longer than that, and they'd had their disagreements and struggles. But they'd met when he was only six—she'd been ten at the time. That was only the first time she'd saved his life.

Edmond swallowed, his arm losing strength, yet somehow, nearly limp, still pressing the sword tip against his throat.

It would be so easy. He could meet her this way. Wasn't that what she believed? The Betrayed Mother would reunite them in the life to come. A hidden city of pearl and opal under undying light—they would be wed in paradise for age after age...

Maybe he had it all wrong. Maybe trying to bring her back was folly. Maybe it was up to him to leave this world behind, and perhaps she would find him in the next. It would have been so easy, too. Just a slight jerk of the wrist or jolt of the head. He'd bled before—pain was an old ally.

Dark thoughts swirled through Edmond's mind and even darker memories flooded his consciousness. The strange cracking sounds from the statue seemed to cry out with a renewed intensity as he stood there, contemplating his mortality and what little say he had in all matters concerning it. How long until he found the location of another God Grave? Was this even a God Grave? The magnificent silver statue, the layer upon layer of defense, the underwater location—it all suggested it to be the case. But nothing here could help him—nothing *would*. The gods were of no use in life, so why should they matter in death, either? His wife had been wrong after all. The Betrayed Mother didn't care. None of them did.

His fists tensed, and he swallowed, trying to steel himself. There was one way to settle the question once and for all. A flick of the wrist, a slow southern voyage—then he'd know for sure.

Another cracking sound. Then, a faint swallowing noise, followed by a quiet breath.

It took Edmond a moment to realize the sound wasn't coming from him. He opened his eyes, a prickling feeling spreading across his skin. He didn't even think to lower the sword from his neck as he turned hesitantly to face the statue.

Except, the gigantic statue was now gone. Instead, a normal-sized woman stood in the middle of a silver pond, naked and pale, staring back at him. Edmond started and dropped the snapped sword to his side. He wiped the tears from his eyes with an aggressive thrust of his wrist. His face flushed with embarrassment, while a simmering anger crept over him for feeling embarrassed. The woman, for her part, didn't seem ashamed at all—her hands stayed loosely at her sides. She watched him, scrutinizing him up and down as if somehow he were the one naked.

For his part, Edmond felt the flush creeping along his cheeks and he forced himself to meet the woman's gaze. But this, rather than honoring her modesty, seemed to exploit it. There was an open, vulnerable quality to her blackened eyes, as if he were staring into a dark well, where the woman's soul had bobbed to the surface, slick with ink and displayed for all to see. It was then that Edmond realized this was the statue—or, rather, she was the woman the statue modeled. Despite her nakedness, or, perhaps, emphasized by it, Edmond could not help but be captivated by her beauty. Her nose, thin and cherubic, turned up in a celestial arch above full lips that parted slightly. Her delicate chin curved up to high cheekbones and flawless, smooth skin. She looked to be in her early twenties and late forties all at once—a combination of age-laden eyes and fresh, lissome features. Edmond found his gaze drawn lower, down the comely curve of her breasts to the sensuous turn of her hips. His eyes lingered at her waist. In the half-light of the underground chamber it seemed to Edmond that the woman had no belly button in the pale, porcelain perfection of her skin.

Catching himself, Edmond shook his head harshly. He tried to only meet her eyes, but found the experience too unnerving, so instead he stared at her feet. The silver pool wasn't just a description of color, but of substance—liquid, melted silver drained away, tracing the sloped ground in rivulets and pouring into the alchemical lights like ink into a pot.

Quicksilver? Edmond's alchemist mind wondered as he stared at the fluid metal.

The cracking sounds had faded. The map, which he'd propped against one of the lights, was brushed aside by a trail of molten silver, and knocked to the ground where it lay, soaked in water and liquid metal. Edmond resisted an urge to reach for the map—he had a feeling he wouldn't be needing it any more.

"Who—who are you?" he said, softly, staring at her feet still. The last of the silver had drained away completely, and the woman's feet were—perhaps unsurprisingly at this point—flawless like the rest of her. There were no calluses or cracks or overgrown toenails. There was no sign of sunstains or weathering.

For a brief moment, his mind was drawn elsewhere. To a small coastal town, his toes buried in the sand, those of his wife intertwined in his. Both of them had been badly burned that day—she had a thin scar all along her right foot—where she'd once stepped on a rusted ox collar while walking barefoot through the shallows. He could almost taste her laughter, her warmth as she'd nuzzled into his shoulder.

He withdrew from the memory, however, as the woman walked slowly towards him. The moment she stopped, two paces between them, Edmond finally looked up to meet her gaze.

"Who are you?" he repeated. As he spoke, he hurriedly removed the jacket from his shoulders and tossed it to her. The woman sniffed as the sodden, ripped fabric arched past her and thumped to the ground.

GRAVEYARD GODS

"Please," Edmond swallowed. "Put that on."

When the woman at last spoke, her voice was soft, nearly faint. She wasn't whispering, but rather her voice itself seemed faded, reluctant even, the sort of voice one had to attend to fully to hear. Edmond found himself leaning in to listen. "Would you have me answer your question or don your garb?"

"I wouldn't oppose either," said Edmond, finding his own voice softening to match hers. He was all too aware of his own loud breathing, echoing in his head as if his ears were plugged. He tried to breathe softly, to match the tone of her voice, but instead cut off his breath prematurely and found himself gasping to draw another to compensate for it.

The woman, almost reluctantly, turned towards his coat, her midnight black hair spilling past her shoulders and shifting with her steps. Edmond looked away quickly as she made to reach for the jacket. He gave it a moment before looking back. Finally, when he did, he was relieved to find that the jacket covered her down to her thighs and she'd buttoned it closed.

"Sand and damp," she said, wrinkling her nose and moving her arms beneath the fabric of her new jacket. "Are we beneath the ocean?"

Edmond nodded. "Now for my first question," he said, meeting her eyes again. "Who are you?"

"Mirastious," she said, without blinking.

Edmond felt the prickle return to his spine. "I—I would ask you if you were joking, but I suspect I know the answer. It isn't often one finds sightly women trapped in underwater crypts. Are you really though? Mirastious, the goddess of secrets?"

He said this last half to himself, and half to the open air. Regardless of what she said she was, her mere presence here told Edmond she was dangerous. Normal women don't rest in magical statues beneath the waves.

The woman nodded once. "I was dead," she said. "Or as close as a goddess can find herself—mindless, powerless, ensnared in silver." She glanced towards the map, then towards the alchemical lights that had drained the molten metal. "And what of you? What is the name of my rescuer?"

At this, Edmond frowned. He'd been struggling to gather his thoughts, to make sense of it all. Now, though, at these words, some of the anger he'd previously felt began to return, seeping into his mind like chilled liquid into a sponge. "I'm no rescuer of gods-er-goddesses," he said. "I didn't—" he licked his lips, and cleared his throat, "I didn't *know* that you would be freed. To be frank, I didn't even know you *could* be freed."

"Well, I am now," she said with a shrug. "You must have spoken the unbinding words—the song crafted in the Godforge itself. I was undone, but you have reforged me. I am in your debt."

"I didn't speak any words," said Edmond. He looked down at the displaced scrap of leather, realization piecing together his words as he spoke. "The alchemical lights shone through the map, reflecting words onto the statue. The statue melted. It was unintentional."

"I see," Mirastious said, looking down at the alchemical lights scattered about the floor. As she looked back up to Edmond she gave a demure smile. "Unintentional heroes are still worthy of reward," she said, softly. "What would you have? Gold?

Land? Titles? Take me from here and I can bestow any of them to you."

Edmond scratched his jaw, eyeing her skeptically. "Don't much care for gold or land. Gold makes enemies. Land makes pretentious enemies." Mirastious turned her head, her eyes narrowing slightly as she appraised Edmond. "Titles I have aplenty, you wouldn't believe the tripe they give away titles for. No, there's really only one title I value. 'Free man'. Accidentally reviving a god? That's one thing. To intentionally free one from her crypt?" Edmond twisted his hands in front of his chest as if they were tied. "Sorry. No thank you. Good luck with your next rescuer."

The woman's jaw stiffened. She stared unblinking at him. "You won't leave me here." It wasn't a question, but neither was it accompanied by god-like wrath. Edmond folded his arms.

"You're a goddess," he said. "I'm sure you can take care of yourself. An immortal can't be killed. I suppose it makes sense. But unless you know how to revive the *truly* dead—a mortal—then you're of no use to me."

The cavalier way in which he said this caused Mirastious to bristle. "I cannot revive the dead," she said. "I'm the goddess of secrets, not death."

Edmond shrugged. As astonishing as this all was, he started to get worried. His moment of darkness had passed, and now he wanted to escape this crypt unscathed. The contents of the squid-monster's stomach suggested that Fiora had suffered a similar fate to her brother, and Edmond didn't want to be the third to fall prey. A resurrected goddess did little to help him. In fact, it worried him. He didn't know what a goddess of secrets was capable of, and he didn't want to stay to find out.

Some stories, no matter how amazing, were meant for other ears. In Edmond's estimation, this was one such tale. The sooner he could extricate himself from the goddess' presence, the better. Seven years he'd spent, but he'd learned some things along the way. The patch-cloak peddler in Trabson who'd sold him *this* map had suggested he might be able to acquire more. Edmond would have to make a return trip. This was a delay—not a dead end. He couldn't afford to think otherwise. And while Edmond had little interest in treasure, the peddler had exhibited no such aversion. Edmond hefted the jeweled sword in his hand, grimacing at the broken blade. The gem-crusted scabbard would go well with it. At the very least it would help pay passage back to Carabas.

As Edmond turned and began extricating the gemmed-scabbard from where he'd kicked it beneath a pitcher of silver, the goddess called after him. "Wait a moment, mortal, you can't leave me here."

Edmond shrugged. "Bet I can."

"No—you don't understand. Don't you know who I am?"

Edmond nodded once, his back still to her. "The familiarity mostly cements my decision."

"Who is your god? It isn't Ageron is it? Nepir? Mercusi? Pardi? Who?" There was a slight sneer to her voice.

"No god," said Edmond. Spotting one of the swords he had thrown on the pile earlier, he dropped the broken blade and sheathed the new sword. As he hefted the scabbard, he found it had a pleasing weightiness to it.

"You're godless—but—but..."

Edmond glanced back at Mirastious. "Who is your god?"

"I—I don't have one. I *am* a goddess."

Edmond shrugged as he picked through the pile of treasure. "Fat good that's done you. Well, I don't have one either. Never found one I much liked, to be honest. My wife did, once, but that did little to help either of us."

"Your wife? She's a beautiful woman, no doubt?" Edmond felt the woman's slender hand slip over his shoulder, her body suddenly very close behind his. Her breath tickled his ear as she whispered, "Is she as beautiful as me?"

"Ten times as beautiful," Edmond said without batting an eyelid, his voice full of sincerity. But as the words left his lips, a cold feeling settled in him. Voices out of memory railed, *fish-licker, drowner, briny-whore.* There had been those who thought her ugly. Shaking loose the goddesses hand with a sudden shrug, he growled, "Don't think to tempt me that way either—it won't work. A Caraban prostitute would be cheaper and leave me feeling less sickened." There was a pause. Behind him, Edmond heard Mirastious's small footfalls on the wet, stone floor as she stepped back from him. Her voice, small, almost hurt, carried none of its previous sensuality.

"You really hate us that much?"

"Yes." The word fell like a hammer, heavy and blunt. There was a pause while Edmond scratched his jaw, letting his eyes explore the shape of the room around him; looking everywhere except back at Mirastious.

"May I ask why?"

Edmond rolled his eyes with a frustrated sigh. "Yes." He squinted up towards a high, dark cranny, but realized it would be too small to make an escape through.

Mirastious waited, but when no answer was forthcoming she said, "Well?"

"Well, what?"

"You said I could ask you why you hate the gods."

"I guess I mispoke. I don't hate 'em. Not really. Just don't trust 'em. And I said you could ask. Never said I would answer. Now if you don't mind, I'm looking for a way out."

"Take me with you."

"We've been over this. No."

"Please."

"In that case, no." Edmond chanced a glance at Mirastious. She had withdrawn her hands into the sleeves of his jacket, and she seemed to be pouting. Her snow white cheeks were dimpled as she pressed her lips in a firm line. Edmond frowned a moment; she didn't seem to be breathing. Her nostrils didn't widen softly with her mouth closed to draw in precious air, nor did her chest rise and fall beneath the stained and frayed coat.

He shuddered. "Use your godly abilities," Edmond said. "If you're so deserving of worship, shouldn't you be able to handle your own escape, hmm?" Edmond made his way to the wall, checking to see if he could find any footholds or handholds. He found a particularly promising patch of rock wall and began rubbing his hands against the driest parts in preparation. His wrist was still cracked, though. Growling, he removed his sword, preparing to cut through the leather on the hem of his pants to wrap his arm.

"I can't," she said. "They're—they're gone."

There was such a note of despair and sadness to the goddess' soft, understated words, that Edmond couldn't help but glance back again, eyebrow raised. "What's gone?"

She stood there staring at the ground, a deep frown crushing her brow. "My secret threads," she whispered. As she spoke she knelt down to the ground and spread her fingers across the stone floor. "I used to know where the centaur roamed and the king of the dragons slept. Now my secret creatures are dead to me. The night would whisper and tell me things. Now I cannot hear its voice." She lifted a pinch of sand from the floor, looking at it closely. "The skeletons in human closets were mine to pillage and resurrect, but now all I find is dust." Letting the sand fall from her fingers, she swallowed and looked up. "I may yet live, but what made me goddess once is now gone. I've been unmade."

Edmond paused a moment, considering the words. "You may no longer be a goddess. These things are beyond my comprehension. But I'm a tomb raider, a grave robber—unless you have something to offer me beyond a pitiable tale, I'll be on my way." He ripped the leather from the hem of his pants and began to wrap it around his wrist.

There was a moment's silence, and for a second Edmond hoped she'd left him to it. But then the unmade goddess was on him, her lips nearly touching his ear. "I may not hear the night, and my will in the dark is lost—but I still *remember*," she said. Up close, her voice no longer felt faint, nor did it require much attention. It was the sort of voice designed to be heard in close quarters or in rooms with shuttered windows. "I know things—things that can help you. You speak of a beautiful wife—yet your voice is laden with bitter balm and tended by a dagger's winnowing edge. She was lost, this woman, this rare beauty—yes?" Edmond didn't stiffen, he didn't gasp. He allowed nothing in his bearing to betray his thoughts, though one hand, out of sight from Mirastious, curled around the pommel of his newly acquired blade. She continued, now her lips actually did touch the top of his ear, grazing down the side as she deposited honeyed words in his furtive mind. "You speak of undoing death. You speak of raising a mortal soul. This—this I cannot do. *But* there is one who can. The gates to the other side are locked and sealed—an abyss stretches from here to there as large as the world is wide. Yet there is one who can cross. The Nameless. The Unspoken. The Black Horseman of Winter Winds."

"Death?" Edmond said, softly.

"The king of our order—the god of gods." She gave a languid shrug. "Allegiances are always shifting in the pantheon," Mirastious said primly, an edge to her voice. "My imprisonment here confirms, I am victim to such shifting sands myself. Who called for my death, I do not know. I was taken while reclining

GRAVEYARD GODS

beneath the Wise Oak, watching the lightning flies of Valeer. My memory is empty from then until now."

"Huh, so the gods are a bunch of infighting traitors," said Edmond. "Little surprise there. I don't see how—"

"Not all of them. Some are conniving and duplicitous, others do care for the mortal kind. But what concerns you need not be the politics of the pantheon, but rather the gifts they give to the mortal world. No—stay your tongue, before your protest. I do not mean boons given in prayer, but rather arrangements. Arrangements that have occurred for nearly fifty years now... hold—what year is it?"

"The five hundred and fifty-fifth year of Agreon's Ire."

Mirastious didn't falter, but corrected herself as she continued. "An arrangement of seventy-five years, then. I've only been in torpor for twenty-five. I suppose I should count myself lucky. Little more than a nap for my kind; but still, my assassin will pay."

"This arrangement of seventy-five years—why should such a thing interest me?" Something in the cadence of her voice lulled him, trance-like, to listen. He held his breath and leaned in close.

She spoke slowly now, savoring her words, tasting each one as it left her mouth. "Every five years, the Emperor of your kingdom is given a gift: one soul from beyond the grey. One mortal. The Nameless has gone to extraordinary lengths to keep the arrangement secret—hidden. Though, I'm Mirastious," here her voice strengthened with a quiet pride. "To hide things from my sight is folly from the offset."

"Maybe that's why you were killed," Edmond murmured. "No one likes a tell-all."

His words seemed to trouble Mirastious and she took a step back. He glanced over to see a frown spread across her flawless features.

"Does it trouble you?" he said. "To be at odds with Death himself, I mean. His reputation isn't exactly for benevolence. In fact, *why* would he grant a mortal anything? Emperor or not—the gods don't care about station. Leastwise, that's what I'm told. Death comes for all of us."

"I know not," said Mirastious. "I was looking into it, in fact, when I was killed." The disturbed look grew, but almost in an effort to pass it off to Edmond, she shot him a look and said, "I do not lie, though. It is true. Every five years The Nameless returns a mortal soul to your emperor."

"A fascinating claim," said Edmond. "But I do not know Baltasar II. He is no friend of mine. A gift given to him is of little use to me."

Mirastious chuckled softly, a sound that sent goosebumps scattering up Edmond's arms. "It is not a boon for Baltasar, but one for the emperor, no matter who holds the throne. But you seem an influential sort. Could you not claim the emperor's ear? Perhaps he'd give you your beloved back?"

Her words seemed to hang in the air, and in one dizzying moment, a million questions erupted through Edmond's mind. Every wheel, every gear in his brain started churning at once. Pieces of plans, fragments of strategy sifted through his mind. Here he stood, speaking to a resurrected god in an undersea crypt. Seven years ago, such an idea would have been

GRAVEYARD GODS

laughable. What other impossibility could be accomplished in seven years time? Could he befriend an emperor? Could he gain the ear of Baltasar II? An invisible ladder began to form in his mind. Ranks and titles piled past each other. Faces and names whirled and coalesced, all of them bringing him higher up the ladder, closer to the Emperor.

Edmond's father had been a minor noble—a reeve, the lowest rank of nobility. Edmond himself had even trained, briefly, as a knight. But the emperor had thousands of knights who bent a knee to his reign. Then what about a Baron? Could Edmond pass off as one of those? But no, Baron's controlled just land. In the Gilded Isles, it was the ship owners who were considered most powerful and who possessed the most sway. Lord Captain, then? Perhaps even Commodore. Admiral—well, admiral was simply out of the question. There were only six islands, each of them run by one of the admirals. He couldn't trick his way into their closed ranks—it was impossible.

But what was impossible? He was standing in the room with a goddess. Even among the devout, few had ever claimed to see the beings they worshiped.

Edmond exhaled softly through his nose. It was two straws short from a half a chance. No betting man would have placed so much as a flea's leg on Edmond's likelihood of success. But, he could scheme—it was his greatest gift. He could plot, and he could trick. He was an alchemist, after all...

"Mira," he said slowly, "You don't mind if I call you Mira, do you?" Mirastious frowned and started to shake her head as Edmond cut her off. "Good. How do I know you're telling the truth? A goddess of secrets would seem to me to be a goddess of guile."

"I want you to help me escape from here," she said, slowly. "But also, if you are able to gain the ear of an emperor; it isn't too much of a stretch to gain purchase in the pantheon itself. Remember, the Nameless wants to keep his arrangement se cret..."

Edmond frowned, peering at her for a moment, but then realization struck him. "I see," he said. "You would use me to get close, then blackmail Nameless Death to return you to your position?"

"All things in this world drift toward their purpose. I am a goddess. I am ill-suited to constraints."

"With a face like that you wouldn't be powerless long—not among the isles. Beauty is its own weapon."

"So you *do* find me attractive?" Mirastious teased. Edmond raised a hand in protest, but the goddess smirked, waving it away. "Don't worry. I am very good at keeping secrets, after all." Her eyes flashed wickedly, and she said, "You are right though. Beauty is a weapon, perhaps one I could use. Yet still, I wish to be restored. And yes, I would use you to do so. As you would use me. As I said, I remember many secrets."

Edmond's lips had suddenly gone dry; he licked them, tracing the cracks with his tongue. "Fine," he said. "I'll help you escape, if what you say is true. Though I'm afraid your insistence is insufficiently convincing."

He reached towards her sharply and Mirastious flinched. Edmond held up a placating hand and gestured towards the jacket's front pocket. "May I?" he said. She inclined her head, hesitantly. Careful not to press too hard, he fished a small cloth pouch from inside the jacket, pulling two green stems boasting bell-shaped leaves from the front pocket. Hurrying over to the scattered loot, he reached for one of the sealed silver jugs. "As long as it has a bite to it," he murmured, before smashing the jar against the ground. It took him another couple of swings, but finally the seal cracked and dark liquid began to dribble from opening.

Edmond held it up and sniffed. Then, he licked at the liquid and smacked his lips. "Far finer fare than necessary, but it'll do." He grabbed the pewter goblet and placed the bell-shaped leaves in it, followed by a healthy measure of the dark liquid spilling from the jar. "Two stems of badger's ear, a finger of whiskey—mead will have to do. Let's say," he paused, his eyes flitting with internal calculations, "three fingers of the mead... And, finally, a drop of blood from someone speaking truest truth."

Edmond reached for his new sword, pulled it an inch from the scabbard, then pressed a finger against the exposed edge of the blade. He inhaled deeply through his nose, then said, "My name is Edmond Mondego—Ailsa's river gift. I would do anything to reclaim her. It's the truest truth I know." Then, he jerked his finger across the blade. Quickly, lest he lose the precious drops, he held his hand over the goblet, collecting the ruby droplets of blood and allowing them to mix with the ancient mead and badger's ear. Once he'd accumulated the desired amount, he gripped the goblet with his bleeding hand and used the pommel of his sword to grind the mixture, swirling it around.

Now for the dangerous bit, Edmond thought, lowering the sword to take the goblet in both hands. All alchemy came from the alchemist themselves, and even the finest potions were useless without intent. No amount of knowledge, secret recipes, or exotic ingredients would matter without the will to achieve. Still gripping the goblet, Edmond focused his mind; a truth serum—simple enough. He could feel his fingers buzzing where they touched the goblet, the contents of the cup bowing to his will, rearranging themselves to meet their maker's desires.

With a rushing hiss, he felt the metal heating in his hands. Edmond opened his eyes, peering through ghostly coils of steam rising from the goblet to the goddess. He extended the cup to her. "Drink," he said. "It will tell me the truth."

"A Serum of True-Telling," Mira said with a note of admiration. "Brave of you to use your own blood, even transmuted in the serum. The things a person can do with someone's blood and a little know-how..." Letting the implication hang, Mira took the goblet, swirling it under her nose, inhaling the scent while she mused.

"Stop stalling," said Edmon. "It's no longer my blood. The alchemy changes it to suit the alchemist. Drink."

Mira raised an eyebrow, "You fancy yourself quite the alchemist, then?" She closed her eyes, holding the goblet close, like a hot cup of tea on a cold winter's night. "I know many hidden formulas, you know—I remember them still. I could teach you, if you—"

"Just drink. If you want me to help you escape this place, to help restore you to the pantheon, I must know the truth of the matter. With an extended finger, he pushed the goblet insistently towards her, watching sharply in case she tried anything at the last minute.

Shrugging, Mira took one final smell off the steaming cup, then tilted it, drinking it whole. Black liquid dribbled from the corners of her lips, spilling down her chin and tracing the slope of her neck. Once she drank the serum in full, she tossed the goblet aside and met Edmond's gaze. As Edmond watched, her eyes flashed, and she said, "Ask me your questions. I spoke only truth."

Meeting her challenging stare, Edmond felt a twinge of...of something welling in his chest. He frowned before realizing what it was: hope. As he peered into Mira's eyes, he realized that he believed her. However incredible it seemed, she was telling the truth about the emperor's boon, about Death's secret pact, about her motives... Had he found an ally in a god? Had he found the next step to his plan?

Instinct alone was insufficient proof, however. Edmond cleared his throat, and said, "Answer every question without hesitation. If you try to deceive me, the potion won't allow it. It will hurt you, badly. Understand?"

Mira nodded, unblinking. "As I said, I spoke only truth. I have nothing to hide."

We'll see about that, Edmond thought, then he launched his inquisition.

Chapter 8

THE GODDESS MIRASTIOUS SAT at the prow of the dogger, and Edmond sat in the center, rowing them steadily towards shore. The frigate could still be glimpsed, but far in the distance, still obscured by fog. They had floated back to the surface far from where Edmond and the pearl divers had initially been sunk. Both Edmond and Mira were sopping wet, and sea water slicked every surface in the dogger. The plug had been returned to the hole in the bottom of the hull, and the capsule of compressed air Edmond released in the overturned boat did a fine job floating her back to the surface with them. The sudden drive to the surface had torn the sail free of the mast, but the oars were still secured where he had tied them.

The goddess was surprisingly good at following directions. She had not questioned him, nor did she hesitate. His new-found companion seemed as eager as he to leave the crypt behind them. Even escaping the labyrinth and the monster within had been easy enough.

GRAVEYARD GODS

When he'd described the creature to Mira, she'd shrugged, nonplussed, and informed him, "I know what you speak of. It's a marid of an ancient line. A hidden, depths-bound fiend that found its way through some crack in failed alchemy hundreds of years ago, long before I was entombed. It tracks mostly by sound, and is incredibly nearsighted. Mortals call it a fourth-tier demon—but the thing knows itself only as—" and here she made a strange moaning noise that set Edmond's teeth together.

He'd been half tempted to ask her how she knew all this, but then quickly remembered who he was speaking to. Perhaps the goddess of secrets, stripped of all her powers save her memory, wouldn't be completely useless to him. Though it was a close thing—in all other aspects, especially physical, she was as useless as an infant. Edmond had tried to instruct her in climbing the rock face to the hole in the ceiling of the silver room, but she lacked every manner of coordination and strength. In the end, he'd been forced to lash her to his back with the scabbard belt and make the climb himself. Had she not been so slight, he never would have managed it. Thankfully, the thirty foot climb to the gash in the ceiling hadn't been too taxing.

Then, they'd set to crawling upwards through the slick chute. Nearly three times, Mira slipped and fell, forcing Edmond to catch her and drag her along like a wetted pup. He supposed it made sense—a goddess likely had servants to do the more physical labor at her behest. Additionally, she'd been ensnared in the silver statue for coming on twenty five years now. That was almost as long as Edmond had been alive. But still, it didn't irk him any less, when she'd asked him to carry her through the water in the tunnels. He'd flat out refused, and she'd pouted—though, still without protest—as they crept quietly through the crypt, up the spiral staircase, and back to the entrance of the tomb.

She hadn't even known how to swim to reach the dogger; Edmond had been forced to drag her along, again like some hapless child, pulling her through the murk.

Now, as they sat gasping in the newly righted boat, Edmond rowing with steady strokes, Mira sat with a poised grace, wringing out her dark hair as if she'd simply stepped out of a bath. The fact that she seemed unperturbed by the morning air while he shivered with cold only irked him further.

"We'll set in before dawn," Edmond said. "I'll find you some proper clothes—something warm. But, we won't be able to stay long... I rented a room in Sile. We'll want to be gone before morning."

Mira nodded as though listening, but did not seem to be paying him much mind. Instead, she scanned the still surface of the sea around them, frowning as she did. A couple of times she yawned as if something were wrong with her ears, but this only deepened her frown.

"What's the matter?" said Edmond.

"It's so very quiet. How come the ocean isn't speaking? How come the wind isn't whispering. The clouds are often chattiest of them all."

Edmond shook his head, but didn't know how to answer this, so he didn't. Forming a friendship with a god wasn't high on his to-do list. However, the truth serum had verified his gut reaction: Mira had been telling the truth. Every five years, the

GRAVEYARD GODS

Nameless One would bestow a mortal soul back to the world at the Emperor's request.

How Edmond would reach the emperor, or convince the man to use his boon for Edmond's sake was beyond him, but it was the surest glimmer of hope he'd had in a long time. Edmond was nothing if not resourceful.

They'd rest a little back at the inn, then leave town before any of the pearl divers' cousins could come calling. After that, he'd start to plan. Already, he could feel schemes formulating at the corners of his mind. But now, all there was to do was row. So row he did.

Chapter 9

Augustin stood at the prow of his ship while the *Intrepid* cut its way through the cold waters. The sails snapped overhead, and he stared up at the Imperial flag as it caught the wind high over the frigate's deck. The flag's red and gold stripes were muted in the early dawn light, but the blue heron stitched into its center couldn't be missed.

Order, Augustin thought as he looked at the Emperor's sigil, a symbol of the dynasty's power over the Gilded Isles. The blue heron was order. It was power; an iron band that held the empire together like a well-fitted barrel. Without it? Chaos. Augustin took a deep breath of the salty air. The Emperor oversaw the Admirals, each to his own island. The Admirals empowered the Commodores to their own coasts and counties. The Commodores to the Lord Captains, and the Lord Captains to their ships to keep the peace in the multitudinous baronies of the Gilded Isles.

Peace. Augustin's thoughts turned to the previous night's events, and he closed his eyes. The image of the robber's dogger slipping away into the mist played behind his eyelids, and Augustin ground his teeth. *A trick. A base and cowardly trick.* To have that thief slip within sight and then disappear into the haze, all while making him believe the dogger was sunk, infuriated him to a degree Augustin had not felt in years. It reminded him of his time as a squire taking lumps from wooden practice swords he was wholly unprepared to parry. He had learned from those bruises and grown with them. He could do the same now.

Unless the Commodore strips you of your office. The thought set Augustin into a firm scowl. It was possible. The nobles frequently exploited each others' failures to promote people of their own choosing; to put some toadie or other into a position of authority. Augustin was reminded of his own mother's contributions in attaining his captainship. The thought did not sooth his wounded pride, and he forced himself to focus on his breath, driving the thought away. No matter the circumstances, he had failed, and he knew what his duty now demanded.

His fingers tightened around the shimmering sheet of alchemical parchment in his hand, setting the crinkling paper popping like the sound of a fireplace, and Augustin had to force himself to relax his grip. A single sheet of mirror paper cost nearly as much as the fine steel sword at his hip, and they had to be made in pairs for their alchemy to work.

Trespassers within the forbidden waters, he had written in ink mixed with quicksilver the previous night, hunched over the sparse desk in his cabin. *Descended into depths before escaping. Please advise.* As he stood from the desk, words had returned, alchemically rearranging the ink on the parchment. The speed of the reply had unnerved him, almost as if Severelle had been waiting for such news.

Your trespassers have robbed a God Grave. Confirmed by alchemical alarm. Come give your report, Lord Captain. The coordinates of the Commodore's flagship appeared in the swirling ink, and Edmond had set out, more troubled than before. A God Grave—beneath the sea? He had heard about such places before, from Isobella. At the time he had hung on every word the alluring hellcatcher told him.

"No, Augustin, it's a poetic title. The god's cannot die," she had told him, lounging beneath an olive tree in one of Gamor's narrow valleys. "It's just a place. Like a temple. The cenobic custodii say—"

"The see-no, what now?" he'd laughed, running a hand through the dark curls of her hair.

"Cenobic custodii. They're like hellcatcher librarians. They keep the order's records and advise the arch-hellcatchers. Anyway, even they can't say what the God Graves were made for, but every instance has *powerful* alchemy attached to it. That means, there is always a chance that some nasty demon will suddenly appear, and we have to be ready."

"Where are they? The God Graves? Sounds like good place for treasure," a younger Augustin said from within the memory.

"Don't you dare," Isobella said, giving him a slap on the arm. "Only the custodii and the Arch's know. For everyone's protection. If a hellcatcher were to let that secret slip, well, let's say demons would be the least of their problems."

"Aww, you're no fun. Think of it. We get to slay some demons, rescue some long lost treasure, and go live the rest of our lives like the Emperor, in a Caraban villa." He waggled his hawkish eyebrows, and Isobella laughed at him, slipping her hand over his chest as she rolled to straddle his waist.

"You are a rebel and a villain, Sir Augustin Mora," she said, pulling open the laces of his shirt.

He smiled back at her. "The others will be here soon," he warned.

"Oh, this is the challenge that frightens you?" she laughed, "I know they'll be back soon. Don't worry," she said leaning down to nip at his ear, "You can make it up to me later."

God Graves. He shook his head, setting down the memory with an almost reverential gentleness.

And what sort of person would dare to desecrate one? So much of the previous night still troubled him. Augustin opened his eyes and gripped his rapier's hilt, the gleaming sweep of the hilt's complex hand-guard felt cool in his fingers.

Ahead, the mist of the sea parted and the sunlight cast a shimmering cloak over the surface of the water. A dark shape, like a rocky island rising out the sea, loomed ahead of them. It cast long shadows from enormous towers that rose from its spine. It was a ship. The gargantuan frame dwarfed the *Intrepid* like a great whale beside a codfish, and even in the dim light, the metallic gleam of the iron plates that lined the massive ship could be seen twinkling against the water.

"Lord Cap'n, titan, ho!" a crewman called from the frigate's crow's nest.

No sense in delaying. Augustin folded his hands behind his back. Turning to the crew he called, in a crisp voice of command, "Mirrors and lanterns. In this dim I want no misunderstandings. Crewmaster Agreo, signal our approach."

As the *Intrepid* drew against the titan, the shadow of the larger vessel fell over the frigate and wrapped it in a darkness. A chill seeped into Augustin's skin as he waited for the larger craft to lower a gangplank. He looked around and saw Cristobal hurrying his way. Past the big man, Catali, the young surgeon, caught Augustin's eye and nodded across the ship. Crewmaster Agreo stood on the far side, where Catali had nodded, and Augustin saw the portly man had a small gathering of crewmen around him. He seemed to be making some joke as most were laughing. When he caught Augustin staring at him, the round crewmaster folded his arms and cocked his head in a bitter grin as if he were daring Augustin to approach. Several of the crew around him followed his gaze, a few looked away hurriedly while others folded their arms in solidarity with Agreo.

That's not good. Augustin thought. He held Agreo's gaze for a long moment until the man turned back to his crewmates. He seemed to say something in a low voice that earned him a few more harsh laughs while the men stole nervous glances at Augustin.

"Lord Cap'n," Cristobal said as he joined Augustin in the shade of the titan. Augustin turned his head, to look for the young surgeon again, but Catali was gone.

"Less than two weeks and I'm already a joke. Isn't that what they are saying?" Augustin felt the exhaustion in his own voice, and Cristobal looked down at him appraisingly. He didn't want the big man's pity, but he needed to know how bad it was. Insubordination cast a dark and unpleasant shadow on any company, whether over land or by sea.

With a resigned sigh, the big man said, "I'd hoped after the cold threat you gave Agreo last night he'd be calmed, but," Cristobal gave a lopsided shrug as his stiff left shoulder drooped, "I think after that dogger got away-well, he's jumped on the chance to undercut the meager respect you've gathered. Sir." This much Augustin expected. He craned his neck to the side stretching it with a series of pops. Cristobal continued, "We need to get the Order back together."

An elaborately engraved wooden stairway descended from the titan's deck. It angled sharply as the vessel's walls stood nearly twice as high as the *Intrepid*'s, and Augustin stepped back to allow it space to land.

"Two days to Carabas," Augustin muttered.

Cristobal nodded thoughtfully, "It's been two days to Carabas for nearly a week." He turned to face Agreo and his cohort of chortling crewmen. "I'll keep an eye on them, but the sooner we can gather the Order the better. When the six of us fought together-"

"I know." Augustin put a foot on the stepped gangplank. "Together, we slew a hundred men at Borgo Tortrugha," he said with a wry smile. "You'd think you and I could handle one pissant sailor."

Cristobal turned up one meaty palm as he said in his flat, heavy voice, "You could always challenge him to a duel. It's worked in the past."

Augustin shook his head and suppressed a laugh as he ascended the gangplank onto the titan. He spared one final glance over his shoulder. He found Agreo casually leaning on a nearby swivel gun, pushing it vaguely in the direction of the gangplank stair. He didn't look at Augustin, but instead angled himself to be pointedly not looking where he aimed the small cannon.

Get to Carabas. Get the Order onboard.

A pair of knights in clean, green linen uniforms met Augustin at the top of the gangplank. They wore gleaming steel helmets with dark green shrouds trailing over their necks and shoulders. Sabres tightly secured at their hips, they clicked their boots together as they saluted him.

"Lord Captain Mora, Commodore Severelle has asked us to escort you to his office."

Augustin nodded, and the knights turned on their heels, leading him at a brisk pace across the deck of the titan.

Their path across the deck turned at several points, broken up by large metal tubes nearly as big around as Augustin was tall. These were mounted into wood and steel bases. Around him, Augustin saw the wood and leather frames of ornithopters. A few of the flying machines had their bat-like wings extended to the full twenty feet and were lined up with painted stripes that ran at a hard angle across the flat deck of the titan. An engineer in a leather apron tinkered with an iron cylinder that hung low in one of the ornithopter frames. Augustin's eyes trailed across the dismantled flying contraption as they passed. The alchemical machines had always intrigued him, but they were so expensive to maintain that he had never seen one actually in use before. The in-land barons could little afford such extravagances and tended to prefer the horse and lance over alchemical machinations.

Drawing his attention back to his escort, the bridge of the ship rose in front of Augustin like a fortress. As they neared wood and iron walls, the knights shuffled him onto a platform framed with a waist-high, metal lattice bound by a strong chain at each corner. One of his escorts reached out and rang a bell that hung from the iron lattice-work, sounding three rapid peals. The chains went taut, and the platform began to rise. The sensation made Augustin's stomach drop, and he clasped his hands in front of his waist to steady himself. As they rose higher and higher, he began to see the true scope of the titan. It stretched out around him like a war camp. Dozens of ornithopters of varying size and shapes lay arranged in orderly lines, while contingents of soldiers bearing spears and muskets marched three abreast between them. From above, the large metal tubes took on the form of gargantuan pepperbox revolvers turned on their sides. Well acquainted with cannon and musket, Augustin was surprised he had not seen it at once. They were spaced along the center of the deck, allowing three lanes of ornithopters to run between them and for the guns to swivel and fire to either side of the ship. From his vantage, the military efficiency of the design and the confident fluidity of the soldiers' movements below gave him a feeling of assurity. It was order made manifest, a clockwork of hearts and minds working in concert for the good of the Empire. Beyond the titan, just slipping in through the edge of the mist, sailed a four-masted galleon. Augustin recognized it as the broad-hulled sort of ship the Empire used for moving gold and silver around the empire, and its hull glimmered in the dewy air almost as brightly as its cargo. Flanking the fat galleon, two Imperial Frigates, like the *Intrepid*, moved like loyal hounds at their master's heels. An underwhelming escort given the state of the seas. Once again, Augustin thought of the pirate clans as he scanned the mist that swirled around the approaching galleon.

When the elevator stopped, Augustin followed his escort through a series of hallways into the fortress core of the ship. At a carved wood door, the knights paused and knocked. A muted voice called out from within, and the knight opened the door, stepping aside to allow Augustin through.

Just give Severelle your report. Tell him you have it under control and get back to your ship. Two days to Carabas. You can fix this before Isobella's father ever finds out. You can capture the tomb-robber before Admiral Morecraft ever need know.

As Augustin stepped through the portal he saw a well appointed room with red carpet and a weighty wooden desk. A large window took up most of the back wall, and he could see the mist of the surrounding sea from his place just inside the door. Beside the desk stood a man so thin and lanky that his silhouette might be mistaken for a wind-stripped birch tree. He wore an embroidered silk shirt with the blue sash of a Commodore about his shoulder. Augustin made a neat bow. .

"Commodore Severelle."

The man turned his rat-like face towards Augustin. His drawn features crinkled, showing every crease and wrinkle across his bald head and cheeks. His jaw carried a feeble attempt at a beard that drew into a sliver of inky black hair hanging like a dark icicle from his chin. Now that Augustin was a

Lord Captain, the man was his direct commander. *And my mother's current plaything.* Augustin coughed to suppress the reflexive gag he always felt in the man's presence. This was his commander. Regardless of how the arrangement had come about and as little as Augustin cared for the man personally, he was still the next link in the chain of command. Severelle nodded to him.

"Lord Captain Mora, a pleasure as always. Are you prepared to give your report?" the Commodore inquired with a voice that was half a whistle. Something lurked in the question that made Augustin hesitate a moment before he spoke.

Just give your report so you can go fix it. "I am, Commodore."

"Good." Severelle gave a crooked smile and gestured behind Augustin to the corner of the room. "I hope you don't mind, but since his Grace, the Admiral of Gamor, was aboard, I invited him to sit in on your report. He says the Emperor has a keen interest in these waters of late." A bolt of nervous energy shot through Augustin. He turned his head to follow Severelle's gesture as the Admiral stepped forward.

"Your Grace." The soldier in him pushed Augustin through the phrase and kept his bow precise and proper, but within, his heart pounded as shock threw his mind into disorder. Why was Morecraft here? Just coincidence? Bad luck? The one man he had hoped to keep the shame of his failure hidden from, the man whose daughter he hoped to wed, and here he stood to hear the account from his own lips.

The aged Admiral waved a calloused hand. "Rise," he said. Augustin stood. Light from the window caught the large golden chain that hung around his neck and set it aflame against the Gamorian red of his doublet. The Admiral's wrinkled face scrunched, pushing a line of scars up from his jaw to stand like furrows in the white field of his beard. He ran an appraising eye over Augustin, and he wondered if the Admiral remembered who he was.

He will remember now, Augustin thought grimly. He'll not forget the young Lord Captain who allowed a God Grave to be robbed from seas the Emperor himself marked as forbidden.

Augustin locked his hands behind his back and fell into the straight backed posture of a professional knight. This apparently pleased the Admiral as his lips cracked in a small smile.

"At ease, Lord Captain. I see that you were not simply knighted in title, isn't that so?"

"Yes, your Grace. I was squired to Baron Colinas and knighted on the battlefield at Trelliman's Folly."

"You're one of Colinas' boys?" The Admiral stepped closer. The scent of oranges and salt wafted from the older man's clothing as he looked at Augustin more carefully. "I know your face."

Severelle spoke up. His nettling voice seemed to spike in the same way a cat meows in search of attention. "Your Grace may remember the Lord Captain from the tournament grounds. He was quite the celebrity several years back." Recognition dawned on the Admiral's face, and his neatly-trimmed, white eyebrows shot up.

"Of course." He clapped Augustin's shoulder and let out an explosive laugh that seemed to fill the entire room. "You're that young spitfire that kept sweeping the prizes in the melee. There was a name they used to call you. What was it again?"

"The Wasp," Augustin said. He managed to keep the excitement from his voice. *Admiral Morecraft knows me. He remembered me.*

"That was it!" Admiral Morecraft pointed a finger from Augustin to Severelle. Augustin was taken aback; he had only met the Admiral once before, but he got the impression he was a singularly severe man. His boisterous laugh shattered the image, and Augustin wondered for a moment if he was thinking of the right person. He lost the thread of the conversation as the Admiral started into a story about tournament jousting from his own youth. His ears were ringing, but Augustin managed a weak chuckle in response to Morecraft's enthusiasm. This was everything he hoped a formal meeting with the Admiral would be. Praise. Admiration. Laughter. Comradery.

And I'm going to destroy all of it. Augustin felt like there was a pistol at his back, and he simply waited for someone to pull the trigger. Commodore Severelle turned back toward Augustin.

"Well, let's have your report," he said. His rat face twitched with irritation, and Augustin felt he must have missed something.

Focus, he told himself. Augustin cleared his throat and started to speak. While he relayed the events of the previous night, it felt as though he detached from his body. He left his anxiety far below and let the soldier take over. He spoke in a clear clip that described each stage in simple detail, telling them everything from the sighting of the dogger in forbidden waters to the sinking, resurrection, and escape of the vessel.

Admiral Morecraft listened. His expressive eyes turned to flint as he watched Augustin with the impassive gaze of a gargoyle. Commodore Severelle interrupted several times to make scoffing noises, but ceased as he too become the subject of the Admiral's frigid gaze.

"He will not have gone far," Augustin concluded. "I believe I can deliver this tomb-thief to you by my next report. I would have gone after him directly, but your orders were quite clear, Commodore."

Severelle sniffed.

"It would be unnecessary to make such clarifications had the grave robber been dealt with. You say they sailed off into the mist. Who's to say where they are now that you've given up the chase." He dragged the words out, as though they left a foul taste in his mouth.

Augustin's feet shifted, and his legs tensed. "Commodore, a dogger is a fishing vessel. It can't handle the high seas."

"So?" The Commodore sneered.

"It can't go far. There is only one settlement that makes sense. Sile. Pearl divers and fishermen mostly. Even if the thief wasn't from there, they had to go through there. They'll be there or I'll have their trail. Either way, I will find them."

Outside the office, a flare of red light shot into the air and exploded in a crackling pop. They all turned and hurried to the window. Peering out, Morecraft pointed to the mist in the distance.

"Black flags," he said, a hint of satisfaction in his voice. Out from the mist several small ships flanked a larger frigate. Dark flags billowed from their masts, though Augustin failed to determine the devices on them. Sunlight glinted off the sides of the ships.

"Their guns are out," Augustin said. "Pirates. Are they trying to ambush us?" He looked to the left and the right. More ships. Dozens of them. Severelle stepped back towards his desk and sat on the edge.

"No, Lord Captain Mora, quite the opposite in fact." Severelle put a dainty hand to his lips and sniggered. "Clan Gallowglass. We knew they'd follow the mist North. They must think themselves rather clever, sneaking up on that ignorant, unsuspecting galleon."

Augustin peered through the window, spotting the treasure ship he'd noticed earlier. The two frigates were still flanking it, the titan waiting off, sails stowed, hidden beyond the horizon of mist.

Severelle seemed entirely unconcerned with the approaching pirates as a metal trumpet sounded from the deck below. A series of blasts beat out a staccato rhythm of orders, and soldiers moved in hurried columns below.

"Lord Captain Mora." The Admiral's voice cut in, bereft of its previous enthusiasm. He continued to stare out at the pirate fleet as it converged on the treasure ship's escort like wolves attacking a downed doe. "How is it you intend to convince the people of Sile to cooperate with your hunt?"

The question confused Augustin, and he struggled a moment to answer. "I'm sorry, your Grace, but why wouldn't they cooperate? I'm hunting a tomb-robber. An enemy of the Empire."

Severelle gave a short derisive snort, but held his tongue. The Admiral clasped his hands behind his back and sighed.

"Empire. Yes, you're a good Emperor's man, aren't you, Lord Captain Mora?"

"Blood and bones, your Grace," Augustin said reflexively, though the question unsettled him. Outside, he heard a whirring sound like a swarm of gigantic crickets. His eyes flicked to the window and for a moment he was mesmerized by the sight of the ornithopters, their wings beating like dragonflies, sweeping across the deck and into the open air. Morecraft pointed to the black-flagged ships.

"And what about them? Your knighthood was inland so the thought may never have occurred to you, but where do you think pirates and raiders go when they finish their raids? To secret caves and mysterious islands?" The Admiral's voice blackened and Augustin felt a charge in the air like a coming lightning strike. "No. They go to the fishing villages; the small hamlets of mud farmers and pearl divers. They go back to being commoners. So I ask you again, how will you convince the villagers to give up their tomb-robbing brother?"

Augustin watched as the black-flagged ships began to turn. They were nearly in range for cannon fire, and they twisted their broadsides towards the distant galleon in a wave. He felt his stomach churning as the sight of the pirates and the weight of the Admiral's question bore down on him.

"I'm sure if I talk with them-if I explain who I am and the sort of person I'm chasing, then our mutual self-interest-"

Severelle interrupted with another sniggering laugh.

Augustin heard the groaning of metal. He strode forward and stood in the window beside the Admiral and saw the deck cannons orienting themselves to face the approaching pirates. At this distance, from their high vantage point, Augustin could distinguish the pirates, approaching the treasure ship, unwittingly setting foot in the mouth of the trap. But, at the same distance, from the lower deck of a regular-sized clipper or sloop, spotting the titan through the thicket of mist would have been difficult unless they were looking for it.

"Mutual self-interest," Morecraft said as he shifted his jaw with a click. "The commoner's interest is in little more than their blood and their bread. They have no respect for duty; no honor. Trust me, Lord Captain, order is not kept with an open hand. It is with iron and bones." The Admiral paused, and the droning of the ornithopters seemed to drown out all other sound for a moment. He inclined an eyebrow, and, in nearly a murmur, he said, "Do you remember how to use that rapier, Lord Captain?"

The titan's cannons roared as gouts of flame sprang from the long barrels. Red flashes reflected in the Admiral's grey, implacable eyes. There was a pause—a long pause—then hellfire rained from the heavens, bearing down on the mistbound ships. As Augustin looked out over the water he saw the ring of pirate vessels erupt into a blasted and burning wood reef. A cascade of musket fire fell from the ornithopters as they finally reached the enemy and strafed over the sinking ships like a flight of birds. Augustin watched the miniscule figure of a distant man run across the deck of his ship. He was wrapped in fire like a cloak and waving his arms wildly, but if he was screaming, the droning of the ornithopters and the ringing in

Augustin's ears swallowed the sound. His chest tightened and Augustin's mind tried to steady him. He thought of battles he'd fought, the blood and chaos of Borgo Tortrugha, but there was nothing to compare this with. He found himself holding his breath and when he wondered why, he realized he had just seen hundreds of men die in less than a single minute. The air grew quiet. The mountain of carnage before him slipped into the sea, releasing black smoke into the air and blacker ash into the waters. The bodies of dead pirates bobbed in the waves. Drifting like leaves on a river, they pushed their clumsy way through the flotsam and floated South. The sight sent a cold feeling in Augustin's stomach. The treasure galleon looked unharmed. The sails of the two frigates that had been escorting it bore a few new rips, but they too were mostly untouched.

Augustin couldn't help but stare in awe at the enormous titan's long guns. To be so accurate and devastating from such a distance—spewing alchemical projectiles like the unrelenting blade of Mercusi himself... Augustin shivered.

"You have one week." Severelle's declaration snapped Augustin's attention back to the office and away from the floor-to-ceiling window. The Admiral had stepped away from him, and the rat-faced Commodore held up one thin finger. "One week to bring me this tomb-robber, if you can."

That's not enough time, Augustin thought, but he couldn't bring himself to argue. Not over the droning of the ornithopters. Once more, the soldier in Augustin puppeted his body through a precise bow as his Commodore dismissed him.

GRAVEYARD GODS

***

Severelle stepped to Admiral Morecraft's elbow. "I am truly sorry, your Grace. I had high hopes for the young man. 'The Wasp'. Phe! 'The Lamb' more like. Did you see him pale at the sight of the pirates? Such a disgrace. I-"

"Silence, Pecha." Morecraft watched the debris in the sea. He would send the men to clean every scrap they could find—the rest would be claimed by Nepir. The ornithopters docked on the titan's deck, and the smoking cannons swiveled back into their original configuration. He felt the edges of a headache and thought any more of the Commodore's sycophantic fawning would cause his ears to bleed.

Morecraft took a deep breath, drawing a peel of orange from his pocket to smell. It was the only thing that seemed to help his headaches anymore. The Lord Captain presented him with an inconvenient problem. Meeting him, the man seemed more capable than the usual toadies and hangers-on that Pecha Severelle uplifted, but nonetheless, he had allowed a tomb raider to access a God Grave and escape. This was not something he could afford to take lightly.

"Pecha," The Admiral said. Severelle stepped forward again.

"Yes, your Grace?"

"No one else can know about this failure."

"Yes, your Grace."

"I want you to personally patrol the forbidden waters while Lord Captain Mora hunts for this tomb-robber. When he finds them, I want it reported to me directly."

"Your Grace, you don't seriously expect him to find the thief?" Severelle said in a tone that danced the edge of sarcasm. Morecraft shot him a dangerous look.

"My orders from the Emperor were that the forbidden waters were to be secured against any vessel. I come here and find you had a lone frigate patrolling them under the command of a Lord Captain who has never commanded a ship before." His white beard quivered as Morecraft's eyes blazed. "You should hope he finds that tomb-thief. You should hope that we can cover this whole mess up. Because if we do not find that thief and quietly float him South, I swear to Nameless Death that I will see you tormented in the deepest dungeon in Gamor for the rest of my days. Your friends and family will have forgotten your face, and your clever tongue will run out of ways to describe the menagerie of horrors that your body has become, and yet I will still be torturing you." Severelle's face blanched and he licked his lips as the Admiral turned to move towards the office's door.

"Do not fail in this."

"I'll send Muergo," Severelle said.

Morecraft stopped by the door. His skin crawled at the mention of the name, and he felt a small wave of disgust roll through his stomach, curling his lips. Severelle coughed and spoke more softly.

"Just in case the Lord Captain should fail," he added.

GRAVEYARD GODS

The Admiral made a slow nod. "Do what you must."

Chapter 10

THE MOON'S GLOW STRUGGLED in the ocean fog. The light that shined down was not quite ripe and fitfully rolled in the blanket of clouds like a sleeper captured by some nightmare. Under this heavy, dreaming mist creaked the hull of a swift sloop. The slim body of the small ship swept along by the anxious pull of invisible sea winds. No lantern hung from her bow or stern. No graceful script proclaimed her name in tall painted letters. Even the taunt, triangular sails that drove her forward could hardly be seen as their black fabric faded to match the night sky. A few men swathed in dark linen clothes crewed the ship and did so with the grave sincerity of a hearse carriage as they cut their solemn path through the night. To the West, thunder rumbled.

From the keel of the ship, a heavy-set man came walking; he stared nervously towards the thunder, but could see nothing through the fog. "Three days. Hrrm, maybe four," he muttered to himself as he scrunched his nose, looking down to inspect the flapping vellum of a map as he crossed the deck. His squinting eyes looked up nervously as he approached the front of the ship. *I'm no miracle worker. I'm a navigator. I don't control the winds and the waves, I just chart them,* he rehearsed in his mind. Swallowing hard to drive back some small bit of the anxiety churning within him, the navigator wiped at his forehead. *Damn him. Changing course again. Didn't even know where Sile was, but suddenly he has to be there? Charting a course isn't easy, you know. Changing your course mid-voyage to some nowhere piss-pot of a town.*

With each step, some small measure of his nervous energy turned to a sort of righteous indignation. *The navigator should be respected on a ship,* he thought. *Without me, there's no voyage at all. What do you think of that?* The man gave an abrupt nod that set his round chin quivering. Another clap of thunder roared, this time closer and louder. The navigator looked up, startled by the sudden sound, and at once felt his vigor melt away into a sensation that he urgently needed to relieve himself.

On the ship's bow, ten feet from the navigator, leaned a hunched figure. The sea winds snapped and pulled at a thin cape about his shoulders as if making up for the absence of a proper flag aboard the dark vessel. A woolen hood obscured the figure's face, and linen strips like bandages wrapped the pale flesh of his wiry arms. In his hands he held the grip of a long, straight stiletto dagger, and he ran the blade over a whetstone with the tender strokes of a lover brushing out his woman's hair. With each pull, the stone whispered to the stiletto, and the point winked with the faint moonlight. The hooded man made no move to acknowledge the navigator's approach, and there passed a momentary pause where the whetstone sang softly as the navigator fretted the map in his hands.

"When do we reach Sile?" the hooded man asked. His flat and stony voice seemed almost a part of the whetstone's rhythm, and a heartbeat lapsed where the navigator questioned if he had actually spoken.

"Three, maybe four days." The momentary confidence in his voice died as the hooded man stopped sharpening his dagger, freezing in place. Around them, the sloop's rigging let out an eerie creak as a brief gust surged the ship forward.

"No," the hooded figure said. "Sooner."

The navigator shook his head and closed his eyes. "Sir Muergo, I'm sorry, but it can't be done." Opening his eyes again, the navigator held up the map, pointing with one thick finger, but the hooded man did not look up. "Even in fair weather I'd say it may take us two days, but we'll have to go around the storm as well, and-"

"I see," Muergo said. Pocketing the whetstone, he held up the stiletto, gingerly pressing the edge to the top of his thumbnail. "In that case, go through the storm." The navigator's mouth hung open, and in his surprise he had to snap his hand shut to stop the map from flying out of his grip.

"Go through the storm? Are you mad? Sir Muergo, if I may-"

Like a whirlwind, Muergo's dark cape swept around him as he stood, appearing in front of the navigator within the blink of an eye. Letting out a cry of fright at Muergo's preternatural speed, the navigator threw his arms up in front of his face, falling to the deck in shock. Above him two luminous eyes, wet and pale like those of a fish, looked down on him, wide with a cold inner light.

"I am no knight." Muergo's voice, coarse as the sound of sawing planks, arrested the navigator, holding him in place like a deer fixed by the sight of a predator in the brush. "Stow your 'sirs.' We go through the storm, and you-" Muergo knelt down, crawling towards the prone man on akimbo limbs like a spider. "-you will lead the way."

***

The storm's rain pelted the deck around him as Muergo held his cape tight to his body. Crashing waves drove through the scuppers of the wildly tilting ship, but he stood as firm as a tree rooted to the planking of the deck. At his back, his crew fought to keep the sails while the wheelman's strong arms contended with the wild waters. The ghost of a smile trailed on his lips. He always looked forward to the moments when Commodore Severelle sent for him. Yes, he would make Sile. No quarry had eluded him yet. The hunt, his beloved, stirred and tugged his slumbering heart, and he quietly danced with her amid the storm's rage. Below him, the sloop's prow drove his former navigator through the water like the edge of a blade, mangled arms and legs tied back against the hull. He would lead the way until nothing of him remained.

Chapter 11

EDMOND SUCKED AIR THROUGH his teeth, chest heaving in an attempt to stave off the pain pulsing through his side. The pearl diver's blade had missed his stomach by a matter of inches. He supposed he was grateful the residents of Sile kept their trade tools in states of good repair. The blade had been sharp—a quick puncture followed by rapid removal. This wasn't the first time the tomb raider had been stabbed, and rusted knives, or hooked knives were far worse; they would rip and tear as they exited. At least this way, the damage was manageable, though no less painful for it.

Mirastious stood by the window of the small houseboat where they'd taken refuge. It was little more than an outhouse stapled into the hull of a dinghy, a comparison only exacerbated by the lingering odor seeping into the splintering wood and molded hull. The goddess stared at Edmond's wounds, her eyes wide in the dull light.

Six of the pearl divers' family members and friends had raided their rented room at the crest of dawn. Judging by their raving shouts, they'd suspected Edmond of murdering Felex and Fiora and absconding with the loot. Edmond had tried to reason with the rabble, but the knife-toting gang hadn't seemed the reasonable sort. So, they'd fought.

Edmond *never* fought fair. It was against his moral compass. Even in his sleep-deprived state, he'd managed to reach his alchemical pouch—and while he hadn't prepared any defensive potions, he had managed to grab a handful of coarse ground pepper seeds and scatter them into the eyes of the attackers. Pearl divers and fisherman had knocked into each other, bumping into walls and tripping over the end table as they hacked and coughed and wiped at their faces, further rubbing the mixture of pepper into their eyeballs.

One of the attackers still had the wherewithal to knock the leather pouch out of Edmond's hands as a couple of the others swiped wildly in his direction. One of them had managed to stab an accomplice as the other slashed Mirastious' arm. But, Mira hadn't reacted in pain, nor had she bled. Her pale flesh had simply opened like a cut through butter. The resurrected goddess had frowned in confusion at the chaos, edging toward the hallway of the inn. With the blinded knives between him and the door, Edmond had given his pouch of alchemist supplies a kick, sending it up into Mira's arms. He soon lost sight of her as the attackers closed in on him again.

Blinded as they were, Edmond wrenched the knife from one of the attacker's hands and shoved the man forward like a human shield, and with a ducking roll he had managed to tumble into the hallway of the inn, practically falling down the steep stairs as he rushed for the door.

More of the ambushers swarmed in, and as Edmond had followed Mira to the exit of the inn, one of the divers got off a lucky jab with his pricker. Gasping in pain, bleeding like a half-butchered hog, Edmond had managed to push off and dart for the door. The man had even thrown the knife at Edmond's retreating back, but by the sound of things it had stuck into one of the low-ceiling's beams.

Now, in the cramped hold of the rotting houseboat, Edmond's shoulders crowded against the rough grain of the wood, his hand clutching his blood-drenched side, his eyes shuttering as he winced against the pain. Mirastious only watched him.

Edmond frantically surveyed his options. "My pouch," he said through gritted teeth. "The one I tossed you on the way out—do you have it?"

Mira stared at him, eyes still wide. "I—No, mortal. I didn't know you wished me to bring it."

He growled, his eyes flashing with panic. "Why would I give it to you if I didn't want you to bring it? What good is a goddess if she can't even carry a sack!"

Mira sniffed and crossed her arms, pointedly turning away from him. As she did, she flashed the arm that had been cut. Again, Edmond glimpsed a bloodless wound. He stared at the goddess' exposed back, a slight chill creeping through him as he did. Despite what she appeared to be; *this* was no human.

And a doubly inhuman thing it was to misplace a man's alchemical pouch. Edmond cursed, then hissed with pain. He frantically scanned the dinghy for any sort of potion ingredients. He needed to close off the wound and fast. The only formula he knew was a tier three incantation—he'd won the formula off a toothless medicine man from Dumas, but he'd never tried it before. He would just have to make sure he was careful, but without his pouch was it even possible? Feeling his blood running between his fingers, he figured, impossible or not, it was now or never. "Rust," he said, puffing his cheeks to temper his breathe. "Find me rust."

Mira hesitated for a moment, casting a glance back at him.

"Look," he seethed. "You may have been a god once—you may become one again. You might think it's slumming it to follow directions from a mortal, but suffice it to say, if you don't, I'll die. If I die, you'll be caught again. Fancy a thousand years snoozing in silver?"

Mira gave him a long, cold look. "I have no qualms with following your lead. However, you're injured and you're asking for *rust*. I can't help but wonder—you're not going to use untreated rust for a potion, are you? Do you know the myriad of problems that could cause? The extra water alone from the damp..." She shook her head, clicking her tongue. "It's not the way one should brew. Not by a mile. Even with treated rust, one must heat the grains for instant healing, or cool them for a slow mending. I can't be sure which you—"

"Mira. Do you *have* any treated rust?"

She hesitated then shook her head.

"Well, I did. In that pouch I threw you. But as it's back in the room where we were nearly murdered, maybe now isn't the time to worry about *treated* or *untreated* rust!"

Mira opened her mouth, paused, then looked around the room. She cast an eye over a discarded hammer, a rusty skillet that seemed to be collecting cobwebs, and a haphazard pile of fresher wood and nails. She muttered something that sounded like, "no proper alchemist..." and "*untreated* rust indeed..." But she grabbed up one of the nails and started scraping rust from the skillet into her waiting palm.

There we go. Finally, someone who listens, Edmond thought, though he didn't say it.

As Mira scratched at the rusty skillet, Edmond tucked his tongue inside his cheek. His head swam. *I'm losing too much blood,* he thought. Biting his tongue, the pain sharpened his focus. "Blood from a body whole," he said, reciting the second ingredient. "I'm injured—we need someone else's blood."

"I do not bleed," Mira said, softly, returning with a small handful of rust scrapings.

"I've noticed." Edmond shifted slightly, sending spasms of pain jolting through his body like the dabbing of hot coals. Despite the sudden flair of agony, he focused on the window set in the door. "We'll need to lure one of them over," he said. "Look out the window—tell me what you see."

The comment concerning her survival seemed to have done it; Mira no longer seemed reluctant to follow his instructions. She hurried over to the door, pressing her face against the dusty, cracked porthole window.

"I... I see a small village," she said. "The inn where we stayed is just over—" She stiffened, her eyes flaring in the reflection of the glass.

"What—what do you see?"

"Men," she said softly. "Nine—no, *ten* of them. Armed. They're checking the small vessels."

"They're coming this way?"

Mira nodded once and swallowed.

Edmond cursed. There was no time for fresh blood; his blood would have to do. Sometimes one could get by with substitutions as long as one's will made up for it. It wasn't like he had a choice.

Edmond gestured frantically at Mira and watched as she took the cue and poured the rust shavings into his waiting palm. Then, he held the cupped hand against his side, allowing some blood to trickle into the mixture.

Mira let out a scandalized cry. "You're injured—you can't use injured blood in a potion of—"

"Do you have any *healthy* blood on you, perchance?"

"No, but—"

"Then, it'll do. Besides, I'm healthy. Right? Yeah, I'm pretty healthy." The room began to tilt. Edmond's head drooped. He couldn't catch his breath, and his hands felt cold. *Not good.*

Mira frowned. "You're insane."

"So I've been told."

The final ingredient of the formula required a devout person's prayer. Edmond wasn't devout, but he figured Mira counted as much as anyone. "I need you to pray!" he said hurriedly. "It can be about anything."

"Your rust is untreated. Your blood isn't whole. And I don't pray," said Mira in a steely voice. "Water cannot be dampened. The sun cannot be brightened."

"You can pray to yourself—I don't care. Just do it!"

Mira looked ready to protest further, but then something seemed to catch her eye and she gasped softly, peering out the window once more. "They're pointing at us—oh dear—they're coming this way."

"Mira—*I'm serious*. Here, whisper it into this."

He held up his cupped hand filled with rust and blood. It was no mortar and pestle, there were no proper containers. Edmond might have brewed in worse circumstances, but at the moment he couldn't think of any. Mira lowered her lips to within an inch of Edmond's knuckles. Hesitantly, she offered up a quick, rehearsed prayer. The words fell out in a rote rhythm, like a children's rhyme. *"Goddess of silence and hidden things, bestow a gift of will and want; grant me the mind to know where shadows dwell, and the heart to stand firm in the black."*

Vaguely, Edmond thought he recognized the prayer as one of Mirastious' own order, but his own mind was too focused on the concoction scraped together in his palms to dwell on it. As the last of Mirastious' words faded, a soft shadow began to pool across the rust and blood. Droplets of crimson seeping through his fingertips turned to ink.

Edmond swallowed, then focused his will. Third tier potions were often difficult, especially for someone like Edmond. He had experience in the craft, but hadn't devoted his whole life to the art like the Brewers of the Signerde, nor did he have the patience of the Underwater Sisters rumored to lurk South of Gamor's coastal villages. Failure to master the formula and enforce one's will could have catastrophic consequences. *Things* lurked in the dark at the edge of every alchemical equation. Things that would watch and wait. Things from a different plane, where the alchemist's will would wander and bring back power. Sometimes, though, one's will brought ba ck...

...other things.

Edmond shivered.

Mira cast him an anxious glance and murmured, "They're coming nearer. Oh dear—I believe one spotted me." She ducked beneath the door, back pressed against the wood, wide, black eyes studying Edmond where he lay bleeding and in pain.

There was nothing for it; if he didn't heal himself soon, he'd bleed out.

Shakily, he began to murmur the potions ingredients beneath his breath—this step wasn't necessary, but it helped him focus. Then, he reached out with his mind, pressing his will into the blood and rust bathed in the goddess' prayer. His will was like warm water, gently soaking everything it touched. Edmond could feel the iron flavor of blood on his lips; all across his body he could sense grit and ground rust rubbing against his skin. The goddess' prayer echoed in his mind, sending chills up and down his chest in electric spurts. He forced the potion to coalesce, to form the healing he needed. He could feel his will taking root, binding to the ingredients.

He reached down, pressing the concoction against his ribs. He could feel the pain fading, his wound closing.

Just then, the door of the small room rattled as something from the outside slammed against it.

His concentration slipped.

As he grasped for it, he felt his will melting, trickling away through his fingers. He could feel *things* on the edge of his consciousness, pressing in on his will, reaching for the untethered power. Edmond cried out, frantically reaching with his mind for the loose strands of power slipping through his grasp. Another blow sounded at the door, sending the decrepit wood splintering inwards.

Edmond's head jerked to face the open door as his focus broke. The ingredients in his hands began to writhe and wriggle like graveyard worms or maggots exposed to sunlight. With a shout, Edmond dropped the squirming, congealed mass. It hit the ground with a splatter, but continued to grow, like the black gum eaten by the salt miners, or squid ink thickened with blood.

"Djinn!" Edmond shouted a warning. "Watch your eyes!"

Mira stumbled further away from the door. Large, hulking figures cut imposing figures in the threshold. Weapons glinted in their clutched fists as they moved into the houseboat, causing the fragile hull to shake and rock in the water.

Edmond, for a moment, didn't know where to look. His left hand was clutched in a fist, and his lithe body tensed for action. He glanced from the pearl divers crowding through the door, to the writhing mass of the failed potion on the floor. The forming djinn continued to grow, like a shadow spilling over a threshold. Soon, it stood as tall as a small child, hunched over, with black, sooty arms and a melting face. The demon blinked with yellow eyes as it glanced furtively around its new surroundings. Edmond had known a hellcatcher once who told him that demons arriving from the distant plane would be discombobulated at first by their unexpected trip. But once they settled... then the carnage would start. He only had moments, and Edmond knew he needed to escape before that happened.

"What is that thing?" shouted a voice from on deck. A couple of other, broad-shouldered figures hesitated in the doorway.

Mirastious had managed to scoot past the djinn as it struggled to catch its bearings. She now stood next to Edmond, eyeing the thing with a look of disgust.

The djinn, though, seemed to sense the scrutiny. Like a frightened animal trapped in the glow from a hunter's lantern, the djinn stiffened, its eyes wide and luminescent. A sulfurous smell erupted from its diminutive body as its lipless mouth stretched open like taffy, and with a keening sound, like a wounded dog, the thing began to reform.

A line of clicking insect legs sprouted from the blackened body, growing hair like a tarantula. A multitude of yellow eyes sprouted from the thing's head like the bubbling seeds of a pomegranate, while pincers and razored ridges grew around its mouth. As fast as thought, the djinn scuttled up the wall and onto the ceiling. It glanced towards Edmond, then towards the men framed in the doorway, the fractal aspect of its burgeoning eyes moving each yellow globe in concert with the others.

"Kill it!" someone shouted. "Kill it now!"

A pistol blast blasted in the small room, and a bullet slammed into the ceiling, scattering dust and splinters. The spider-demon was already on the move though, scuttling rapidly towards Edmond and Mirastious crouched in the back of the house boat.

"Edmond!" Mira called, her voice shrill. "Kill it! I command you!"

"Yes, your highness," Edmond muttered. He reached frantically about for a weapon. There were some old boards nailed against some side-panelling, but no sign of the hammer. He felt around blindly laying hold of the rusty old skillet leaning against the wall and coated with cobwebs. Still, something was better than nothing.

Another pistol blast resounded from outside, and this time Edmond didn't spot the bullet's impact. He could smell gunpowder now and could still hear the shouts of the pearl divers as those at the front tried to warn the ones in the rear.

"Some huge spider—disgusting bugger. Fast too!"

"Magical summonings. The lady is a witch—I told ye she were! Don' let her touch yer pecker!"

"Pecker? What does that have ter do with nothin?"

"Witchy things, Ermos! It'll give ye the rot, and thrice curse ye fer your trouble. Mark me words!"

Edmond only vaguely heard the shouts. He didn't know much about 'witchy things' or 'the rot' but he did know a thing or two about swinging heavy items. He tucked his tongue inside of one cheek, aimed, and as the djinn leapt from the ceiling, he grunted, putting his full might into the swing.

The djinn twisted in the air. Its legs fanned around its tar colored body to form a hundred-pointed star, as the poisonous mandibles flared like an evil flower at its center.

Edmond slammed his skillet into the creature, sending it screeching and hissing through the air. Edmond's aim was true; the demon landed at the feet of the pearl divers in the door. Some of the others seemed to be pushing the leaders, ushering them deeper into the boat.

Meanwhile, the tough-looking Silians in the front shook their heads and kicked out with heavy booted feet. The effort caused the boat to rock even more and creak with the motion.

"Flimsy hull," Edmond murmured, his eyes scanning the darkness around them.

"What was that?" Mira said.

Edmond ignored her, frantically scanning the corners and shelves and dusty crevices for some type of—

There. That's what he needed. Edmond reached out and grabbed hold of a hammer. It was no small relief to Edmond that whoever last worked on the old houseboat had left their tools behind to finish the job.

He hefted the hammer—a good, solid grip, his hands grazing against banded wood. He took a couple of practice swipes, then eyed the door.

The demon had bitten one of the pearl divers, and the man was on the ground, clutching his ankle and howling in pain.

Edmond winced. He'd heard of djinn bites before. They would lead to excruciating tremors all throughout one's body, then, the next day, the person would turn... They'd become soulless, mindless, no more than beasts themselves. Inevitably, grieving families would have to put down bite victims.

It was no way to go.

Edmond felt a surge of pity for the bitten man.

But the pity was short lasted as he spotted the glinting weapons of the man's accomplices. There were more pistol shots and the sound of swiping blades as the demon made its way, crawling along the doorframe, onto the deck.

Edmond lost sight for a moment, but heard tapping sounds like raindrops. The djinn had reached the roof. The hellcatchers would have to be sent from the main harbor. They had ways of tracking this sort of thing. By the time they arrived, though, Edmond planned to be long gone.

"Hey!" someone was shouting. "He's got a weapon, careful!"

The attention of the pearl divers was split. A few of them were still focused on the djinn. A cloud of moldering dust fell from the beams above with a sudden crack.

It's getting bigger, Edmond thought. Blinking the debris from his eyes he lifted the hammer.

The others, though, minus the one rolling in the doorway, clutching his ankle, seemed to have regained their original focus. Three men and one woman, all carrying knives—two of them carrying pistols—began to make their way into the houseboat.

GRAVEYARD GODS

Edmond didn't wait. Tightening his grip on the hammer, he brought it crashing down.

Chapter 12

"Human!" Mira shouted in alarm as Edmond slammed the hammer into the thin hull of the boat. A satisfying crunch issued from the splintering wood.

Edmond grinned, lifted his hammer, then brought it swinging down a second time. Then, a third.

"Oy!" one of the pistol wielders shouted in alarm, aiming at him.

Edmond eyed the barrel, frowned in thought, then shook his head. "You fired already," he said.

"I didn't—you can't know that!" The woman said, her hand trembling, still pointing the pistol at him. "Now stop hitting—"

Edmond shook his head. "I am a really good guesser."

He brought the hammer slamming back down again. There was another crunching noise, and water began to trickle through the cracks in the hull. *Wham! Wham! Wham!* Three more hammer blows. Edmond's side throbbed with pain, but no shots were forthcoming. He'd guessed correctly.

The woman's two accomplices were approaching on either side of Edmond, as best they could given their narrow confines, their daggers raised.

Edmond ignored them. The patchwork on the boat with the nails and board had told him the sort of repair this houseboat was in. Just by looking at the hull, he could tell this thing was held together by little more than spit and prayers.

He raised his hammer and brought it down once more.

At that moment, one of the men, a fellow with short, stubby hair and an underbite, lunged in, knife at the ready.

At that moment, a sudden jet of water gushed through the holes in the hull, and sent the short man to his knees. The sudden movement of two heavy men towards the side of the boat with the punctures had increased the pressure, also increasing the burst of liquid.

Edmond had been counting on this.

There was a crack.

"Get back!" the woman shouted, her eyes widening. "Get away from him!"

One man took a swipe at Edmond and scored a slice across his palm. The other one lunged at Mira and managed to grab hold of her wrist. He tried to yank her towards him, but received a couple of good kicks to the wristbone by Edmond for his effort. Mira just stared, scandalized, at the man touching her as if she hadn't thought such desecration were even fathomable.

Water gushed into the boat, the cracks in the poorly maintained hull widening from the pressure. The fragile houseboat was sinking. The water rose to ankle height, then knee height.

Others from outside the boat were shouting. They also realized they were sinking.

"Get off!" someone called. "It's going down—where's that blasted critter!"

"In the water!" someone shouted. "Turned into a shark."

"Over there," cried another voice. "It's hiding behind them barrels! Has claws now."

Edmond sincerely hoped the second voice had the way of it.

"What's the plan?" Mira demanded, staring wild-eyed at Edmond and his hammer.

He glanced at the tool then tossed it aside. "Sink," he said simply. "Do what I'm doing, quickly." With one hand, he reached out and grabbed a wooden shelf. Then, he started hyperventilating, filling his blood with as much oxygen as possible before the inevitable submersion. He closed his eyes, inhaling, exhaling rapidly.

The water reached his chest now, soaking through his shirt. He cracked an eye and managed to spot a thin trail of gossamer red against the murky wet. His side still throbbed with pain.

He also noticed Mira eyeing him, incredulous.

"Do what I'm doing," he repeated, with a growl.

GRAVEYARD GODS

"I'm not like one of your expendable lackeys," Mira snapped. "I don't *need* to breathe."

As if to prove her point, she closed her mouth and pinched her nose, then fixed him with a would-be imperious glare. The regal effect was slightly ruined, however, by her ridiculous appearance. Edmond wasn't sure if this were true. Mira hadn't bled when she'd been cut, so perhaps she could breathe underwater—or, perhaps, she didn't need to breathe at all. He, on the other hand, was no Signerde, and was flush out of Depths Draughts.

He closed his eyes again, drawing deep breaths until his head started to ache from the excess oxygen. The cold water tickled his neck, then chin, then moved past his ears, and, finally, the entire house cabin was submerged, taking Edmond along with it.

He could feel the sucking sensation at his feet and body as the houseboat drifted towards the bottom of the bay, creating a vacuum in the water. He opened his eyes now, mouth clenched shut. He had two, maybe three minutes at best. He needed to resurface as *far* away from the pier as possible if he wanted even a chance of escape.

Edmond groped blindly through the water, orienting himself. But there was a reason he'd snagged hold of the wall as they'd submerged. It was a sign post. Sometimes, sinking vessels would turn upside down, or sideways, completely jarring the sense of direction for their unfortunate occupants. Now, though, he held the shelf against the port wall. The exit was only a few feet in front of...

...there.

He reached it, in the murk, and gripped the door frame with his hand. Then, he glanced over his shoulder, his head swishing through the churning, bubbling water. The longer he waited, the worse his vision would get. Soon, disturbed silt would be taken up by escaping air bubbles from beneath the hull, mixing silt with water until he was practically swimming in mud.

He spotted a dark shape in the water, coming towards him. For a moment, he nearly squeaked, and a couple of precious bubbles burst from his lips and tickled past his chin in their ascent. He tracked the direction the bubbles went, orienting himself accordingly. The houseboat was leaning left against the ocean floor.

The dark shape was too large to be the djinn— he hoped

He reached out, and grabbed hold of a small, female hand. Then, with an insistent tug, he guided the goddess out through the doorway. Once she was safely outside, he followed after her, pulling himself through the door.

Mira, meanwhile, was already kicking her legs and moving towards the surface.

Edmond didn't roll his eyes—to do so underwater could sometimes allow silt into one's tear ducts—but he did come close. He reached up, snagging the goddess by the ankle and pulling her back down. Then, pulling her alongside him, he kicked through the murk, pushing off the houseboat's hull and propelling himself through the turbid bay.

As he swam, he tried to keep an eye out for any approaching sharks. But there was no sign of them or the demon. There was no sign of anything. He could barely see ten feet in front of himself now.

A couple of times, swishing strands of seaweed touched at his exposed skin, sending him into a convulsive panic, but each time he managed to calm himself and continue his swim.

A minute passed. Two.

It still didn't feel as if enough distance were between them.

His lungs ached at this point. Mira, however, didn't seem concerned. She also didn't seem to know how to swim, and was content to allow Edmond drag her through the water, though this only served to further slow them down.

Thinking grudging thoughts, Edmond continued their momentum, dragging the goddess of secrets like dead weight through the bottom of the bay. He didn't stop until his lungs were fit to burst, his chest throbbing with pain. Edmond was a man used to pain. It didn't bother him much anymore.

Still, drowning himself was no way to go. So, slowly, he released a couple more bubbles from his lips. He watched as the air snaked past him. He reoriented himself slightly until he was facing 'up' the direction the bubbles had fled, and then began to kick, heading towards the surface, his vial bouncing against his chest.

He kicked once, twice more, then, his head broke the surface of the water.

He gasped, inhaling deeply, kicking to stay afloat and reaching up with his free hand to wipe his eyes. His other hand dragged Mira to the surface. The goddess didn't gasp, she didn't even breathe. Almost threateningly, she kept her mouth closed and her fingers clasping her nostrils. She glared at Edmond, though, at least, she had finally seemed to figure out how to keep herself afloat by watching him.

She kicked a couple of times, both times striking Edmond's kneecap.

"I get it," he said, ruefully. "You can hold your breath longer than me. Good for you." He glanced around, trying to catch his bearings.

Then, he stiffened.

They were in the shadow of a boat. No—not a boat. They'd left the small pier a good distance behind them. Edmond could still see dark shapes moving about on the docks and peering into the bay. None of them seemed to be looking this direction though.

With good reason.

No pearl diver wanted to be caught casting too long a glance in the direction of an imperial ship.

And that's where Edmond and Mira found themselves. They were treading water in the shadow of an imperial frigate by the looks of it.

Edmond glanced up at the railing, but was relieved to find no face returning his look. He pulled at Mira, making a shushing sound as he guided her deeper into the shadow of the ship.

As he did, he spotted men moving on the jetty. One such man cut an intimidating figure. He was nearly seven feet tall by the look of him, though it was a difficult thing to determine from where Edmond bobbed in the surf.

But compared to the others, this man stood a head and shoulders taller. The sun caught the white scar tissue where an ear should have been, and small shadows outlined the giant's bulging muscles. Next to the man was his lord captain, judging by the uniform. The lord captain wore a rapier on his hip, which he clutched with one hand even as he walked, as if it gave him some sort of comfort.

The two men were accompanied by a third and were speaking quietly to each other, but Edmond couldn't quite make out what they were saying.

He licked his lips.

"What now?" Mira said. "Our deal is for you to restore me to my powers. Or did you forget?"

Edmond glanced at her, then shook his head. "No—I didn't forget." He spat a couple of times, emptying his mouth of bitter sea water.

"First things first—I need new supplies."

"I didn't know you wanted me to bring your bag."

"I didn't say anything."

"No, but you thought it."

"Oh?" Edmond inhaled deeply as he gripped the lowest framing of a ladder fixture on the side of the frigate. "Are your powers back? Guess you don't need me after all."

"I can see now why you're godless," Mira said. The way she spoke, calmly and without any indication of being out of breath, set Edmond at unease. Even treading water, she didn't seem to be exerting herself. "No god would have you."

"They don't know what they're missing out on, my dear," said Edmond. And with that, he pushed off the frigate and moved towards Sile's main dock. A ladder built into the side of the slippery, barnacle-covered support beams led back onto the jetty.

Edmond pulled himself up, with no swift movements. He reached the top and helped Mira up behind him, pulling insistently on her arm. Then, with a couple more quick glances back towards the distant pier where he'd left the pearl divers, he began to move, quickly, but casually in the opposite direction, dripping seawater with every step. He held Mira's arm, hooking his through hers, despite the glare he received for the familiarity.

"Now," he said, "We go to Carabas. After I fill my supplies—we'll start planning. There's much we need to discuss."

"Carabas?" Mirastious wrinkled her nose. "I suppose if we must... I—I don't quite recall... But I seem to remember one of my devotees runs a brothel there. They offer fine wine at their altar every first week to keep their business secret."

Edmond raised an eyebrow and glanced at Mira. "An underground brothel? They're not uncommon."

"Yes," said Mira. "But the owner also dealt in illicit materials. I may not have my powers, but I am at least left with some of my memories. You're an alchemist, yes—though a reckless one."

"I dabble."

"I know recipes too," said Mira. "The sort of recipes *long* forbidden and kept hidden."

Edmond glanced at her again, but this time with a renewed interest. He picked up their pace, guiding the goddess of secrets further along. "Perhaps you divines aren't as useless as you appear."

"You think you're so much better than the thousands of souls who attend me and my brethren?"

Edmond hesitated. Almost involuntarily, his hand reached up, stroking the small vial dangling from his throat. "No," he said, softly. "You're not useless. My apologies."

"I'm half tempted to believe you mean that."

"I do," he said, simply. "And if what you tell me is true... If Death can return my wife to me... Well, perhaps I've severely underestimated the lot of you."

"It won't be simple. I told you, only the emperor—"

"Only the emperor can request the return of a soul. I get it." Edmond wet his lips, his eyes narrowed slightly as he stared straight ahead to the vague shadows of tradesmen tending their small ships. "All that means is we have work to do. Come, now—we're going to have to swing back through the inn and hope none of those maniacs swiped the sword." Edmond drew his lips into a hard line as he thought about the gilded blade and gem encrusted scabbard that he'd taken from the God Grave. "That should be enough to get one of these boats to get us underway to Carabas within the hour. That is, unless you threw that away too."

Mira rolled her eyes, but allowed Edmond to guide her along the jetty, up the nearest street, down an alley and away from the distant clamor of their would-be hunters.

Chapter 13

During the voyage from Commodore Severelle's titan to Sile, Augustin kept the crew busy by running them through drills and exercises. Agreo protested when the Lord Captain ordered him to take inventory of the ship's stores, but a heavy scowl from Cristobal sent him about the work, albeit, with a grumble.

"A good idea to make him do it alone," the giant Gamorian said. "It will take him some time and he'll have less chance to poison the crew with his talk."

"That is the hope," Augustin replied. He could already see some of the crew scowling his way as Agreo whined like an angry gull and descended below deck. "We had best keep the rest busy as well. I'll have one group inspect the rigging. Take shifts below for drills with the cannons."

"Aye, Lord Captain." Cristobal nodded and stepped out to organize the crew.

Two days to Carabas, Augustin thought with a brooding sigh. The course for Sile would bring him no closer to reforming the order, but at least it wouldn't bring him any further away. He hoped that it would be as easy as sailing into the village and securing their tomb-thief. He didn't like the idea of chasing them all over the isles. *I won't have time to chase them,* he remembered. *One week. Severelle, you snake.* Anger boiled under Augustin's collar as he thought of the rat-faced Commodore's declaration. The time limit was as arbitrary as it was cruel. *He's looking for a way to justify my removal.* The thought sprang to his mind like a sudden thunderbolt. *That's why he sent me to guard the forbidden waters alone. Why he insisted on my reporting personally. Why he insisted on a ridiculous time limit. He wants me to fail so he can remove me.* The leather of his gloves creaked as Augustin gripped his rapier, his jaw clenched as he scanned the horizon around him. The feeling of betrayal sat in his stomach like a wound. He pressed on it, coaxing the pain into a hot, defiant fury. *Well,* he thought. *I suppose, I'll just have to succeed.*

***

"I'm so sorry, m'lord cap'n," the dockmaster said as he folded his hands over the floppy, woolen hat gripped in front of his chest. The melodic island accent undercut the harsh quality of the man's voice, and his bushy black beard scraped across his chest as he shook his head. "The doggers you see docked there are just the village fishermen. I don't know anything about any stranger or tomb-thief." The dockmaster's sun-wrinkled face blushed beneath the dark tan and thick tangle of his hair. He had not met Augustin's eyes since he had approached the man, though he had given Agreo and Cristobal a suspicious look and taken off his hat as Augustin introduced himself.

Augustin's lips pulled into a thin line as he scanned the boats again. The night had been dark and full of mist. Each of the three doggers that lay nestled amid the small walkways and rafts of the moldering dock were remarkably like the one he had encountered in the forbidden waters. Any or none of them could be the one he was after. He wanted to ask Cristobal his opinion, but he knew that the big man had as little experience with ships as he had himself. As he weighed the benefit of asking Agreo for his thoughts, he turned his attention back to the dockmaster.

At that moment, he spotted a group of large men, carrying weapons moving up a distant pier. They disappeared from sight, obscured by the thatch roofs of two hunched buildings. As the dockmaster turned to follow Augustin's gaze, a clamor of distant shouting and pistol shots rose up from their direction.

Cristobal stepped forward, positioning himself between Augustin and the distant sounds.

"Don't you worry," the dockmaster said quickly. "Just a few rat hunters I hired yesterday. Lazy louts took twice as long to find the vermin." Another pistol blast reported from the far off pier. "Shouldn't be much longer now."

Augustin frowned, but the sounds had already faded. Before he could question the dockmaster further, though, Agreo grunted over Augustin's shoulder.

"You are saying that no one has come through Sile with a dogger? No one you didn't know?"

The man nodded and touched his cheek. "By Nepir, may her eyes be blessed, no one, I swear."

Agreo snorted. "Bastard's lying."

The dockmaster started and looked at the round crewmaster with an angry scowl.

"I do not lie," he insisted, but Augustin saw his eyes flit around the dock in anxious desperation.

Agreo stepped forward, brushing past Augustin with his wide hip. He drew a large curved dagger from his belt. "Why don't I slice open your Silian belly and see what other secrets you're hiding from us?"

The man's eyes flared, and he opened his mouth as the blood drained from his face.

"Enough." Augustin's voice cracked like a whip, and Agreo looked over his shoulder with a curious expression. "Crewmaster, Agreo. Sheathe your blade."

The crewmaster's jowls flushed as a look of disdain spread across his lips.

"That is an order, crewmaster." Augustin's patience with the man was already thin. When he had insisted the crewmaster join him and Cristobal in going ashore, Agreo had moved at a snail's pace. He hovered just shy of insubordination as he delayed their departure from the docked ship by a quarter hour. Nonetheless, Augustin was loathe to leave him behind while he and Cristobal went ashore. He knew in his bones that he couldn't trust the man enough for that. Agreo sheathed the wicked looking blade and took a step back, making a curt bow to Augustin.

"Aye, m'lord cap'n," he muttered. Augustin turned his attention back to the dockmaster. He knew that the man was holding something back, that much of what Agreo said was true.

'Do you remember how to use that rapier?' Admiral Morecraft's words echoed in Augustin's mind as he looked at the frightened man. Could he be in league with the tomb-thief? What if the person he was after lived on this island? *No,* his inner voice contested. Augustin put a hand to his breast. *I'm more than a blade.* "I apologize for my crewman's behavior. The person we are searching for used a dogger to infiltrate forbidden waters and commit grave robbery, a most heinous crime in the eyes of the gods and the emperor. If you know anything, please tell us." The dockmaster seemed taken aback. He licked his sun-cracked lips and scratched his bushy beard while he looked down at Agreo's sheathed knife. Augustin sighed. "Can you tell us who those doggers belong to? I wish to speak with them. If one was perhaps rented temporarily, then the tomb-robber may have committed his crime without their knowing. That would be no fault of the boat's owner." The man seemed to consider this and relaxed slightly. He rubbed the back of his neck as he looked up into Augustin's eyes.

"They're good men, each of them. Good Emperor's men," he muttered.

"I'm sure they are," Augustin replied, careful to keep his impatience in check.

"They didn't have nothing to do with any grave-robber." The man twisted his hat; wringing it between nervous hands while Augustin stood silent. "There maybe was a man. Came through recent. Stayed at the inn. Might ask about him up there." The dockmaster pointed further inland towards a cluster of wooden buildings that huddled on a nearby hilltop. Augustin smiled and gave the man a quick nod.

"What is the inn called?"

The dockmaster gave Augustin a lopsided smile, showing a gap of missing teeth. "No name. Not some fancy inn, just a few rooms with some beds."

In a village as small as Sile, that made sense to Augustin. "My thanks. If I find what I'm seeking there then I'll have no reason to trouble the fishermen." The man nodded in response and stepped aside as Augustin led the way.

Agreo grumbled as they trudged up the hill towards the ramshackle inn. "Now he'll go warn his fishermen friends. This is a damned fool's errand he sent you on."

Cristobal glared at Agreo, his eyes dark like a bull about to charge. "You seem to forget that you speak to your Lord Captain," he said. His face flushed as Augustin saw frustration boiling in the giant Dumasian.

Agreo sneered back. "Just talking to myself. Or am I not allowed to speak now either?"

Augustin frowned. He was growing more resistant to Cristobal's intimidations. Just another reason to keep him close.

"Quiet, both of you," Augustin cut in. He shot a glance to Cristobal. Agreo was irritating, but he hoped that by taking him along they might be able to understand the man a little better. For the moment though, he would settle for a little peace. "We can't focus on finding the tomb-thief if you two are at each other's throats. Focus on our investigation." Cristobal and Agreo both fell to a sullen silence that was nearly as disagreeable as their bickering.

As they crossed into the cluster of buildings at Sile's heart, Augustin saw few people. Sile was not a populous village by any means, but it seemed to him that the few people who were there were going out of their way to avoid them. Windows shuttered and doors closed as they walked towards the large building Augustin presumed to be the inn.

"Friendly place," Agreo said as they entered the open doorway. Within, a bald-headed man wiped down heavy, ceramic mugs behind a bar. A soot-blackened fireplace held the charred remains of a fire, and tables and benches were haphazardly arranged. A back stair led to the second story. The innkeeper set down the mug as they approached and threw the cloth over his shoulder. The sun hung low in the morning sky, and apart from a colorful bird that sat in a nearby window, the only other person in the inn was a young woman at one of the tables, sewing the frayed end of a shirt sleeve. The bird squawked loudly as they walked in and made a series of melodic whistles that drew a smile from the woman which tugged a loose thread of desire from Augustin. *You went to sea to get away from such pursuits,* he reminded himself, struggling to maintain his focus. The woman's full lips moved to some silent song, and her dark hair tumbled across one bare shoulder. It was with great difficulty that Augustin turned to approach the innkeeper.

The innkeeper said nothing but stared at the three of them in an expression of sober assessment. Augustin folded his hands behind his back. "We're here to investigate a tomb-robber. He was spotted in the forbidden waters sailing a dogger and we've reason to believe he fled here. Do you know anything about that?"

The innkeeper looked at them, his eyes narrowing. "Don't know anything about a tomb-robber," he said, picking back up a new mug to clean. Agreo snorted and flashed a snide smile. Augustin ignored him and stepped closer to the bar.

"We don't want to cause trouble. Have you had any strangers staying at the inn recently?"

The man continued to clean the mug. "It's an inn. Most folk who stay are strangers."

Augustin felt his patience thinning. Why would no one talk to him about the tomb-thief? Something strange was happening. The innkeeper looked nervous. He seemed to be sweating now, though a cool breeze cut through the windows of the inn.

"We don't want any trouble with the Empire," the innkeeper said, coughing into his shoulder.

"Sile is part of the Empire. You've nothing to fear from us."

"As you say, m'lord." The innkeeper's eyes flitted to Augustin then back to his mug. In that moment, Augustin realized he was clenching his rapier's hilt. With a sigh, he stretched his fingers and folded his hands at his waist.

I don't need that, he told himself as he took a slow breath. The innkeeper still seemed nervous and Augustin felt a small stirring of pity. *He doesn't know what's happening. He just cares about his blood and bread. He would do just about anything to get me to leave.* The thought gave Augustin an idea and he sat down at the bar. "Listen, I know you want me to leave." The innkeeper started to protest, but Augustin held up a hand to silence him. "I don't want to trouble you, but someone broke the Emperor's law. Someone sailed into forbidden waters, and I need to find them. The dockmaster trusted me to keep my word and be on my way as soon as I find what I need. He said I should talk to you."

The innkeeper froze. His eyes flicked as he took in Augustin's words. "Ol' Jaq sent you my way?" he asked.

Augustin nodded. "He seemed to think well of you and thought if I spoke with you that I could find the person I'm looking for; then I can leave." It was only a little bit of embellishment, but it felt strange on his tongue and Augustin hoped the innkeeper wouldn't take it amiss. The man ran a hand over his bald head, giving the stubbly hairs at the back a fretful rub. Setting down the mug, he leaned forward.

"Maybe there was a stranger here, maybe a little stranger than most," he said. His eyes looked to the doorway before continuing, as if he were on the lookout for someone. "He came in and took up a room. Kept mainly to himself. This is a small village and I'm no gossip. I can't tell you what deals he did or didn't do, but-" Here the innkeeper ran a rough hand over his face and scratched his nose like he was clearing his head. Augustin waved backward at Cristobal, and the big man kept himself and Agreo a respectful distance back. "The man kept a room here. That I don't mind telling, because it's my roof and my room. He left in a, er, *hurry* this morning, but if you want to look at the room." The innkeeper leaned back and shrugged.

Augustin smiled. This had to be him. The tomb-robber. His chance at redemption. "Where did he go? Did he say? What did the man look like?" His voice was urgent, and the innkeeper seemed a little startled. Augustin sat back, trying to quell his excitement.

"No. He didn't say, and I don't know." The innkeeper pointed to the stair. "If you want to see his room it's the first on the right at the top of the stair. As for his face," The innkeeper shivered and his lip curled. "He looked like a drowned dog. All dark, matted hair, a beard, a crooked nose." Shaking his head, the innkeeper slapped the counter. "The last time he was here, when he left that is, he had a woman with him."

"A woman?" That made sense. They had seen three people on the dogger that night, though he was unsure how many were on the vessel when it slipped away. The innkeeper nodded.

"True. As shining a beauty as I've ever seen. Eyes as dark as midnight. Skin a smooth as silk and as pale as silver. I'd not forget a woman like her." For a moment, the innkeeper's voice relaxed into a more conversational tone.

Agreo said, "Doesn't sound like a tomb-robber to me." He eyed the innkeeper suspiciously.

"I tell you the truth," the man replied as he waved the cleaning rag in protest. "As true a beauty as you've ever seen. Like no woman in Sile."

Augustin stood. "I believe you," he said in a calm tone that ended the argument. "You have my thanks for your aid. Once we inspect the room we will be gone." The innkeeper nodded and went back to cleaning his mug.

As Augustin led the way to the stairs, he saw the young woman in the corner sneaking a glance at him. Their eyes met, and she winked in his direction. Augustin felt his blood beginning to warm. When he had been a younger man, travelling with the Order or fencing at tournaments, women had given him that look a lot. It called to him as clear as a horn marking the start of a hunt, and Augustin felt his mouth twist into a charming smile as reflexive and precise as his sword drills.

The jab of a finger in his back drew his attention as Cristobal mumbled, "Stay focused. Remember?"

Augustin suppressed a spurt of irritation. He cleared his throat and turned away from the woman's inviting look as he reluctantly mounted the stairs.

The room the innkeeper had directed them to was unlocked and as the door swung open, Cristobal let out a soft curse.

"Blue fire and black fish, what happened here?" The room was somewhat spacious. The bed seemed to have been shoved and sat crooked to the room's corner. A small dresser was knocked on its side with the drawers tumbled out across the floor. The remains of a footstool lay smashed to flinders in the center of the room, and a chamberpot, with its contents, lay dented and upended against a wall.

"A fight," Agreo said with a scoffing sneer. "What else?"

Ignoring the comment, Augustin stepped into the room. He and Cristobal began to inspect the scene while Agreo leaned on the doorframe like an overstuffed scarecrow.

"Huh," Cristobal murmured. He stood and reached up one long arm. A thin knife was stuck in the wooden ceiling of the room, and with a quick levering of the blade, he pulled it free. He looked over the steel carefully. "No blood." Augustin looked at the knife then turned his gaze to the rest of the room.

"You're right. No blood anywhere. How do you have a fight that destroys the furniture, but with no one bleeding by the end?" Augustin turned over the puzzle in his mind. It didn't make sense. Not yet.

Agreo laughed. "Maybe your tomb raider is a master of combat; one of the Ghost Warriors of Salamaron. That's why he doesn't bleed." Augustin shook his head, irritation burning at his cheeks.

"Crewmaster Agreo, why don't you check that corner and make sure we don't miss anything?" Augustin pointed to the wall with the upturned chamberpot.

"Oh, come on, that's-"

"That's an order, crewmaster."

Agreo's nose curled in disgust and his face flushed with a storm of anger as he stared back at Augustin. His fingers twitched and it seemed to Augustin that he might go for his knife. Augustin put a hand onto his own rapier's hilt, and the soft rattle of the blade in the scabbard drew the crewmaster's eyes. With a snort he turned and stalked towards the overturned chamberpot.

Cristobal walked over to Augustin, eyeing Agreo as he passed. He pointed down to the floor. "Look here, Lord Captain. Burn marks." Augustin knelt down to look closer. He was right, there were blackened lines like scorch marks on the ground. "I don't see a candle or coal anywhere," Cristobal added.

"No." Augustin took off one of his gloves to trail his fingers across the black marks. "These are alchemical burns, sulfurous. See how they blister the wood like that?"

Cristobal squinted then let out a groan of comprehension.

Augustin rubbed his fingers together to wipe off the charcoal-like residue. "Our tomb-robbers, the man or the lady, is an alchemist." A pause hung in the air, while Augustin stood. A tomb-robber with some skill in alchemy could be a dangerous target. Though it did explain, at least in part, how he managed to evade them so effectively. Augustin, up to this point, had only been thinking of the culprit as "the tomb robber." Singular. There had been something about the posture of those silhouettes that night. Two of them frantic, gesticulating, one standing tall, firm-footed, balanced in the water like one of the Signerde. *This* had been the tomb raider—the others, his lackeys. Augustin had an eye for authority and he would stake his reputation that the straight-postured silhouette—the one who *hadn't* spoken was the real threat—the real tomb robber. An icy discomfort condensed in Augustin's gut. How could he hope to catch such a man in little under a week?

"I wish that we had Serenia with us," Augustin said. "She would know more about what happened here; what sort of alchemy was performed."

Cristobal nodded in agreement. "Carabas," he said quietly.

Augustin sighed. Serenia had been part of the Order with him and Cristobal; one of the last to leave. He remembered the way her eyes would shine whenever she was at her alchemy; the way she loved to explain all the ingredients and effects in a hurried voice that neither waited on one's understanding nor cared if her companions were listening. The alchemy itself was what mattered to her. Commanding, arrogant even. A woman who knew what she thought; who knew what she wanted. They continued to inspect the room, but could find little else. The innkeeper was right, whoever had been staying here had left in a hurry and, apparently, taken everything with them.

There has to be something else, Augustin thought. He couldn't believe that the trail would leave them nothing to follow. His eyes fell on the crooked bed. Laying down on his stomach, Augustin looked underneath the small wooden frame. With a curious tilt of his head, he pulled free a second knife. This one was red with dried blood. A meager hope began to form in his mind. "Cristobal." Augustin called the big man over and he looked down at the blade. Agreo, finished with his own task, turned and approached as well.

"That's a diver's knife," the crewmaster said pointing to the thin, wide blade. Cristobal nodded.

"But whose blood is it?"

Augustin wondered the same. Turning the blade over in his hand, he said, "It's clear our tomb-thief had a fight here. It must have been quite a few people to shift the room this way." He gestured to the broken stool and drawers. "There is no blood anywhere else. That says to me that he took some care and had some skill to avoid killing his attackers."

Agreo rolled his eyes. "Or he has Dulomora's own luck," he said.

Augustin shrugged and turned the blade again. "I don't think so. I think that this is his blood, and that means-"

"We have a lead," Cristobal said. The big man let out a heavy chuckle and rubbed his rough hands together with a clap. Augustin stowed the knife in a pouch at his belt as Agreo held up a skeptical hand.

"You have a bloody knife. What good does that do you? You don't know where he went."

"True," Augustin admitted. "But I know someone who can find out for us." Augustin stood and looked over to Cristobal with a knowing grin. "Vicente."

The big man smiled back, nodding in understanding. "To Carabas."

When Augustin turned away from Cristobal, he saw the dark haired young woman standing at the doorway of the room. Her slender hand held the door frame, and she peeked around the side with one eye, keeping most of her body hidden. As Augustin looked her way, she disappeared around the corner. Cristobal and Agreo had their backs to the door, and now they had a lead. Excitement burned in his veins. They had a trail to follow, and quickly too. Surely, he wouldn't be missed for just a little while?

As Augustin stepped towards the door, he called over his shoulder, "Ah, keep searching the room. I'll, ahem," he cleared his throat. "I'll return in a bit."

Cristobal gave him a curious expression, but shrugged and turned to appraise the overturned drawers.

Augustin felt certain of their next move. They would go to Carabas. He could reunite with the Order, with his friends. He would find the tomb-thief using his own blood, and he would redeem himself in the eyes of Admiral Morecraft. His sure confidence put energy into his stride as he rounded the corner.

Down the hallway, half-hidden in shadow, the young woman stood. Her arms were folded about the waist of her skirt, and she shook her shining black hair over her bare shoulders. She waved him forward, biting her lip in a shy way that sent a quiver of excitement through Augustin as he approached.

"I heard you talking downstairs," she said. Her voice was smooth with the melodic tones of the small island's accent, and Augustin found himself watching her lips as she spoke. "Is is true that you are hunting that grave robber? You mean to capture him?"

Augustin nodded, putting on a semi-formal air. When he had travelled with the Order, he found that local girls always seemed to like him more when he acted the part of the noble knight. "Yes, lady. I am duty bound to find and bring him to justice." Augustin paused. There was something in her question that prodded him from behind his desire. "Do you know something about it?" he asked almost reluctantly.

The young woman seemed to shiver and looked down towards the ground. She bat her eyelashes as she looked back up to him and Augustin's smile returned. "Yes. When he first came to Sile he hired two people from the village, twins, a brother and sister. He took them to sea, but when he returned the next day he had only a woman with him, a new woman. The twins were nowhere to be seen."

This was new. The man was now up to three accomplices by his count, and Augustin nodded, urging the young woman on. "The cousins of the twins demanded to know where they had gone, but soon it was clear that the grave robber had murdered them, making up a story about how they had died to escape the blame. The cousins were not fooled. They attacked the grave robber. Blood must repay blood." She shook her head, her eyes growing moist.

As the desire to comfort the young woman swelled within him, Augustin raised a hand to her cheek, and her watering eyes met his.

"I promise, I will find him and make him pay for what he has done," Augustin said to the woman. She placed her own hand over the one he had put to her cheek.

"You misunderstand. I don't want you to help. I want you to understand why you have to stop."

Augustin frowned in confusion.

"You need to stop," she continued. "Blood must repay blood. My kin cannot be interrupted until they find and kill this grave robber. Until they avenge their blood."

It made a certain amount of sense to him. Augustin had no real family to speak of apart from his mother, but he felt a stirring of sympathy. Would he want any less in their situation, he wondered. It was a difficult question.

Augustin furrowed his eyebrows. "My lady, I cannot stop," he said. "I'm duty bound to find this man."

The woman took hold of Augustin's hand. Sliding it down from her cheek to her shoulder, she stepped forward until the linen of her shirt scraped Augustin's uniform. He felt the warmth of her breasts pressed against his own chest, and his breath caught for a moment.

"Surely, I can do something to convince you to give up this foolish search." She pulled his hand down the curve of her waist until it rested on the firm slope of her hip. The mounting desire flared within him, and Augustin pulled the fabric of her dress between his fingers as the woman tilted her head up and pressed her lips against his. His other hand sought her waist and held her. They held together in a warm and insistent kiss, and for a moment Augustin lost himself as he stirred with yearning. When their lips parted, the woman smiled at him, invitation written large in her eyes.

Augustin knew what he wanted. He felt his body betraying him. His mind grew muddled as he tried to see through the fire of the moment to the plans that had seemed so clear a minute before. He had been with many women. His appetite had overwhelmed his better judgement many times in the past, but this felt wrong. As much as he wanted it, as much as he wanted her, the warning in his heart told him to turn away. With an inward groan, Augustin closed his eyes. "I can't. I'm sorry, lady. I cannot lie to you and tell you that I would give up this hunt."

A sudden sharp pain dragged a cry from his lips as Augustin felt cold steel plunge between his ribs. His eyes flared open, and he looked down to his side. The woman's slender hand held the handle of a knife. The heel of her palm pressed against his uniform as blood welled up and stained her wrist.

"You should have at least lied," the woman said as she leaned on the blade, pressing it deeper. "Your last moments would have been far more pleasant, you Imperial pig."

CHAPTER 14

CRISTOBAL SPUN AS HE oriented his good ear to catch the sound of Augustin's cry. He shouldered roughly past Agreo, sending him reeling against the wall.

"Depths below!" the paunchy crewmaster cursed as he caught himself.

Cristobal ignored him as he cleared the door and looked down the hallway. He saw Augustin standing with his hands around a young woman's waist. She looked at Cristobal over the Lord Captain's shoulder, and the glare of her dark eyes checked his stride as his stomach tightened with anxiety. Augustin began to sway drunkenly, and Cristobal took a hesitant step forward trying to understand what he was seeing. Jerking her hand back, the woman sent a spray of blood sprinkling from Augustin's side across the floor.

"No!" Cristobal shouted. He dashed forward as Augustin slumped against the hallway wall and slid to the ground.

The woman raised the bloody knife, leveling the point at Cristobal. "Death to tyrants, Imperial-"

Cristobal's enormous hand swatted her wrist, receiving a bleeding scratch across his forearm as he knocked the knife from her grip. He lowered his shoulder into her chest, his full force behind the blow. The woman's dark hair flew past him in a wave as she thudded to the ground with a gasping cry. Leaving the woman, Cristobal dropped frantically next to Augustin. It was bad. The Lord Captain's eyes were squeezed shut, and blood welled from between his fingers as he clutched the gash.

"The Lord Captain's been wounded," Cristobal shouted over his shoulder to Agreo, who had stepped into the hall. The crewmaster looked from Augustin to the woman sprawled on the ground. She began to cough and gasp as she fought to catch her breath, and Agreo snickered.

"What? This little doxy?" he strode over to the woman as she rolled onto her side. "Oh, aye. I can see she's a real killer. Tell me now, does the cap'n always need you to help him put a woman on her back?"

Cristobal barely heard. He pulled his shirt off his back and tore a sleeve off as if it were paper. "Easy now, captain," he said as he moved Augustin's hands.

Augustin winced as the giant Dumasian cinched the sleeve of linen around his ribs to bandage the wound. "My fault, Cris. I got distracted," Augustin said. His voice hissed with pain, coming out weak.

Cristobal adjusted the bandage with a grunt, shooting his friend a sideways smirk. "I'm going to remind you of this, the next time I catch you trying to slink off with some woman."

Augustin tried to laugh, but clenched his teeth instead. With the bandage in place, he pressed his hands back over the wound. It soaked through in red almost immediately.

"Damn it," Cristobal muttered. He couldn't deal with this here. The wound was too deep. He needed a surgeon. "Agreo, I'm taking the captain back to the ship. Follow as soon as you can."

The woman let out a pained squeal, and Cristobal glanced over his shoulder. Agreo had a fist full of her dark hair, and she grasped wildly at the wooden floor as he made to pull her up. He leaned down next to her ear.

"So what then? Our cap'n try to give you a poke, and you decided to give him a poke instead? I have a friend name'o Matimeo Navara who'd *really* like you." Agreo gave a predatory sniffing sound, which sent the woman thrashing, and the crewmaster laughed, shaking the woman by her hair.

Cristobal felt heat rise in his face as his hatred for the crewmaster boiled over. They didn't have time for this. Augustin was bleeding out.

"Agreo!" Cristobal snapped in a voice that sounded like the bark of a wild dog. The crewmaster swiveled his head to look back, bored irritation on his face as he met Cristobal's glare. "We don't have time. Bring her–"

The woman twisted like a cobra in Agreo's grip as her seeking hand brought the knife up from the floor towards his stomach. The crewmaster let go and jumped back with surprising alacrity. In a flash, his own curved knife came out, and Cristobal watched as the blade slashed across the woman's throat. Her eyes went wide with surprise, and she dropped her knife for a second time as her fingers clutched at her bleeding neck. Augustin let out a choked cry, one blood covered hand reaching out toward them with impotent anguish. The woman slumped to the ground as she began to sputter and gurgle, drowning in her own blood.

"Bitch," said Agreo. He spat on the collapsed woman as he knelt to wipe the blood off his knife with her skirt. Almost as a second thought, Agreo's hand inched towards the woman's angling towards a silver band wrapped around her index finger, but he stiffened at the look on the first mate's face.

Cristobal growled as his disgust for the crewmaster rose to meet his anger, but then Augustin gasped. The Lord Captain's skin was pale and his breathing came rapidly. Cristobal closed his eyes. His hate for Agreo would have to wait. Right now, he needed to get his Lord Captain to the ship's surgeon. He needed to save his friend.

With his giant arms, Cristobal scooped up Augustin like a sleepy child, lifting him effortlessly. He did not spare a look at the dying woman. He had seen people bleed to death before and listened to their death rattles. With a wound like hers, there was nothing to be done. She would die, but Augustin didn't have to. Not yet. The wood of the inn creaked and groaned as Cristobal rocketed down the stairwell. His face hardened into a grim mask of determination as he took the steps five at a time and crossed into the common room.

The innkeeper stepped out from behind the bar and stood in front of the entrance. He held a musket, and when he saw

Cristobal charging towards the door, he lifted the barrel and fired. A gout of smoke erupted from the shot and filled the space in front of the bald innkeeper. Cristobal felt the musket ball punch a ribbon of pain through his chest, striking the right of his pectoral muscle just below the armpit. He didn't stop or even slow. The only reaction the giant Dumasian gave was a slight twitching in his eye against the gunsmoke as he broke free.

The innkeeper cried out in fear as he reeled back with the musket, attempting to use the spent gun as a club. Cristobal lifted one large boot and kicked the innkeeper squarely in the chest, sending the man flying through the inn's door and rolling across the ground outside. Cristobal's broad strides carried him over the innkeeper as the bald man curled up in retching pain.

The giant knight spotted the *Intrepid* docked ahead of him. Free of the inn's confining hallways, Cristobal put his strong legs to speed. Clouds of dust kicked up behind him, and the ground seemed to shake as his boots slapped the dirt road with a sound like a galloping horse. Racing down the hill toward the docks, he felt his hand grow slick with blood running through the bandage he had set.

Hold on, he thought to his friend. *Ververiona, giver of life, just a little further.* Augustin's hands slipped from his side. His arms jangled and his body went limp as a ragdoll in Cristobal's hand. *No! Not yet!*

"Surgeon! Surgeon!" the giant called as he hurtled across the dock. He crossed the gangplank to the frigate's deck in two great leaps that threatened to snap the wooden boards beneath his feet. Crewmen gasped and called out to each other as excited alarm swept across the vessel. They rushed forward and formed a close circle around Cristobal.

"The Lord Captain has been stabbed! Where is Catali?" Cristobal roared.

"Here. Make room." The young surgeon pushed her way through the press of crewmen. With one look at the blood running down Cristobal's fingers, her eyes narrowed and she pointed a finger towards the stern of the ship. "Carry him to his quarters."

Cristobal nodded and hurried to carry out the order. Augustin's soft mewls of pain urging him forward like daggers at his heart.

Chapter 15

Augustin's head swam. He felt at once the sensation of standing and lying on his back in a pool of water. Shadows flitted at the edge of his vision. Demonic, grinning djinn and cavorting marid swirled in the fog of his perception. Fear gripped him. He wanted to move, to flee, to draw his sword and fight, but his muscles refused to answer his demands. A figure appeared at his side, a woman, a sweep of brown hair as a hand lightly pressed his chest.

"It's alright, I've got you," she said.

"Isobella," he murmured. Of course, she was a hellcatcher. She knew these demons. She would save him. She could protect him.

Mercusi, be just, why can't I move?

The woman leaned closer. He saw the glare of glass lenses before her eyes. "It's alright," she said. "I have you."

"Serenia?"

The woman pressed her lips to his, taking his black hair in her fingers as she pulled him close; sliding her body over his in the weightless space he drifted in. He couldn't breathe. He couldn't think. As her tongue slipped into his mouth, he lost all sense of himself, drinking in a wave of pleasure.

***

As Cristobal laid Augustin down on his bed, Catali dropped her leather bag of tools at the headboard. Augustin's quarters were sparse compared to the sumptuous accommodations onboard the Commodore's titan. There was the bed, of course, and a desk where he could log their voyage. A dressing table with a wash basin provided some comfort, but Augustin had not crowded the room with luxuries the way other captains did at times. The room had a direct efficiency to it. A one-man barrack kept in clean order. Cristobal started to pull off Augustin's coat and shirt.

"Let him lie." Catali's voice was firm and cool, arresting Cristobal in place. Catali drew a clear glass bottle of transparent liquid from her bag. "You'll just aggravate the wound more if you try to undress him. Let him lie on the bed."

Gently, the large man let Augustin down onto the hard mattress. Catali pulled the wash basin from the dressing table. She poured the contents of the clear bottle over her hands, letting the excess run off into the basin. The strong, stinging scent of alcohol and other herbal scents he could not recognize filled the cabin, and Cristobal held up a hand to his face as his eyes began to sting. When the bottle was more than half emptied, Catali withdrew a set of delicate looking metal tools from her bag and set them into the wash basin, letting the alcohol soak over them.

"Is all of that his blood?" Catali asked.

Cristobal cocked his head in confusion, then Catali pointed a thin finger at Cristobal's chest, and he looked down at himself. His torn shirt left behind at the inn, Cristobal's bare stomach glistened, smeared with red. He passed a hand over the torn flesh at the edge of his armpit where the musket ball had passed through. Just a flesh wound; not even bleeding anymore he noted with a small wince as he pushed his finger tips over the ripped skin. His hands and forearms were crimson from carrying Augustin, disguising the knick the lady's knife had given him.

"I'm fine." Cristobal murmured.

The young woman raised a disbelieving eyebrow, but turned back to Augustin and drew a small pair of scissors from the wash basin. She began to cut away the bandage. "Was this the crewmaster?"

The question caught Cristobal off guard and at first he didn't respond.

Catali poured some more of the clear alcohol over Augustin's wound, and a pained expression passed over the unconscious man's face. "I'm sorry. Might not be my place to ask, but when

I saw he wasn't with you and the Lord Captain being like this-" She let an exaggerated shrug carry the rest of her implication.

"No. Agreo will be here soon. We were attacked at the inn, and I ran on ahead."

The young surgeon nodded, and Cristobal stretched his neck. The adrenaline of his run from the inn had left his body shaking, and he fought to control his fidgeting hands.

"As you say." There was a pause while Catali worked. Without looking to Cristobal, she said, "I had hoped that when you both went out with just him that you'd settle things, but no. I should have known he doesn't think that way. The Lord Captain is an honorable man." She fetched a small ceramic jar from her bag and drew out a length of suture. Her hands seemed to move on their own, without distraction as she spoke. "But I know what a man like Agreo does to honorable men."

Catali next drew a metal needle from the wash basin and threaded the suture into it with a deft twist. "And I know what it does to a crew when an agitator like Agreo enjoys the indulgence of honorable men." As Catali stuck the needle into Augustin's skin, threading the gut suture around the red wound, her fingers moved in a tight efficient pattern that was as mesmerizing to Cristobal as it was grotesque. "You're both trying to do the right thing. So am I. If you were to tell me that Agreo attacked the captain, well-" The surgeon gave another elaborate shrug, "Perhaps I could back up that assertion. I have a feeling that, like me, you wouldn't miss the old ball of spite." With this last, the surgeon looked up at Cristobal, her thin face drawn in tired lines of cynical appraisal.

Unease crept into his heart as he met the surgeon's eyes. Cristobal looked down at Augustin, Catali drew her mouth into a grimace and said, "He'll be out for hours. I wouldn't try to wake him up unless it was the direst emergency. He trusts you though. You protect him. You have a chance to protect him now, before the danger grows even greater."

Cristobal folded his arms. The thought hadn't occurred to him before, but Catali was right. The woman was dead. Augustin would be unconscious for some time. If he lied, said Agreo attacked his Lord Captain and tried to kill him, would that be enough? His lip twisted in agitation. Agreo was cruel and conniving. Cristobal thought of the way he had threatened the man at the dock, and the way he had spat on the dying woman at the inn, and he snorted in revulsion. The man was poison to the crew; that much Cristobal was certain about, but he hadn't crossed a line they could punish him for, not severely. He couldn't just let Agreo be, but could he really murder him? The word stuck in his mind and Cristobal felt his stomach twist. That's what it would be. If he lied and had Agreo hanged from the yardarm for a crime he didn't commit, it would be murder.

Cristobal held up a hand, and his fingers twisted into a sign against evil as he muttered, "Mercusi, protect us." Looking from Augustin's pale face back to Catali, he said, "No. I can't do that." The young surgeon's expression seemed to grey as she sunk into a look of jaded disappointment.

"As you say, sir." She opened a jar of pungent gel and began to spread it over the sutured wound.

At that moment the ship shook as a rapid succession of thunderclaps announced cannonfire. Cristobal fell into a defensive stance as Catali looked to the door in confusion.

"Blue fire and black fish, what now?" Cristobal growled as the initial shock wore off, and he stormed to the door.

His eyes drew immediately toward Sile. As he looked towards the small village, he saw the black smoke of fire and debris where cannon shots had landed amid the cluster of wooden buildings. He expected to see an angry mob of villagers or a pirate clan sweeping in on them, but he saw none of it. The *Intrepid* was not under attack. Looking around him, he saw crewmen moving to load the smoking bores of the deck guns. The *Intrepid* itself had opened fire. Augustin's ship was bombarding a village of civilians. The horror of the moment sunk in Cristobal's chest like a cold stone. He frantically cupped his hands around his mouth.

"Cease fire!" Cristobal roared. His deep voice thundered across the deck. The crew who manned the top guns all turned and stared at him, pausing in the midst of reloading. "Who told you to open fire?" He bellowed, fury straining his voice, his neck taut.

The replies of the crewmen were drowned out as a second volley of cannon fire erupted from the gundeck below them. The wood walls of Sile's inn exploded inward as the heavy iron shot found its target. Cristobal did not wait for the crew to repeat their answer. He had a feeling he knew where the order came from. Stepping below deck, he saw Agreo marching up and down the gundeck barking orders. The crew were in the process of reloading for a third volley.

"Take aim!" Agreo shouted.

Cristobal's booming voice filled the gundeck "Belay that order!"

The crewmen froze, looking from Agreo to Cristobal. The crewmaster rounded on the blood covered giant and pointed an accusing finger.

"Don't you belay my commands, you dumb ox," he said with a venomous scowl. "I'm the crewmaster, and with the lord cap'n wounded, that means I'm in charge during military efforts."

"There are civilians in Sile. People who had nothing to do with the attack!" Cristobal countered.

"Oh, boo-hoo. Listen up, you coward. For all we know everyone in that piss stain of a town is out to get us. Even if they didn't hold the knife, they let it happen. You can't attack Imperial sailors, especially an officer, and get away with it. So you can take your bleeding heart and shove it right up your soft Dumasian arse, because I'm not about to let this stand. Now, take aim, you-"

Cristobal's fist slammed into Agreo's cheek like a mallet.

Agreo teetered as his hands spun, trying to catch his balance. Crashing to the deck, he groaned and spat out a bloody tooth that clacked across the gundeck. "Oh, you've done it now, boy," Agreo said as he stood and drew his curved knife from his belt. "I'm going to carve you up like a side of beef."

Cristobal wasted no words. Instead, he dove for Agreo. The blade flashed as Agreo squatted down on his thick legs and swiped for Cristobal's stomach. Spinning to dodge the knife,

Cristobal felt the edge slice across his waist. It was a shallow cut, not nearly as bad as it could have been, but a warm line of blood welled up immediately. In the dim light of the gundeck, the crewmen rushed closer. Their inarticulate shouts punctuated cries of: "Show that landwalker how a sailor fights!", "Send 'em South!", and "Twelve coppers on Cristobal!"

Agreo didn't let Cristobal get his footing. He stepped forward, menacing the bigger man with the knife. Cristobal held up his hands, testing Agreo with small grabs and jabs, but the pudgy crewmaster's eyes glinted with a crafty light. He refused to be baited and held his knife close until he was ready to send out a jab of his own. Another line of red spread across Cristobal's arm, just above the elbow, and he bared his teeth. The pain was nothing new. He was used to pain. Cristobal rolled his shoulders as the circle of crewmen tightened around them.

I need to get that knife, he thought as the blade lashed out at him again. The press of men pushed them closer and closer together. If he didn't try something soon, he knew that Agreo would get lucky, and he would be dead.

Agreo swiped out with the knife, aiming for Cristobal's shoulder. The big man jumped back, bringing his hands up to either side of Agreo's slash. He leaned backward into the ring of sailors behind him, and the crewmen let out a string of curses as they fell back under his weight. Agreo's arm extended, and the blade sliced down onto Cristobal's muscular chest. Cristobal's hands flew together and clamped down on the back of the blade, pressing it against him. His strong grip held the metal tight as Agreo tried to pull it back. The crewmaster's eyes bulged as he jerked with his shoulders, and pain shot through Cristobal's chest with each attempt, but the blade would not come free.

The knife stung as it nestled its sharp edge into the skin and flesh of Cristobal's pectoral muscle, but he held it tightly, not allowing the blade to saw or slide in his grip.

Now I've got you. Cristobal let out a booming laugh that startled the sailors around him into silence. His leg shot up in a kick to Agreo's stomach. The crewmaster curled over, his trembling fingers released the knife handle as he clutched his ample middle. Cristobal pulled the bloody blade from the shallow slice in his chest, turning it around to grasp the handle.

Seeing the red-edged blade, Agreo put up his palms and shouted for help, but the roiling noise of the crew drowned out the cry.

Cristobal took long, deep breaths. He felt his hate and disgust beginning to bubble, churning in his chest like a violent surf. His knuckles went white around the handle of the knife. As he stared at the pleading figure of Agreo in front of him, murderous voices in his head deliberated where he should cut the man first.

A pistol shot rang out from the upper deck stairway.

All shouting ceased as Cristobal and the crew whirled to face the sudden noise. At the top of the stair stood Augustin. His shirt and coat stood out, bright and bloody, against pallid skin, and he stood with his hand on the hilt of his rapier. He held a pistol towards the sky that trailed smoke like some dark incense. Cristobal craned his head in disbelief. Hadn't Catali said he would be unconscious for hours?

"What is the meaning of this?" Augustin's voice had the firm iron of wrathful command behind it. Cristobal looked down at the knife in his hand. The bloodlust drained from him, and he felt hot shame flushing his face. When no one replied, Augustin closed his eyes and snapped. "I will have order on this vessel." He opened his eyes again, looking around to each of the silent crewmen. Finally, he said, "Cristobal, follow me. Crewmaster Agreo, get us underway."

In shock, Agreo simply nodded.

Cristobal stepped through the parting circle of crewmen and up the stairs. He gave one last glance to Agreo, dropping the stunned crewmaster's knife to the deck as he took the first stair.

When he reached the top of the staircase, Cristobal saw Catali standing just to the side of the stairway, out of sight. Augustin said nothing, but turned stiffly and strode toward his cabin with a deliberate slowness. The crew watched as Cristobal walked beside their Lord Captain.

As the three of them crossed the threshold of the captain's quarters, Catali closed the door with a firm shove. Augustin stood rigid for a moment, looking at Cristobal. He licked his lips, and Cristobal noticed that sweat drenched Augustin's pale forehead.

"Just get us to Carabas," Augustin said. At that moment, Augustin's eyes rolled up to their whites and he collapsed to the cabin's floor like a sack of flour.

"Shark shite, help me get him in the bed," Catali said, kneeling by Augustin's head.

Cristobal hurried to grab his friend's legs. "How did he-He looked half dead when I left."

They laid Augustin on the bed and Catali pushed open his eyelids, looking at each closely before she stood up again. The young surgeon stretched her neck and scratched her shaved head with a relieved sigh. She then held up a small vial of bright orange pebbles.

"I gave him some of this," Catali said. As Cristobal looked closer he thought the pebbles looked jagged, like salt. "It's my own tweak on an old formula."

"Alchemy?" Cristobal asked.

"No. Nothing that dangerous. Just medicine. A substance that incites the breath. I had just got him fully bandaged when I heard the crew shouting. I thought maybe they had mutinied." She pocketed the orange salts, giving Augustin a remorseful look. "I didn't want him to be killed without a fight, if that happened."

"Mercusi, be just," Cristobal cursed. Mutiny. As he looked down at the unconscious body of his friend, Cristobal wondered if they would even make it to Carabas. *No.* He shook his head to clear away the thought. They had to make it. Clenching his jaw, he put a hand on Augustin's shoulder. "Rest well, old friend. I'll get you there."

Turning to Catali, Cristobal said, "Thank you. I'm sure he'd be dead without you."

Catali shrugged in reluctant acceptance of the compliment. "Don't thank me yet. He really shouldn't have been walking around like that with his wound. He's going to be sore as hell when he wakes up."

CHAPTER 16

THE TRADE CITY OF Carabas nestled in the Bay of Bianchetto like a ruby burrowed into the pommel of a sword. Approaching ships greeted a white-stone lighthouse illuminating a trailing line of reef and sandbar like submerged battlements in the bay. A quarter-mile stretch of deep water allowed ships to pass between the lighthouse and a high, rocky cliff upon which was situated Castle Fantalco, a seaside fortress overlooking the bay as well as the city of Carabas itself.

Fitted stone blocks supported the docks and stretched along the coast from the shadow of Castle Fantalco—home of the Commodore of Carabas—to the rocky base of Verian Hill on the western side of the city. Ships of various sizes and sails clogged the harbor with their coming and going, the swish of cloth and heaving anchors rattling the breeze ahead of the sound of shouting voices in a dozen different languages. The choir of hagglers and merchants resounded over the bay, preceding the wares offloading from the ships to nearby warehouses, or to the carters prepared to transport the merchandise further into the city.

Few merchants recognized the Man-of-Faces or his veiled companion. Some stopped or glanced in the odd couple's direction as they disembarked a large fishing vessel, bidding farewell to the captain with a toss of a small coin pouch—by the sour look of the man and the reluctant way his arm hung after the toss, it was coin he could ill afford to part with.

The man wore a simple vial of blackened glass which dangled on his chest and his disheveled clothes looked as if they'd only recently dried. Tanned, with a muscular form and a crooked smile, the more keen-eyed observers might have noticed the man favoring his left hand—and the more superstitious among them waved their fingers in a warding gesture against the cursed presence of one who leads with their left. If one looked even closer, they might have described this man's gaze as permanently melancholic. The man was of average appearance and average height; but his movements were anything other than pedestrian. He moved like one of the Signerde, who called themselves The Children. And though he was no Signerde, his body rolled like the ocean waves coming in to shore; he took surefooted steps and danced his way through the crowds on the wharf, guiding his veiled companion into the city. He had dancer's feet, but the forearms of a sailor.

Burglars and latchlads might have spotted some similarities in the man's physique and movement. Nobles and dignitaries might have recognized the poise and confidence in the man's bearing. Brewers and alchemists would certainly have recognized the scorch marks and stains on the man's fingertips and knuckles.

GRAVEYARD GODS

But few would have recognized the look in his eye.

It was the look of a resurrected soul. A dead, shriveled, husk of a spirit given life by the breath of hope; by the promise of a new heading.

Edmond Mondego was a man with renewed purpose.

"I still don't see why I have to wear this," muttered Mirastious. Tugging at her new dress. It was a simple, cotton affair, with thick laces dipped in goat's milk and dehydrated sap, pretending to be silk.

"Yes, well not everyone is as comfortable walking around starkers as you seem to be. Besides, I paid the captain a good coin for that—and your veil."

"My face is not meant to be hidden."

Edmond glanced over, and gave a half shrug. "And if one of your acolytes recognizes you? How long till word reaches your friends in the pantheon? Do you want them to know you're alive before you found out who killed you to begin with? You'd end up at the bottom of the sea again. Don't think I don't know why you're still with me."

"Oh?" Mirastious inclined an eyebrow. "And why is that?"

"Because, you'll never find another man like me."

Mirastious snorted. "Your humility is dizzying. You're not so skilled that you're irreplaceable."

"Oh, aye, there are those more talented than me. But how many of them are godless? How many of them avoid offering prayers every hour of the day? Prayers to your once-friends.

Prayers to the waiting ears of the gods or goddesses who murdered you. Oh, aye. You may find another of greater talents in your quest, but you'll never find one who will keep your resurrection secret from divine ears."

Mirastious frowned behind her veil, but said nothing, only further confirming what Edmond had suspected. Mirastious *needed* him.

As they moved up the broad avenue that led from the docks, through the city gates, Mirastious nodded towards a couple of the guards watching the tradesmen enter and exit Carabas. "I remember a prayer I once heard. A guard offered me their soul in exchange for vengeance. They wished for the identity and location of their child's murderer."

Edmond cast his companion a sidelong glance, tilting an eyebrow towards the sun. "What a lovely story."

"If I still had my powers, I could discern *who* betrayed me. No secret would be safe."

"Yes, well, you don't have your powers, but you do have me." He flashed a winsome smile.

This declaration only seemed to further sour Mira's mood. "I know an apothecary or two who barter in favors," she said. "You can resupply there."

But Edmond shook his head. "You *knew* apothecaries. After twenty-five years, they could have moved or died. No, I have my own hole-in-the-wall outfit that can help us out. Might not be fit for the toes of a goddess, but the smell will certainly distract you well enough. First, though, I need coin. Then, I'll resupply. Then, I'll change my face."

Mirastious eyed him up and down from behind her veil, turning her face towards him as they walked. "You're a face changer?"

"Alchemy has granted me more boons than the gods."

"Perhaps you don't ask nicely."

Edmond chuckled. "There's some truth to that, I warrant."

"This coin? People will give it to you? Do you have prayer wells, also?"

"Prayer wells? What—no—us mortals aren't just showered with offerings and teenths. We have to earn our living the hard way."

"And that would be?"

But in answer, Edmond suddenly veered off the wide avenue, and ducked up a side street. He maneuvered down another alley, narrowly avoiding a carter carrying a stack of foul-smelling boxes. Two more turns, and a long stretch of cobblestoned road later, Edmond and Mirastious found themselves in a dimmer, darker part of the city, hidden on the cusp of the wharf. Here, the streets were less crowded. Figures that moved up and down the street did so quickly, with purpose in their strides as if wanting to avoid lingering.

A couple of men behind a grimy window made eyes at Mirastious and mouthed obscenities through the glass. Edmond flicked his nose at them and caught Mira's arm, guiding her quickly away.

Instead of looking scared in the dark alley beneath the crowded, looming buildings, Mira's eyes were wide with delight.

"What is this place?" she said, breathily. "In all the prayers offered me by mine, I don't think this has ever come up. It's beautiful! Can you imagine the stories hidden beneath these stones?"

"It's only really been built up in the last fifty or so years. Maybe you missed it. This is Crawler's Way," Edmond said in a quiet voice, glancing up and down the street. "The only things you'll find hidden here are bodies and pools of piss. Here, this way." Frowning at Mira's reaction, he guided her beneath the overhang of a dilapidated, disjointed building. It appeared as if someone had glued together the floors of four different buildings, and the assemblage gave the dizzying impression that it swayed with every step they took towards it. A sign out front read, "Maiden's Doubt." Beneath the sign, the painted red emblem of a crowing rooster languished in the chipped wood of the doorframe. Loud noises, even louder than the sound of milling pedestrians and carts, echoed from inside.

"Keep your veil on," said Edmond, his voice low. "No sense sending the place into a stampede."

"What do you mean?"

"Just keep it on."

He pushed into the establishment.

The Kindly Roosts of Carabas were well known throughout the Gilded Islands. Islanders from all around the archipelago would travel to the great city to partake in the never-ending fountain of drinks and the equally bottomless pit of debt one could accrue at the cards and dice tables. Nestled in every district of the city, the Kindly Roosts contained all manner of gambler's delights. There were games requiring pool cues and balls, others that had tin cups and darts. There were competitions of strength and other competitions of drinking. The whole place smelled of stale food and fresh urine, punctuated by barking laughs and shouts of joy—or fury—while revelers invoked fervent prayers to Tempa, the goddess of luck.

The Kindly Roosts could be vicious, but indiscriminate. All manner of customers were welcome in these self-described establishments of fortune. Even Edmond didn't need the goddess of secrets to know the worst kept secret in Carabas: the Roosts were allowed to operate due to their ties to the Commodore's family. The Commodore's own aunt, Sofia Di'ladrion ran one of the most efficient and ruthless crime families in all of the archipelago. Recently, Edmond had heard rumors that a new upstart family was trying to edge their way in on Rooster territory, but the kind ones weren't the sort to take insult lightly. Already, if the rumors were to be trusted, more than one body, eyes painted red in warning, had been fished out from beneath the piers.

Mirastious' expression of delight beneath her veil only seemed to increase with each step. For a goddess of secrets, a place like the Maiden's Doubt was a treasure trove of illicit thoughts, hidden motives and shameful indiscretion. Normally, Edmond liked to draw as little attention to himself as possible. But visiting a place like this with a beauty such as Mira went a long way in undermining his clandestine efforts.

"Keep your head down," he muttered. "Don't touch that! That either!" The first comment was directed at Mira's hand venturing towards a handful of colored shells which were used as currency in the Roosts; the second was prompted by the thrusting hips of an old, wizened man with a leer stretching his sallow lips.

"Touch someone's shells and they'll likely stab you," he said, guiding her quickly along the room towards a door at the back. "Or me."

"This is how you earn your coin then? Through games of luck?"

Edmond shook his head. "Can't gamble if you don't have coin. No—the roosts are serving of *all* customers. My source of enrichment comes from *below*."

He pushed through a door at the back and pulled up short.

Two brutish figures blocked the top of a staircase. They each looked like worse versions of the other, with thick jaws and fingers the size of imported bananas. They each had a tattoo of a red rooster on the sides of their necks marking them as kind ones. Judging by their mean gazes and their position at the top of the stairs, they were relatively low on the totem pole, which, in Edmond's experience meant they were more dangerous. Criminals with nothing to lose and a desire to prove themselves would go bounds beyond what normal gangsters considered decent.

And it was with indecent gazes that the men were examining the duo. Though, an uncomfortable moment passed before Edmond realized the leers were indifferent to Mira and, instead, were leveled on him.

"You know the password?" said one of the apes.

Edmond frowned. "Since when is there a password?"

The other gorilla chuckled and waggled a finger, gesturing Edmond should lean in. "I can whisper it to ye if yer like. I'd be happy ter whisper other things, if ye know what I mean."

Both kind ones chuckled—it sounded like a couple of clacking boulders trying to escape their chests.

"As charming as I'm sure you find yourselves, I'd like to be on my way. If you don't mind..." Edmond tried to move past the guards, but they placed their hands on his chest, impeding his progress. They didn't lower their hands until Edmond took a hasty step back.

"Weren't jokin' bout the password," said one of the Roosters. "New policy."

"On account o' disturbances from the Yellowbacks," said the other guard.

"The upstarts? Their family is affecting Rooster policy? Since when?" By the sound of things, the feuding between the families had gotten worse since Edmond had last been here. "Sofia isn't the type to cow lightly," he said. "Or have things changed?"

The guards grunted, eyeing Edmond with a new interest. "What do you know about the boss?" said one.

"Sofia Di'ladrion? Oh, she's an old acquaintance of mine. I was there when she lost her eye, you know. I know she likes to say an assassin tried to gouge it out, but really," here Edmond dropped his voice to a conspiratorial whisper, "it was her own doing. She tripped."

Of course, Edmond *did* know Sofia Di'ladrion, and he had been there when the mother of the Rooster crime family had lost her eye—especially since he'd been the one she blamed for its loss. It was a small matter of detail that Sofia *hated* him, and had hired more than one killer to try and hunt him down. The guards didn't need to know that part.

"Truth told," said the guard, "I always suspected as much. But I don' care if ye know the pucker'a the emperor's own ass. Yer not comin' down without the password."

"Wise," said Mirastious, nodding.

The Roosters and Edmond glanced towards her.

"It's only, I know a thing or two about your organization as well," she said smoothly. "There are more devout in your ranks than you might think. And the things they tell me," she shook her head softly. "Would make your hair curl."

Both men frowned slightly. Neither of them had any hair.

"For one," she said, "Did you know every new hire has to steal something from a family member? It's a well-guarded secret, but the goal is to break ties outside the gang. What am I saying? Of course, you knew that. Did you steal your mother's pearls? Perhaps something from beneath your father's bed? Though, Roosters are rarely the sort to have fathers... Maybe you only robbed your brother while he was sleeping, or—I heard this once too—perhaps you punched out the golden teeth of an uncle and sold them for a handful of d'oro."

The guards stared at Mira as all interest in Edmond faded.

"How do you know that?" said one, shaking his head. He took a threatening step forward. "You shouldn't know that!"

"The golden teeth—I heard that story too," said the other, a slight quaver in his voice. "That was ol' Gui. He was the one what recruited me." He dropped his voice to a trembling hiss. "How do you know that!"

Mira maintained her composure, despite the looming threats. "The same way I know that those tattoos aren't the only identifying marks on your bodies."

The guards shared another stunned look. Now, the one who'd been moving threateningly forward, took a cowed step back.

"Who are you?" he demanded. "What witchery is this? How do you know about the branding?"

"Beneath the toes, where no one can see? How do you think I know," said Mira.

The men shook their heads wildly.

"Now," said Mira. "You will let us pass, or, I'll tell our *dear friend* Sofia that you were causing trouble for paying clients. You wouldn't like that, would you? Remember what she did to Renal?" Mira winced, shaking her head. "Stripping his flesh like that? All for what, making eyes at her daughter? Pity that."

Judging by the mens' expressions they *had* heard what happened to Renal. Edmond, though, didn't know half of what Mira was talking about, but gauging the reaction, he supposed having a goddess of secrets along for the ride wasn't the *most* useless thing he could imagine.

He watched, trying to hide his amusement as the guards stepped aside, fawning over Mira and shooting doubtful looks at Edmond, gesturing down the stairs.

Mira kept her chin tilted, her eyes ahead beneath her veil as she stepped down the stairs with elegance and poise. Edmond, allowed her to lead, then, with a nod and a grin at the guards, he fell into step behind her.

"Not bad," he muttered as they reached the bottom of the stairs.

"My patience is wearing thin," Mira said. "When will we start planning? I miss my true self. Memory alone is a poor substitute for true power."

Edmond sidled past the goddess, stepping further into the dingy basement. "Just because those two upstairs were bending over for you, doesn't mean I will. Don't forget who got you out of that crypt. I told you: I need coin, then I need to resupply and change my face. After *that* we can plan."

The stairwell brought them to a wide basement. Alchemical lanterns hung from grey timbers, illuminating a circular sand pit. Men and women shook clenched fists at the circle, and their commingled shouting filled the room with an intense heat that brought a bead of sweat to Edmond's face. Within the circle two men grappled, and the sound of slapping flesh skipped over the crowd in a staccato of punches and kicks.

Mira gave Edmond a skeptical look. "And this coin? You'll get it betting on the fighters?" Looking past Edmond, Mira examined the pair of fighting men. A rough looking fellow with cauliflower ears and a tapestry of scars across his face moved very little, dragging his leg with a bit of a limp, but when he did strike, his arms snapped forward with blistering speed. Every time he landed a blow, the crowd would either cheer or grumble, depending on which way their coins had exchanged hands. A lender, who doubled as a referee, sat behind a pile of red-gold d'oros, counting out the winnings of a short line of betters from the previous fight. Every so often, the lender would mutter things like, "Watch the eyes," or, "no weapons," then he'd wave disinterestedly in the direction of the fight.

Edmond had been here enough times to know that seeming attention to fighter-safety was only for show. Down in the basement of the Maiden's Doubt, there were only two rules: no weapons, and anyone could fight as long as they could front the coin.

Edmond watched the two men batter each other, nodding in approval as the scar-faced gent knocked low a boyish youth with a sandy crop of hair. The young fellow clattered to the ground, a couple of his teeth skittering away across the dusty floor.

The lender looked up and, with a heavy sigh, said, "Wagers on Timnus' victory come collect your winnings. Those backing Fernard, better luck next time."

Nearly half the room muttered darkly, shooting shifty-eyed glances towards the lender. A couple more brutes with tattoos of red Roosters stood against the walls, though, deterring anything beyond malicious glances.

"Our champion will challenge a bold soul soon enough," said the lender, calling across his desk at the two-score assembled spectators. "For now, next on the dockets, we have Elrid the

Hammerfist. Any takers? Remember, the purse is fifty d'oro, free and clear!"

A few reluctant hands rose into the air. The lender scanned the volunteers until his gaze settled on a scrawny, middle-aged man with a dusting of pale hair. "You sir!" said the lender. "Fancy your chances against Elrid?"

The small man—who had clearly had more than his fair share of something strong—tried to nod, but couldn't seem to manage the motion. So, instead, he bowed slightly at the waist, stumbling with the gesture.

"Oh come on, Grerald! The Hammerfist will make rubble out of the geezer!"

A few more grumbles.

"Always picking the sure thing," someone growled. "No sense in even wagering..."

"I'll offer ten to one odds," the lender cried, pointing towards the frail, white-haired man. "Takers?"

Reluctantly, a few takers lined up and made their payments, collecting their ticket stubs.

"Any takers for Elrid?" said the lender.

Immediately, a line formed from one end of the room to the other as men fished handfuls of coin or painted shells from their pockets. Once they reached the front of the line, they cast sympathetic glances in the old man's direction, but then wagered months of salary on his imminent demise.

"Who is this Hammerfist?" said Mira.

"I thought you knew all things."

"I'm not omniscient; I'm attentive. Also, I can't help but notice you still don't have any coin. How are you going to win anything down here?"

"Just wait," said Edmond. "I know what I'm doing. I've visited this place a good few times. They don't recognize me on account of..." He waved a hand across his face.

Mira mimicked the gesture. "What does this mean?"

Edmond ignored her simply to annoy her.

Mira sighed, but turned her attention back towards the rest of the room. She seemed entirely disinterested in the fighting and preferred to watch men and a few women approach the lender and, muttering their wager, shove piles of coin they likely couldn't afford into the waiting hands of Grerald.

"Ooh, look at the way she's glancing over her shoulder," said Mira, practically salivating. "I bet her husband doesn't know. Oh—*no* ring. Doubly interesting; what I wouldn't give to pry into her skull and examine the dark corners."

Edmond swallowed slightly and gave a shake of his head. "Maybe restoring your powers isn't such a great idea."

Mira, however, didn't seem to hear him on account of the fight commencing once more. Scar-face had retreated into a back room, and, from the same dark hallway, emerged a thick-shouldered man with fists twice the normal size. If Edmond didn't know better, he would have assumed some sort of alchemical affects at play. But, physical defect was the more likely cause in a place like this. Not even the Roosters would be so bold as to employ an obvious alchemical advantage on one of their fighters.

Mira glanced pityingly at the old, wizened fellow who'd already stepped into the circle. The old man eyed the approaching, ham-fisted fighter. "It won't end well," she murmured.

Edmond glanced from the lender, to the fighters. He then glanced towards the crowd. A couple of the men who'd been complaining loudly about Grerald's choice of fighter were now smirking in the gloom. They also, he'd noticed, hadn't placed any bets.

Plants then. Edmond smiled slightly. "I wouldn't be so sure," he said.

Mira coughed. "Excuse me? You think that wizened fool has a chance?"

Edmond glanced at the lender again who was counting stacks of d'oro. "I think he's going to win."

Mira scoffed at him, but then nearly swallowed the sound as the fight commenced, and the old man came out swinging. Suddenly, he didn't look half so old. He moved with the speed of someone seemingly half his age and caught Hammerfist with two quick jabs. Before Elrid could recover, the old man kicked out, catching him on the knee.

"Alchemy might be disallowed, but a little bit of makeup and hair dye goes a long way," Edmond murmured. "Likely as not, Elrid is in on it. The Roosters always win—a slogan worth remembering."

GRAVEYARD GODS

It didn't take long for Elrid to hit the ground, either unconscious or faking it, and the old, wizened man hurried off, down the fighter's hall without collecting his fifty d'oro winnings.

A shellshocked crowd turned on the lender, their shouts of disbelief and anger reverberating in the air and dislodging streams of dust which trickled from the rafters to the ground. A couple of red-faced men moved towards the lender, but were caught by the guards who pushed off the back wall and surged forward faster than Edmond would have guessed.

One of the guards dragged the aggressors to the bottom of the stairs by the ears, and sent them tumbling up. The guard called out to his colleagues at the top of the stairs, and a few strangled cries later, the agitators had disappeared.

"Well," said the Lender. "What a surprise." He didn't seem surprised in the least. "Our champion is up next—any takers?"

This time, no one raised their hand.

Mira murmured, "Are we just going to sit around all day inhaling body odor and blood?"

But Edmond ignored Mirastious' mutterings. This time, he stepped forward. "Who's the champion?" he called out.

A few heads turned towards him, and the lender frowned at the question. But, after a moment, he called back, "I'll remind you, everyone is welcome in the Kindly Roosts. We are no respecters of persons."

"That's not what I'm saying," said Edmond, starting to grin. The answer was what he'd been hoping for. "I don't mind strange competition. I'm just asking for a name."

"The current champion," the lender said, clearing his throat. "Is Calder the Shark."

Now, Edmond was practically beaming. His hand shot in the air. "Fifty d'oros, free and clear?"

The lender hid a smirk behind a cough and quickly covered by saying, "If you *win*, yes."

That was the thing with the Maiden's Doubt. Sometimes, the fighters would be ringers. Other times, the audience members would be "randomly chosen." And, other times, it would all be above board.

"I'll fight him," said Edmond, still smiling.

Mira clapped a hand to his shoulder, squeezing him tight until he winced. "What are you doing?" she hissed.

"Earning us some coin," he muttered back. "Like I said."

"I've seen you fight! You were useless—you were also stabbed."

Edmond waved away her protest with a shrug. At a nod from the lender, he approached the fighting circle, stepping beneath the swinging alchemical lanterns dangling from the rafters above.

"Alright, gents, we have a new challenger," the lender cried. "Now, introducing the reigning champion—give it up for Calder the Shark!"

Some of the crowd muttered darkly as the champion emerged from down the hall. Others glanced pityingly in Edmond's direction. Edmond knew his chances in a fair fight against the pit fighter were slim at best. He'd once trained in a knight's academy, but that had been a lifetime ago— and he had been kicked out. What little he knew about hand-to-hand combat usually came while he was trying to break away from his assailant and flee. So, no, in a contest of combat, Edmond rarely overcame his fellow men.

Which meant it was a good thing that Calder was an exception. The fighter standing across from him, emerging from the shadows of the hall was no man at all. In fact, he wasn't even human.

Chapter 17

Muergo held his pale hand in front of him, staring down at the curling ember that had landed in his palm. The dirty linen strips that wrapped his arms clung to him as a thin sheen of sweat beaded under his dark cape. The heat from the fires behind him drove smoke high into the air, and he watched as the ember he held turned to ash and blew away in the sea breeze.

The crying villagers had simmered to a low whimpering punctuated by the occasional sob, and his mind filtered the convoluted and conflicting stories they had told him, distilling truth from panic and fear.

An old fishwife had told him about an obscene payment in the form of a gilded sword that her husband took to sail a stranger to Carabas without delay, along with the promise of future coin upon arrival. Others told him about a writhing black demon that had torn men limb from limb before disappearing into the small island's forest. Yet others said that a family of pearl divers had run amok, killing their neighbors, but most agreed that the fires had started when an Imperial Frigate opened fire on the village.

Augustin, Muergo thought. Severelle had been clear about who else hunted this tomb raider. Had only one person told him the ship opened fire, he would have dismissed it. The thought of Sir Augustin Mora opening fire on a defenseless village struck him as the height of absurdity, but then again, *Perhaps, the lad has finally cracked.*

Muergo's mind drifted then, and he lost himself in the memory of another burning city. The sea breeze vanished into pines that roasted like torches, the wood huts were replaced with cracked brick and stucco, but the smell remained. The smell of burnt flesh and blood, shot through with the acrid scent of spent gunpowder. *Borgo Tortrugha.*

"Muergo, we've loaded what provisions we could find at the inn." One of his crewmen said from behind him, breaking Muergo from his reverie. "This shit-smear of a village didn't have much in the way of gold, but what we could find has been sent to your cabin."

"Very well. We leave." Muergo strode across the dock towards his black sloop.

"And what of the villagers?"

Muergo halted. Turning his head, he looked at the long beam he'd ordered erected. The dozen or so men and women who had not fled stood on a haphazard line of boxes, chairs, and footstools, their faces shimmered as streaking tears caught the setting sun, while nooses loosely roped them to the beam above. He appraised them, his pale eyes scanning the line with flinty disinterest. Turning back to the ship, he said simply, "I'm done with them."

A series of panicked cries went up, as the crewmen approached the gallows, but by the time Muergo reached the sloop, he heard only the distant cawing of the gulls.

CHAPTER 18

"BLUE FIRE AND BLACK fish, let me up! I'm still your Lord Captain, dammit." Augustin said, pushing against Cristobal's thick forearm. The strong man stood to the side of his bed and held him by the shoulder, keeping Augustin from standing. Behind Cristobal, Catali crushed dried herbs into a mortar with what smelled like honey and garlic.

"Hold him still, Cristobal," the surgeon said. "He's been walking around too much already these last couple days." Augustin stopped struggling for the moment, though his dark mustache shook as he ground his teeth.

"That's because I'm fine. I've had much worse before."

"I know," Catali said, shaking her head in astonishment. "I see the scars when I change your bandages. You've been lucky so far. Haven't lost anything to infection yet."

"And there's no sign of infection now either," Augustin interjected.

Catali lifted the stone pestle out of the mortar and let the thick, sticky mixture drip back into the receptacle. She grunted in approval.

"And that's good, m'lord captain, but if you want to keep it that way-Cristobal, what have I been telling him?"

"Stop moving around and reopening the wound." The big man's voice rumbled in the small cabin. He scratched the scar of his missing ear with his free hand. "Catali's right, sir. After what Agreo already pulled, I don't want to think about what he'd do if you were down with a fever."

Augustin scowled, the anger hot in his chest. Agreo was most of the reason why he felt he could not stay in bed. After he collapsed in his cabin, Augustin had slept for the majority of the day. Cristobal told him that Agreo was behaving himself, mostly, and that they were en route to Carabas, but it irked Augustin that the man was still on the ship. He thought again about when he stood looking down into the gundeck. Had he not been about to pass out from the strain, he would have been able to find out what had happened and dealt with Agreo right then and there. When he did wake up, it had taken both Catali and Cristobal together to calm him down. The man was a monster, and Augustin wanted nothing less than to drag Agreo behind the ship and let the sharks have him. Catali had liked the idea too, but pointed out that technically Agreo had done nothing wrong. If Augustin took any action, Agreo could argue that with Augustin injured, he stepped into command and defended the ship against an unknown threat. In fact, stirring the pot likely would end with Agreo's seal baron brother stirring up trouble against Cristobal for striking a superior officer. That culminated with the large Dumasian's neck at the end of a long noose.

It only fueled Augustin's anger further to realize that Commodore Severelle would probably accept Agreo's version of the events. There was nothing, honorably, that Augustin could do, but nothing about the situation made him comfortable enough to rest in bed.

Catali knelt by the bedside and gingerly peeled back the bandages. She sniffed a few times, pausing, then giving a satisfied nod before she stripped the rest of the bandage. Cristobal let go of Augustin's shoulder and leaned against the wall of the cabin. While Catali applied her poultice to the wound, Cristobal took a small whittling knife from his belt pouch and began to work a small piece of wood, letting the shavings fall to the floor. Augustin thought he had seen him carving on the small block yesterday as well and asked, "What are you working on?"

Cristobal turned the shapeless block in his hand. "It's a totem to Ververiona. For your healing." Augustin raised his head in sudden recognition. Now the strange knobby turn of the wood started to make sense. It was a knotted tangle of branches and roots, crudely done —the gods had not given Cristobal the delicate hands of an artist— but with the proper number and dimension.

"I haven't seen you make a totem in a long time," Augustin said.

Cristobal shrugged, then looked over to Augustin with a smile. "Well, you haven't travelled with me in a long time."

"No, I suppose I haven't," Augustin said. His gaze drifted in thought as Cristobal turned back to carving the small offering. It was strange to think. He hadn't seen the big man in nearly five years, but here they were. The old bonds between them were still strong. Augustin wondered if it would be the same with the other members of the Order. Catali gave a short snort.

"Oh, sure. Ververiona, mother of life, a fine choice. I'm sure she'll answer your call, just as soon as she's done tending the needs of some poor codfish or a beech tree that's having a particularly hard time of it." The surgeon drew out a length of bandage as she muttered, "Mirastious, save us from ignorance."

Augustin twisted to allow the surgeon a better angle for re-bandaging his wound. He gave Cristobal an amused look, but the big man only scoffed, then went back to whittling, peeling off a thick curl of the wood with an aggressive push of the tiny knife.

"Mirastious?" said Augustin. "I'd have thought you'd pray to Cinae, being a surgeon."

Catali shook her head in a non-committal bob. "Cinae of the healing herb is a fine patron, and some in the calling go for Pardi of the Sun, but my nan prayed to Mirastious. Claimed she appeared to her once when she was a girl." Catali gave a small chuckle as she turned the bandage. "Guess, it's just old habit now."

Augustin's lip cracked into a smile.

"Cristobal and I had a companion, back when we were knights in Gamor. She used to burn blackroot during the new moon for Mirastious." The nostalgia in his voice was enhanced by the cool numbing sensation of the poultice as the bandage pressed it to his wound. Catali's own smile broadened.

"My nan used to do that too. Was your friend an alchemist?"

"She was," Augustin said, scratching at his neck. He had not had a chance for a shave in a few days and the skin around his throat was beginning to itch. "Serenia was one of the best I knew. She wasn't just an alchemist, though that would have been enough. She was a knight. She was actually in the Order with me and Cristobal, and a few others."

"The order?" Catali asked.

"The Honorable Order of the Lily," Cristobal intoned in his deep voice. Catali looked over to the big man. Cristobal moved his large hands as if he were handing the words over to the kneeling surgeon, one by one, with the totem and whittling knife carried along for the ride. "There were six of us. Some, like the Lord Captain and myself, were former knights of the Baron Colinas of Gamor. When we left his service we did not wish to be like so many former knights who fall into banditry or crude mercenary work. So we drew up an accord and founded our knightly order."

"Just the two of you?" Catali asked. She cinched the bandage with an incredulous laugh. "Doesn't sound like much of an order." Cristobal frowned, but Augustin laughed along with the surgeon.

"No," Augustin said as he pushed at the fresh bandage. "It wasn't much of an order, but it is much easier to find honorable work as a freelance when you can convince the local reeve that you are not some random sellsword, but belong to a prestigious order. Besides, once we started travelling, we acquired some new members."

"So what happened to everyone?" Catali asked. Augustin looked at the young surgeon. For the first time he realized that the woman must be about the same age he had been when he left the Baron to become a freelance nearly ten years ago. Augustin coughed and looked away.

"Well, things changed. Some people decided they wanted to do other things." The answer felt lame as it left his mouth, but Augustin made no move to say any more.

Catali raised a confused eyebrow and turned her head as if she would ask more, when Cristobal interjected, "It does not matter. What matters is that the Order is reuniting. That is why we sail for Carabas."

Catali looked from the Lord Captain to the big man, now looking even more perplexed. "I thought we were going there to hunt the tomb raider," she said.

"We are," replied Cristobal. "But to better hunt him, and to better-erm, control the ship, we are reuniting with our former Order."

"Will your friend, Serenia, be there?"

Augustin nodded. "At least, that is my hope. We are nearly a month past when I had hoped to meet them there, and I've had no way to get them a message." Augustin thought again of the one week time limit Commodore Severelle had imposed on them. It was the third day. *They'll be there*, he thought. *They have to be.*

A long pause slipped by before Catali pushed herself to her feet, and turned to the dressing table. "Well, I hope that they are still waiting for you, for all our sakes. Now here, take this."

Reaching into her bag, Catali handed Augustin a glass bottle with a cork stopper.

"Senza?" Augustin asked, looking at the honeyed liquid.

As Catali washed her hands, she spoke over his shoulder. "Yes. For the pain, since you won't listen to your surgeon. Just have a taste at a time and only if the pain gets unbearable." She gave him one more admonishing look as she folded her arms and leaned back against the cabin wall. "So, m'lord captain, with us docking in Carabas within the next few hours, can you stay off your feet till then, or do I need to sedate you?"

Chapter 19

THE SUN WAS BEGINNING to set as the *Intrepid* entered the Bay of Bianchetto. Augustin clutched the railing of the ship's prow with one hand while the other held the handle of his rapier. Once the lookout sighted Carabas' white-stone lighthouse, not even Cristobal could keep him confined to the bed. To port, the lighthouse illuminated a trailing line of reef and sandbar that guarded the bay like an underwater wall. On the starboard side of the frigate, a high, rocky shelf held the roundels and towers of a seaside fortress that overlooked the bay as well as the city of Carabas itself.

Cristobal joined Augustin at the railing as the *Intrepid* passed a merchant carrack. Other ships soon followed as the bay grew choked with the myriad of designs and sizes that maneuvered for access in and out of the harbor. A massive hill on the Western side of the city lay its shadow over most of the dockways, but light from hanging lanterns and windows soon bathed the steep hill in a warm glow that etched out its streets and buildings like a gigantic, haphazard stairway built into its side. "Verian Hill, how I've missed her," the big man said as he breathed in the breeze. Augustin gave a soft murmur of agreement.

"Feels like we were here yesterday," said Augustin. The scent of grilling fish teased his nose for a scant moment before being swept off by the salt air. "I wonder if the Brass Wheel is still open."

Cristobal snorted. "Are you sure you'd want to go back if it was?"

"What?" Augustin asked with mock indignity. "The place was clean; they didn't dilute their wine ... that mackerel with the garlic they used to serve there?" Augustin tilted his head back in fond memory.

"True, but I was more thinking of the serving girls."

Augustin's smile widened with pleasant memories of another sort. "If you're trying to dissuade me from going, you're doing an exceedingly poor job of it."

Cristobal shook his head in mock severity.

"Fine, but don't say I didn't warn you when you're knee deep in brown eyed brats named 'Gus.'"

Augustin's eyes popped wide as the big man laughed.

"You should see your face right now," Cristobal said with a rumbling guffaw.

Behind them, Agreo barked orders to the crew, and the *Intrepid* began its final approach toward an open dock. The throng of people walking the stone harbor let out a cacophony of voices speaking a dozen different languages. They filled the air with argument and haggling over the wares they were offloading to the nearby warehouses or to carters.

Once they were docked and anchored, Augustin and Cristobal set off into the city. Under the shadow of Verian Hill, the streets of Carabas ran in a tangle of cobblestone winds and mazes. Stone gutters, cut into the sides of these streets, carried waste water down the sloping terrain of ramps and narrow stairways to the bay. Men and women in colorful tunics swirled with the unspoken currents of the city's living heartbeat. Soon, even the titanic mound of Verian Hill slipped into shadow, obscured by the buildings around them. Compact boxes of plastered brickwork rose like helter-skelter walls to frame the alleys and byways of the city. As night rose, the light from diamond shaped windows of colored glass illuminated their path and Verian Hill glittered like a second sky under the rising constellations.

Soon, they were climbing the lowest twists in Verian Hill, and came to stop in front of an inn. Beside the door, a squat statue of a priest held a cluster of granite grapes and a small keg that was worn smooth across its top. Cristobal turned his good ear and listened to a nearby busker plucking out a jangling melody on a guitar, while Augustin drew a creased and crinkled letter from his breast pocket.

"This is it," Augustin said, tucking away the letter. "The Stone Priest. Vicente said in his letter that he'd hire out a room until we were all together again. Hopefully, they are still here."

Augustin felt anxiety nip at his heart. It had been more than five years. Vicente. Odo. Tristan. *Serenia.* He reached up and touched the small fleck of grey in his dark beard. The Order, reunited. But, would it really be the same?

Cristobal looked at the wide glass window of the inn behind the little priest statue. "It's been so long. Do you think Vicente will recognize us?"

At that moment, the glass exploded, and a man crashed through the inn's window, spilling out into the street at their feet. He let out a groan as he twisted on his back, blinking up at the sky like a man coming out of a dream.

"Gus?" the man asked. His voice, raw, like sandpaper on glass, tilted with the question. "Cris?"

There was a pause while they each looked down at the prone man. Black dreadlocks spread out behind his head. His face was covered in a rough stubble, interrupted by pale scars running between his jaw and the corner of his eye. The frock coat around his shoulders was so dust-washed and patched that the original red had faded to a muddy brick color. Augustin absorbed all this, but his attention was most drawn to the man's eyes. One reflected a deep, oak brown while the other was yellow, like a curled wasp.

"Vicente?" Augustin asked.

"Vicente!" Cristobal leaned down and grabbed hold of the prone man, pulling him to his feet in one swift motion. Vicente wrapped his arms around the big Dumasian, slapping his back and releasing a mad laugh that fell out of him all at once, like tumbling copper pots. A shuffling of motion rolled from beyond the smashed window, and Augustin's hawk eyes locked onto the figures of five men as they rushed for the door of the inn.

"Cris," Vicente said, stepping back and planting his hands on his hips. Small bits of glass let out a tinkling chime as they fell from his coat and hair to the stone street. "You crazy-jack-ass-mountain-of-a-man, it is pleasing to see you again." Almost at once, his mismatched eyes jumped to Augustin, and he stumbled forward. Throwing his arms wide, the ragged man hugged Augustin in a tight embrace as he said, "And you too, Gus. Or should I say, m'lord cap'n?"

Before Augustin could reply, the five men he had been tracking, burst through the door of the inn and spilled out into the street. Each held their palm to the pommel of a sabre at his belt, and their hands were heavy with brass rings and bangles. Their hair was cut short on one side with the rest tied in numerous braids that dangled with polished stones and glittering glass baubles, while flashy, silk scarves were tied at various places around their bodies.

Bravos, Augustin thought, gripping the hilt of his rapier. Sell-swords and sometime pirates, the bravos of Carabas had a reputation in the isles for their prodigious appetites for wine and violence as well as their immeasurable pride. As the five men stormed closer, Vicente released his hug and turned to follow Augustin's gaze.

"Oh, right," said Vicente with the weary groan of a man who has just remembered some forgotten chore.

"Friends of yours?" Cristobal asked, stretching his neck with a series of loud cracks.

The foremost bravo, a tall man in a green tunic adorned with embroidery of yellow birds, sneered at Augustin, then seeing

GRAVEYARD GODS

Cristobal, he held his hands to the side and brought his group to a halt.

"Step aside, we have business with the honey-snake," he said, jabbing one finger up to his own eye as he gave Vicente a venomous glare.

Augustin drew back his shoulders and spoke with the commanding voice he used with the crew. "Stand down. I am an officer of the Empire, and I have business with this man."

The aggressor licked his lips as his four companions behind him began to speak in rattling Chelleck. Augustin only knew a few words in the western tongue, but he could see their animated gesturing and the way the lead bravo's face reddened even deeper, baring his teeth in an angry scowl.

"You can have the honey-snake when we are done with him. The dog is a thief and a card-cheat. Move aside Imperial, you're not in Godshaven today." With this, the bravo drew his sabre, taking a wide stance and swiping the blade in front of him like he was attacking an invisible enemy while the others at his side did the same.

Augustin blinked, suppressing the urge to roll his eyes at the show of bravado, and looked over to Vicente, who gave a sheepish smile, like a child who'd been caught misbehaving. The busker's guitar had stopped its merry tune, and the street around them clogged as a circle of onlookers formed around the front of the Stone Priest Inn. As Augustin looked back to the bravos, he could see the excitement rising in their breath. They wanted blood.

"How much?" he asked. The lead bravo cocked his head in confusion, so Augustin elaborated. "You said he stole from you. How much?" Again, the bravos behind their leader spoke in rapid Chellek, the explosive words rattling like a bag of coins, while the leader slowly lowered his sword. He shot back what sounded like a question and another bravo tucked his sabre under his armpit while he rapidly counted across his fingers.

The exchange was brief, and with a smirk the leader of the bravos said, "The honey-snake owes us three hundred d'oro."

Augustin inhaled sharply. That much gold could pay his whole crew for a week. It was not insignificant, but possibly-

"Oh, that is shark shite, you drownin' peacock!" Vicente exclaimed. Putting one hand on Augustin's shoulder he spoke in a mock whisper that did nothing to lower his voice. "Bero there is just mad because I went *pearl divin'* with his sister. You'd like her, Gus. A real 'man-eater', if you catch my meaning." Vicente grabbed his crotch with a sly grin while Augustin watched the faces of the five bravos go from shocked disbelief to outrage.

"What did you say?" screamed the leader, Bero apparently. Froth flew from his lips.

"Oh, did you not know that bit?" Vicente asked innocently.

With an animal-like cry, Bero raised his sabre over his head and charged forward, bringing the blade down on Vicente. A clang of steel rang out as Augustin drew his sword into the path of the bravo's slash and caught the blade.

Vicente laughed like a cackling crow as the two locked blades strained a hand's breadth away from his face. "Oh, Bero. You have no idea how bad a mistake you just made."

Cristobal lunged forward to stand to Augustin's right. He raised his arms, as the remaining four bravos surged ahead to stand alongside their leader, two on each side of Augustin. The giant Dumasian twisted his body in a calamitous hook that caught the nearest of the two bravos across the jaw and sent him twisting back as a tooth popped from his jaw like corn from a kettle. His companion shoved the reeling man aside, sending him tumbling to the ground with a wet thud as his sword fell from his nerveless fingers.

At the same time, Vicente stepped backward and tossed open his frock coat, revealing a brace of flintlock pistols hanging from a leather bandolier across his yellowed linen shirt. With one hand he drew a pistol while the other went to his hip and pulled free a thin, steel rapier. Still laughing, Vicente stepped to Augustin's left and levelled the weapons at the other two approaching attackers. He crossed his wrists to present the flintlock in the same motion. Seeing the pistol, the two bravos flinched as if they were trying to take cover behind their sabres, eliciting yet more of Vicente's raspy cackling.

Bero shoved forward with his sabre. With a twist of his blade, Augustin pushed aside the attack and brought down a cut to a green tunicked shoulder. It was a quick, efficient move that left a red slash in the fabric as the bravo skirted back. Augustin watched the man's movements with a stern expression, meeting every slash and cut with a curt parry, waiting till the last moment to turn the strikes aside. He could see the mounting frustration in Bero's tanned face as the man skipped left and right, arcing his blade in wild patterns. It didn't matter though. Bero moved his body quickly, but he didn't fight with it. All his strikes came from his elbow, everything else was just flare and noise. Augustin gave him a light cut across the other shoulder, and the man's eyes flew wide with shock that quickly gave way to indignity.

"You are toying with me, aren't you?" he said, clapping a hand to his bleeding shoulder and looking at the blood.

"No. I'm giving you a chance to run away," Augustin said calmly. He kept his voice low in an effort to spare the man's dignity. He glanced to his left. Vicente's battered frock coat swept around him as he lunged with his rapier, using the cocked pistol almost like a shield. Whenever one of the bravos tried to come at him from the side, Vicente checked him with the pistol while he repositioned himself. To his right, Cristobal had his hands up in a boxer's posture, drawing wild swings from his remaining attacker as he danced out of reach.

Augustin looked back to the leader. "So what will it be?"

In answer, the bravo leapt forward, bringing his sabre to bear in an upward sweep. Augustin stepped out of the path of the blade, and his muscles tensed as he fell into an aggressive posture. He brought his rapier up and gave a thrust that slid three inches into the bravo's chest. The man dropped his sword as he fell back, grabbing the open wound. Leaving him, Augustin lunged towards the bravo harassing Cristobal and landed two succinct cuts across the back of his legs. The man's knees buckled as his severed hamstrings went limp within his body, and he crumpled with a scream of pain. One of the bravos fighting Vicente broke off, jumping for Augustin, but the lord captain brought his rapier down on the enemy blade and knocked it aside as he stepped forward and kicked the man in the chest, feeling the impact rock through his boot and up into his chest. He toppled to the street, and Augustin lowered his sword's point over the man's throat. The man froze as the keen edge hovered over him, and Augustin glanced up to see Vicente playfully turn his rapier and point his pistol at the remaining sellsword.

"Go on. Shimmie on home," he said as he bounced the barrel of the pistol, his yellow eye staring at the man gleefully.

The last two bravos didn't need convincing. As soon as Augustin lifted his sabre, they turned and ran, leaving their companions writhing in the street. Vicente whooped loudly as he sheathed his rapier, but Augustin paid him no mind. Reaching to his side, he could feel the warm wet of his wound as fresh blood began to seep through the bandage.

"Damn it," Augustin muttered, clutching his side as the pain of the tear rose in his ribs.

Chapter 20

THE AROMA OF GRILLED fish and bright lemon rising from the kitchens downstairs helped to distract Augustin from the pain in his ribs. He sat on the edge of the bed doing his best to ignore the angry wound, while Cristobal stoked up a small brazier of coals for warmth. The fresh bindings around his torso were still white, save for a few dark splotches in the clean fabric. The bleeding had mostly stopped by the time they reached the inn. Vicente swatted aside the small coil of used bandages that lay on the bed, knocking them to the ground like a mass of writhing red snakes, and sat beside Augustin. As the bed jostled, a twinge of pain shivered through his ribs, and Augustin considered drinking the pain-killing senza that Catali had given him.

"Just like old times, eh Gus?" Vicente said, pulling a stranded bit of glass from his dreadlocks and tossing it out of the room's window. "Putting some villains in their place. Binding up a wound or two at the nearest inn while we drown ourselves in ale. Hah!"

GRAVEYARD GODS

After their fight against the bravos, Cristobal did not think it wise to stay at the Stone Priest. While the sell-swords had been cowed for the moment, their pride would no doubt bring them back for blood, but Vicente had insisted on staying, saying he'd won credit to the room in a game of cards the night before. The room was of good quality, if not extravagant. The beds smelled clean, excepting the one Vicente had claimed which smelled of sweat, old fish and sugarcane rum tinged with lime, and they stood raised off the floor by sturdy bedposts. A single window with a clear glass pane looked down the hill over the glinting lights of the lower city, and a pewter ewer of clean water sat on a small table beside a wash bowl. Broken glass bottles were scattered in one corner of the room, and two sabres and a couple of knives rested on the floor by the window.

While Cristobal helped Augustin change his bandages, Vicente went down to the bar and returned to the room with three tall glasses of the establishment's stiff ale pinched in his calloused hands. He finished his own glass and was halfway through Augustin's before Cristobal finished redressing the wound.

Speaking around the lip of the glass, Vicente said, "Yes, indeed, indeed. Feels like...coming home. The only thing missing is some poor girl with stars in her eyes fawning over that scratch of yours." He pointed to the fresh bandage as Augustin pulled down his shirt. "I think you might be losing your charms. Finally," Vicente chortled. "Or did you finally make the hellcatcher an honest woman? Just asking because you have the look of a man tied down."

Augustin winced as he remembered the dark haired woman from Sile who had given him the wound.

"No. Isobella and I are still— well, no." Augustin coughed and put on a false smile as he pressed ahead. "You might be right, about me losing my charms though. I definitely don't get the same reactions I used to." Augustin looked up to his companion with a grim smile, and a moment's pause passed between them as the three appraised each other. The lines of age in Vicente's face creased like dark furrows and gave him a texture like cracked leather. His yellow eye wandered a little, following the ale running through him. Only five years had passed since they had last seen each other. Sure, Augustin had a few grey hairs in his beard now and Vicente was nearly ten years his senior, and as he looked at the haggard man sitting beside him, Augustin wondered just how much of the energetic knight he remembered was left.

"Don't look at me like that," Vicente said. His voice fell as he spoke, tired, but not harsh.

Augustin started and lowered his eyes. "I'm sorry, Vicente. It's just—well, it's been a long time since we've seen you." Augustin looked to Cristobal for support and the giant Dumasian nodded solemnly. "I wonder how you've been keeping since the Order dissolved."

"Dissolved." Vicente hung on the word a moment before releasing a bitter chuckle and taking another pull from the ale. "That's one way to put it." Meeting Augustin's eye, Vicente seemed on the edge of speaking when he simply shrugged and gulped the drink down like water. "How have I been keeping? Just fine. Getting work where I can. Keeping ol' scratch quiet when I can." Vicente pointed to the coiled yellow in his eye with a gallows grin.

Cristobal leaned forward and asked, "It has not changed? Same as before?"

"Same as the day he came aboard." Vicente snapped a hand to his temple, closing his eyes in a sudden grimace. The look of pain on his face made Augustin think of a dog who has just been struck across the head. It was a look he had nearly forgotten, and seeing it sent an upwelling of sorrow to his chest.

Vicente groaned and banged his fist against the bedpost, fracturing the sound into a malicious chortle. "He knows I'm talking about him."

"He's still putting visions in your head?" Augustin asked, folding his hands in front of him.

"Yeah. Ol' scratch is still a right bastard, but I've got him under control. When I don't use the sight, he's much more docile."

Augustin thought about the bloody dagger carefully tucked away at his hip. Shame weighed at his heart. He had spent so much of the last month in eager anticipation; waiting to be reunited with his comrades. Then, when the tomb-robber escaped and Agreo's machinations escalated, he felt the desperate need of his former friends and the urgency to return to them. He thought of Vicente's golden eye, but had forgotten where it came from. He had remembered how incredibly useful Vicente's alchemically enchanted sight had been to them, but not how Vicente suffered for it. He recognized now that he wasn't simply coming to ask for help. He had come here to ask his friend to step back into fire for him, and the realization stung. Augustin smoothed his mustache, pushing the rising unease back down.

"The night is getting on," Augustin said. "Are the others staying here at the Stone Priest as well, or are they somewhere else in the city?"

Vicente seemed surprised at the question. A breathless pause carried between them, before he gestured to Augustin and Cristobal. "You are a month late in coming, Gus."

Augustin felt his heart sink as he realized what Vicente was implying.

"The others left. Depths below, I was a few days from leaving myself. Serenia left after the first ten days, said you probably forgot you even asked us to gather. You know how she gets sometimes."

Augustin looked down at the smoldering coals in the room's small brazier as Vicente continued, "Odo took up with a caravan the week after. Didn't even say goodbye. Tristan held out the longest, but after three weeks he decided you had either changed your mind or were dead. Not a bad guess, given the state of the Western Sea lately. Last I heard, there was a pirate fleet making trouble up the Dumasian coast. Gallowglass is what they're saying."

Augustin gave a stiff nod. "You heard right. Commodore Severelle laid a trap for them and sent the whole lot South."

"Well and good, I suppose, but there's always someone to fill the gap. When I left Crook they were already talking about some new company that had formed out of Trabson." Vicente shrugged.

Outwardly, Augustin sat listening, still as a statue, his hand resting stiffly on his bandaged ribs. But he wasn't paying much attention to Vicente's grumbling about pirates. In his gut, he felt the cold teeth of regret nibbling at his liver. In the catalogue of his recent missteps, this last trumped them all. *Damnation,* he cursed, closing his eyes quietly. He had missed them. They had come. They had answered his call and came, and he let them down. Would they come again if he called? The hot flush of embarrassment began to rise in his collar, and Augustin forced himself to his feet. He turned to face the window, letting out a groan as his wounded ribs protested. They ached and throbbed and his forehead felt hot. Reaching into the pouch at his side, Augustin drew out the glass bottle of senza, uncorked it and swallowed a small mouthful of the thick liquid. The mellow smell of the syrup filled the room like a mixture of pine needles and mulled wine.

Cristobal stepped to his side. "You should lie down if your wound pains you," he cautioned.

The numbing warmth of the senza began to spread through his body, and Augustin took a deep breath, nodding in agreement.

There was nothing else for it. The others had left, and he could not bring himself to be angry with them.

Turning back to Vicente, Augustin thought, *So, this is my last chance, to ask my remaining companion to walk back into the fire for me.* He stared at Vicente from his place at the window. He did not want to cause his friend pain, and yet—*We are knights of the Empire,* Augustin thought. *Our lives are pain and sacrifice for the good of all.* Augustin's hand gripped his sword. He felt the strong muscles of his forearm tense and strain against the sleeves of his uniform. Looking down at Vicente's ragged clothing and bedraggled hair, he did not know what to say, but when Vicente's mismatched eyes met his gaze, he knew what he felt. *Some of us have sacrificed much more than others.*

"You want to ask me a question," said Vicente, his voice low.

Augustin nodded, though he still felt unsure what it was precisely he wanted to ask.

Vicente rose from his seat on the bed and stepped in front of Augustin. "I hope you're not going to insult me, by askin' if I still want to join your crew." When Augustin remained silent, Vicente continued. "And I know you're not going to ask if I'm still fit for the life. Five years haven't stolen my edge."

Augustin remembered the wild enthusiasm of Vicente's swordplay in front of the Stone Priest. He had watched him thrown through a window onto a cobblestone street, then get up and fight like a man twenty years younger. No, he felt certain that Vicente could still handle the dangers of the life. Augustin glanced down at the three empty ale glasses that sat nearby. Licking his own lips in thoughtful deliberation, he turned back to Vicente. The older man's face seemed to grow grey, the boisterous energy draining from it like a leaking wineskin.

"Ah, I see," Vicente said. "It's about my eye then."

"I need your sight," Augustin said. He folded his hands behind his back, his posture straight and professional. It was easier this way somehow.

Vicente turned to pace the room. "Good old Vicente with his golden eye. The demon-sight. Bah!" Vicente waved a hand through the air as if he were shooing a fly—his voice agitated and coarse, his pacing foot-falls stamped a staccato against the wood floor. "And if I say 'no'? What then, eh? What if I don't want to open my eye anymore?" Now, his voice carried a bitter weight that was almost petulant. "What if I say, you can have my sword, my pistol, my arms, but not my eye? What if I say I'd rather pluck the damned thing from my head before I'd use the sight again?"

Cristobal held up a placating hand, "Calm yourself, my friend. We were there the first time you tried that. It grew back. All that pain for nothing."

Vicente scowled, continuing to pace, but throwing a defiant finger up towards Cristobal. "Then, I'll pour molten lead in and fill the gap! Or, burn it out with fire." He rubbed at his stubbled chin fiercely while Cristobal and Augustin looked on.

Augustin forced himself to remain reactionless. He watched on implacably as Vicente paced the floor of their room. He could not imagine what his friend saw or felt. To try and pretend otherwise would be as patronizing as it was untrue.

And yet, I still need him. With or without his eye, I need help. I need my comrades.

"Do you want me at your side, Lord Captain Mora?" Vicente spat the title out, stopping in front of Augustin and glaring at him out of the small yellow coil. "Or my eye?"

Augustin looked down at Vicente, fighting to keep his face a mask of calm confidence. "You are my friend, Vicente. I would be honored to have you at my side. With or without the use of your sight."

Vicente blinked and his hands went to his eyes, rubbing them furiously. "Shut up," he growled. Augustin pursed his lips, disappointment blooming in him. He felt hollow at the thought of losing the one companion who had stayed. If he lost him, if Vicente left now, the Order would truly be dead.

"Vicente, I'm sorry. I'm not sure-"

"Not you," Vicente said, turning himself to face the wall. "Shut up. Shut up." He muttered the words in a low voice that half lost itself in the wooden paneling.

Letting out a small moan, Vicente struck his forehead against the wall with a dull crack that made Augustin wince. Augustin took a step towards Vicente's back, when the old knight abruptly spun around. With one hand held to his head, he reached out with his other. "Give me the senza."

At first, Augustin didn't know what to make of the demand and squinted in confusion. Vicente gave an exasperated sigh and flailed his reaching hand. "I saw you take out the bottle a moment ago for your wound. If we're doing this, then I'm going to need something a hellovalot stronger than ale."

"You mean to join with us then?" Augustin asked.

"Yes. Nameless Death drag'ye South, but yes."

Augustin fished out the glass bottle and Vicente snatched it up, dragging the cork free with his teeth and letting it bounce to the floor. He took a heavy pull from the bottle that made Augustin's stomach turn.

"Easy with that. The surgeon says to only use a taste at a time," Augustin said.

Vicente lowered the bottle with a look of relief on his face that spread into a lopsided smile. "I know what the surgeon's say. But they've never had to treat what's wrong with me."

Vicente knelt down and fetched up the bottle's cork with an almost dainty grace, smiling like a man just waking up from a very pleasant dream. In that moment, Augustin felt he saw some of his old friend return. His features seemed to smooth, and his voice lost much of its harsh rasp. The years of pain and suffering from his cursed eye appeared to melt away from him, leaving only the bright and vigorous man within. The sight filled Augustin with a mingling of warm relief and dull agony.

"Now," Vicente said, stoppering the bottle. "I, and my eye, are at your service. What are you looking for that has you so desperate you need me?"

Shoving aside the feeling of unease, Augustin drew out the knife from his pouch. Vicente stowed the bottle of senza in the voluminous pocket of his frock-coat and took the bloody blade with both hands.

"Are you looking for the owner of the knife or the blood?"

Augustin replied, "We believe this blood belongs to a man who robbed a God Grave in the forbidden waters. He's dangerous, possibly an alchemist. That's who we need to find."

Vicente wiped a palm on his coat and adjusted the lay of the bandolier underneath. He scrunched his nose at the mention of alchemy, but otherwise his attention seemed entirely bent to the knife as he turned it over in his hands.

Augustin knew it wouldn't take long. His eyes followed Vicente's fingers as they prodded the dried blood on the blade.

"Oh-ho-ho, there you are," Vicente said. His voice rose in a menacing rasp as he looked down at the blood with mischievous glee.

Augustin looked up and saw the small yellow coil of Vicente's left eye. It glowed like a dim star in the night sky, the banded iris spinning around the black of his pupil like the rim of a carriage wheel. He remembered the first time he'd seen Vicente use the sight. He had looked more closely then. He had been so close that he'd seen the yellow band forming into minute letters. He'd watched then, even as the letters spun into words of some demonic language. It had been beautiful in a way, like watching a lightning storm or a perfectly executed sword stroke.

His attention jumped back to the knife as Vicente closed his hand around the grip like the snap of a bear-trap.

"I have him," Vicente said. When he opened his eyes again, the yellow of his left pupil was a simple solid band once more. "He's in Carabas."

Chapter 21

Pale skin seemed to shimmer like silver in the dancing torch light. Ridges of opalescent bone mantled and twisted about Calder's limbs like coiling vines. His ears would have tapered to points, Edmond knew, had they not been absent completely. The scarred ridges where Calder's ears had once perched were testament to the brutality of Carabas' under-slums. The Signerde weren't welcome in polite society, but they were *loathed* among the common folk. They were seen as cursed—scourges who brought the ire of Nameless Death, and who worshiped the tyrant goddess known as the Betrayed Mother. In contrast to the disgust levied at the beings themselves, their ears were considered a valuable alchemical component. Whether the ears were harvested from corpse or not was entirely up to the dispositions of the collectors.

Low mutterings and growls emitted from the surrounding spectators. But in the Kindly Roosts, all manner were welcome as long as they carried coin or, as sometimes the case, had a penchant for earning d'oro for the Roosters. To name a

Signerde one's "champion" meant that Calder the Shark had likely won the Maiden's Doubt more than his weight in d'oro.

The scars and rough skin of the Signerde were testament to the number of bouts he'd participated in. As with all his kind, the Signerde was shorter than the human patrons of the Roost's basement. But he moved with a grace and poise, scraping one bare foot across the lacquered wood as he approached. Edmond glanced down at the foot. Calder required neither sock nor boot on account of the rigid, pearlescent layer on the bottoms of his feet.

Edmond ran the tip of his tongue along his dry bottom lip. He nodded his head towards the shorter being, and gave a half smile. "Greetings, *kardesh. Gunduz ak geldi, bize.*"

The others in the room didn't hear Edmond on account of their raucous cries and thudding boots against the floor. But Calder hesitated as he drew close, frowning. The Signerde's eyes danced over Edmond, lingering on the potion vial that hung from his neck.

"*Annenin gulu seni bulsun,*" he said slowly. As he opened his mouth, he revealed a set of teeth that had been filed to points. The teeth, like the ridges on his body and the layer on the soles of his feet glinted like pearl. "And what does an alchemist know of The Children's blessings?"

Edmond inclined his head in a slight, but intentional bow of respect. A few of the shouting patrons quieted at this, grumbling beneath their breaths at the seeming familiarity. The lender, however, hadn't noticed—or didn't care. He'd likely seen Calder the Shark's work enough to know Edmond had little chance of walking from the arena.

GRAVEYARD GODS

As the lender shouted odds and final bets were placed, emphasized by the sound of metal coin scraping on wooden desks or jangling in loose pockets, Edmond stretched his back, dancing from foot to foot.

Calder eyed him with interest. The Signerde had scowled as he'd entered the room, but at Edmond's words the scowl had faded somewhat. Now, though, the cries of the surrounding men and women increased in volume, beckoning the bout.

"No eye gougin', Calder," said the lender, his high, lisping voice piercing the cacophony. "No crushin' the man's testicles neither."

Edmond raised an eyebrow towards Calder. The Signerde grinned back, flashing his sharpened teeth. And then, with a shout from the lender, the bout began.

The Signerde covered the distance between them faster than any human could have managed. Edmond, though, responded with nearly equal speed, lurching to the side. He shifted his left foot, pivoting and ducking in the same motion, allowing his shoulder to catch Calder on the hip.

The Signerde took to the air, rolling, back-to-back over Edmond, lest his leg crack from the change in direction, and landed on the other side with a thud. In the same motion, as he landed, he kicked out with his heel, trying to hook Edmond's foot. But the tomb raider, again moving with pace, skirted to the side.

The crowd cheered.

Calder looked up, teeth glinting in the torchlight, pearlescent ridges across his body stretching with each steady breath.

"Spent some time among the Eldest, did you? Know a thing or two about *savo-kahn*, I see?"

Edmond nodded once, balancing on the balls of his feet. He'd never gone beyond a novice's level with the Signerde martial art, but in a literal sense, he did know a thing or two. "My brother-in-law was third brethren. Last I spoke with him, he was on track to master his matriarch proving."

Some of the cries and shouts quieted at this. A few of the spectators leaned in, trying to catch the odd exchange between the even odder coupling. Others, though, shook their cupped fists, sloshing their drinks and booing at the rafters.

"Your brother-in-law?" Calder frowned now, rising slowly to his feet, his hand dangling against his thighs. "You married a Signerde? The Eldest allowed such a thing?"

"It's a rare man to catch storm wind and keep it near his chest. A doubly rare man to find the heart of a crashing wave."

"You know our poetry too? And you, you're such a man? Rare indeed." Calder hesitated. By now, the booing had reached a crescendo. The lender had left his table under the supervision of the Roosters at the back of the room and approached the circle to see what the commotion was about.

Calder eyed Edmond up and down. "You move like one of us," he said. "I give you that. You know a word or two, and you quote our poetry. However..." Here his eyes narrowed. "I'm neither Brewer nor Remnant. I'm an Eldest..."

"I see," said Edmond, swallowing. "The man who told me a Signerde now worked in the Maiden's Doubt forgot to mention that tidbit."

Calder flashed his shark-like grin. "I get to beat the bloody shite out of mudthumpers for fun. Round-ears are always looking for a shot at the champion." He winked, then dashed forward again.

This time, when Edmond tried to pull the same maneuver as before, the Signerde caught himself and brought a knee thudding into Edmond's ribs.

The tomb raider cried out in pain, reeling, but before he could process what had happened, Calder was on him again, fists flying. Edmond had spent enough time around Signerde to know they never tired. *Savo-kahn* was meant to be used underwater where the sea slowed down your movements. When moving through thin air, a trained Signerde could strike like a thunderbolt. In fact, most he'd tussled with or seen in a fight only seemed to grow more energetic as their fights went on.

Calder was no exception. His punches came faster, his kicks quicker. Edmond rolled back, dodging one way, then another, but for each blow he evaded, he received two more to the face or gut.

Soon, he was gasping, bleeding from a cracked nose and peering out from behind a hooded eye that felt like it was already starting to bruise. *This* hadn't been the plan. Calder paused for a moment, tilting his head like a painter examining their handiwork. He wasn't even breathing hard.

Edmond, on the other hand, gasped, each effort of breath a venture in pain. He glanced through bleary eyes towards Mira at the back of the room. She clapped slowly, leaning against the wall. Her veil was thrown back, Edmond suspected, so she could get a better look at him as he had the living daylight kicked out of him. Judging by her shining eyes and bright smile, what she saw gave her great pleasure.

Edmond had thought to use his connection with the Signerde to gain a quick handful of coins. The previous year, he'd heard that the Maiden's Doubt now had a Signerde fighter working for them, one said to deal in alchemical ingredients no less. What *hadn't* been told to him was that Calder the Shark was an Eldest. Of the three main factions among the Signerde, none hated humankind more than the Eldest did. They were a violent, rebellious group—which Edmond quite liked in theory—who delighted in the suffering of round-ears.

And, one of them was leering at him across a bloodstained floor, preparing for another attack.

Another swift charge, which Edmond would have missed had he blinked, followed by two more blows to the ribs and a swift right to the chin. Blood flew from Edmond's lips as he stumbled back, clutching his face, unsure whether to defend his stomach or his head.

Calder nodded in appreciation as some of the crowd cheered—grudgingly for the Signerde earning them coin—and others booed. The boos were louder and more heartfelt than before. More than d'oro was at stake for many of the patrons.

"Come on!" someone screamed. "Put the drowner in his place!"

"Skin the fish," shouted another.

Still a third, cried, "Beat the storm brewer until it cries!"

Edmond glanced with a narrowed gaze at the agitators. He spat, blood dribbling down his chin, mixing with saliva and falling in globules to the floor.

He caught another jab to the nose, and then a swift kick to the groin. Edmond groaned, creaking like a felled tree and toppled to the floor.

"Calder!" shouted the lender's voice. "What did I say about the testicles?"

"I didn't crush them!" Calder shouted back. "It was a tap." The Signerde sounded like he was enjoying himself, which set more of the spectators into dark, stormy growls and muttering. One patron even grew so bold as to toss the contents of his drink at him. Calder, again, moving with rapid pace, darted out of the way of the spray. He flashed his teeth at the offending customer and pointed at him.

"I don't mind settling this off-hours with you."

The man—clearly drunk—tried to respond, but didn't manage to get a word out before one of the Roosters from the back wall strolled over, grabbed him by the scruff and started dragging him towards the base of the stairs.

Edmond used this distraction to rise to his feet. He approached Calder's exposed back, aimed for his head and swung with all his might.

The Signerde ducked beneath the blow, spun on his heel and slammed a fist into Edmond's jaw, sending him tumbling to the ground with a crack.

Now, his vision faded in and out, dancing with bright spots. Edmond swallowed from where he lay on the floor, his own blood and saliva pooling beneath a cheek.

"*Orda kal, deniz dost,*" said Calder, which roughly translated, meant, "Stay down, sea friend."

But, Edmond wasn't particularly lauded for his ability at following instructions. So, grunting, Edmond pushed off his hand, shakily. His muscles strained, his chest heaved with the effort, but he managed to regain his feet.

And, promptly, received a haymaker to the face.

"Think I'll respect you for not quitting when you should?" said Calder. "Think that's how this story plays, eh? Rise again, *dost*. I enjoy the stubborn ones and their dramatic gestures!"

Edmond did rise once more, and again, amid chuckling, Calder sent him tumbling to the ground.

By now, the bloody mess that had once been a tomb raider lay shuddering on the floor, but Edmond still wasn't done. Most men were afraid of their faces being mauled in a fight. Edmond had no such reservation. His faces were temporary. His injuries were, too—pending a good dose of treated rust, uninjured blood, and the prayer of a devout. Besides, as much as he loved the Signerde and what they represented—what they had meant to him as a child—he was growing quite weary of Calder the Shark.

"Blue fire and black fish," Edmond gasped. "Is that the best you can do?"

He rose again and tumbled again. This time, Calder kicked him twice for good measure. Now, the cheering quieted somewhat. The lender shouted something across the room, which Calder waved away.

"Fight ends when he stays down," said Calder.

Edmond got up again. A heelstomp caught his nose, splintering it. The pain was immense, but nothing compared to the next. A vicious kick popped his left eye out of the socket. With a mangled face, one eye dangling by his cheek, his tongue bitten in half, blood pouring. Edmond tried to smile, but couldn't manage it. He clung to consciousness with sheer will. Calder hadn't recognized an ally. The Eldest were always causing trouble. If they had come through that day—all those years ago. This could have been avoided. Edmond's pain would have been alleviated in more ways than one.

If only the Eldest had done their duty... If only his wife had... had...

His thoughts slowed now, coming like gossamer strands adrift in a murky swamp. He tried to follow the trail of consideration, but lost himself in the bog of foolhardiness. And so, looking like some sort of torture victim fallen prey to the hellcatchers' whims, Edmond raised his fists and squared off once more. A tide of nausea rolled in him as his brain tried to reconcile the disjointed vision from his dangling eye. *This is gonna hurt. This is gonna hurt.* Taking a few quick breaths, Edmond let out a defiant scream, and tore the loose eye from its socket. In the flash of pain that followed, he launched it at Calder's head. The rogue organ bounced off of Calder with a silent wobble as it fell to the sandy floor of the fighting pit.

Calder stared in astonishment at Edmond, then glanced down in disgust at the eye, now coated with a fine layer of sand. "Are you insane, round-ears?"

Edmond shifted on his foot, allowing his ankle to show beneath the hem of his now blood-stained pants. He couldn't quite see the expression on Calder's face, the bed of bruising on his face was quickly swallowing his remaining eye, but he did determine that Calder's gaze turned towards his ankle.

Immediately, the Signerde's tone changed. "Why didn't you say?" he hissed sharply.

Edmond shifted again, feeling the weight of his wife's anklet moving as he did.

Through, blood-crusted, split lips, with a mangled tongue, Edmond managed to choke out the words, "You never g-gave me a chance, you seaweed-brained p-prick."

Despite the slurred insult, Calder's tone remained somber. "I—I'm—my sincerest apologies. I didn't know. I didn't..." Calder swallowed then dropped to a knee, shaking his head. "I concede!" he called out. "I concede!"

The crowd, which had started turning away out of disgust and diminished interest, immediately turned back. A few people even thudded back down the stairs, peering over the railing.

"What?" said someone. "You can't concede," said another. "Lender! This is a farce worthy of the Crook! The cad is throwing the fight!"

"I concede!" Calder said, his tone as firm as tempered iron.

"The rules are clear, Signerde," the lender called out. "An uninjured fighter must defend themselves to the best of their ability."

"That's not a rule," Calder growled.

"Well, you can't just give up... Imagine how that would look to our fine, respectable clients... Who, I'm sure, have found this whole thing quite distressing."

"I won't keep hitting him," said Calder. He glanced up at Edmond who, miraculously, was still—if just barely—on his feet.

"Why not?" shouted a particularly large audience member. "You just beat him near half to death, didn'tja?"

"Fine," Calder said, frowning.

Edmond watched through a bleary, tear-streaked eye, as the Signerde stiffened his jaw and lashed out with a fist, slamming into his own chin and sending his head snapping back.

"Now who's gesturing dramatically?" Edmond said, his voice creaking. "Here. Let me help." He hesitated for a moment, eyeing Calder's kneeling form. The Signerde was showing him great respect—a respect Edmond didn't deserve. An inherited honor in the form of a strand of golden pearls settled in rigid twine. Each pearl bore a letter in bone, signifying one of the names of the Betrayed Mother. His wife had been devout, but not only that, she had been a noble among her kind. The golden pearls glinted and flickered with a trapped light like strands of moonbeam caught beneath the waves, reflecting off the sand.

But then, a flash of pain jolted through his ribs and blood dripped down his forehead. Any thoughts of a reciprocation of noble gesture vanished amidst the agony. Edmond wound up and swung, connecting *hard* with Calder where he knelt. Edmond cursed, nearly choking on his tongue as he felt his knuckle crack, a finger dislodging.

Calder keeled over, laying on the bloodstained floor. He did not fall unconscious. His wide-open eyes remained affixed on the jewelry wrapped around Edmond's ankle.

The lender cleared his throat. The room had fallen into silence, waiting on the ruling. "Bets will be returned," the lender said in a bitter tone. "Next fight is postponed until after refreshments."

"Excuse me," Mira said, her voice calling out from the corner.

A good number of patrons joined the lender in turning towards the goddess, their eyes lingering on her veiled face and form. Mira seemed quite indifferent to the attention. She waved a hand in Edmond's direction. "What about his winnings? Fifty d'oro, you said."

"I certainly can't be expected, after that odd showing, to—"

"Renege on your deal?" said Mira, raising a severe eyebrow.

The lender glanced at her, then looked at Edmond. A small note of pity crept into his voice as he said, "I suppose he did win. It'll come out of Calder's earnings anyway. Fine—collect your winnings."

Mira smirked and approached the lender's table. Meanwhile, Edmond's legs buckled out from under him and he collapsed, leaning against Calder's prone form, using the Signerde's stomach as a pillow.

"All according to plan," Edmond said through a mouthful of blood, then he groaned and closed his eye.

Chapter 22

It turned out, Calder *was* a stockpiler and dealer in various alchemical supplies. His stock was modest in selection, only the essentials that Edmond recognized from dozens of formulas, but made up for it in quantity. A keg of treated rust lay stacked with clay jugs of varied honeys against the walls, and bushels of mushrooms dangled from the fighter's dingy room. Various plants grew in dark corners from terra cotta pots, and a fine brass alembic sat disassembled over a cleaning rag. It had taken some doing, with Mira's help, due to Edmond's cracked fingers, but they had managed to brew a decent healing draught, which Edmond was currently nursing amidst a throbbing headache.

"Repeat after me," Mirastious said, her tone clipped. "Regrowing an eye takes hours and hurts—as it should."

"Regrowing an eye," Edmond muttered, testing his newly healed tongue against his teeth, "takes... takes—what was the rest?"

Mira rolled her eyes, and Calder glanced between them, eyeing them both up and down.

The tomb raider leaned against a musty, damp wall, his shoulder pressing into the soft wood. The Signerde's basement room smelled of the ocean. Instead of a cot or a bed, a pile of sand had been scattered in one corner. Various shells dangled from reeds in the ceiling, and a piece of driftwood bore a carving of two shackles dripping with tears.

Edmond recognized the symbol. He nodded to it. "Didn't realize the Eldest collected icons too."

"The Eldest are faithful," said Calder, frowning. "You should know this *deniz dostu.*" He pointed at Edmond's ankle. "How did you come by that?"

"I told you," said Edmond, quietly. He kept his expression impassive. "I married well."

"An heiress chose a round-ear? This is a story I'd like to hear."

Edmond sighed softly, pushing past the sudden surge of emotions that pulled into this chest like the tide. He rushed the same swell from his belly with a gusting breath and shook his head. "We knew each other since we were children."

"Is it common where you're from for human children to play with The Children of the Betrayed Mother?"

Edmond hesitated, then shook his head. "She and her brothers... They saved my life." He smiled, staring at his hands. Then, he glanced up, watching Mira. "Feast your ears secret keeper—that one is for free on account of securing those d'oro."

But Mira was ignoring him, preferring to keep an eye on the two separate potions she was brewing over a soft flame from a worker's candle. Two onion bottles percolated their brewed ingredients, exuding strange aromas. Edmond's natural alchemical skill would be required to complete the part of the brew that drew on forces from another plane, but Mira had insisted on performing the initial preparations. A healing potion bubbled with brownish-red liquid, exuding a smell much like iron and rust. The second potion, a silvery substance like a crystal solvent, didn't bubble so much as it spun, swirling softly in the bottle like a whirlpool over the flame.

Since spotting Edmond's wife's golden pearl anklet, Calder's attitude had completely shifted. Now, instead of outright hostility and aggression, the fighter was the picture of accommodation. He'd allowed them into his rooms and even had offered a discount for any ingredients they had needed.

This was the Signerde hospitality Edmond had initially counted on. Now, though, as his wounds continued to heal, and he sipped on his healing drought, he allowed his mind to wander. Mirastious had gifted him hope. But the emperor in Godhaven was surrounded by thousands of soldiers, tucked away in the imperial palace, guarded by some of the most renowned knights in all the archipelago. Only the most respected of nobles or highest officials were allowed audience with the Grand Emperor Baltasar the II. Somehow, Edmond, a lowly commoner with no title to his name had to convince the Emperor to use his boon to restore his wife's soul to the land of the living. Most sorts would have quailed at the prospect, but Edmond wasn't most. Standing there in a room with a Signerde and a powerless goddess, he knew that the impossibilities of the world were simply riddles meant to be solved for the correctly oriented mind. But this particular riddle would take concentration like never before. One misstep, one error would cost them dearly, and all would be lost.

To start, Edmond needed gold, and lots of it. No proper mission could be accomplished without funding, but the forty or so d'oro remaining—after paying Calder's discounted rates—wouldn't provide much more than a couple of rooms at a cheap inn for a week or so.

Edmond needed more coin than that.

"What sort of opportunities might there be for a man of my talents?" he said, pleased to find his tongue fully working as the potion continued to take effect, tingling across his skin.

"And what talents are those?" Calder asked, inclining a ridged brow.

"The skills of a latchboy, but the conscience of a priest."

"And the ego of a commodore," Mira murmured, while dousing the flames and wafting the smoke towards her, sniffing the contents.

Calder twisted his mouth into a sort of shrug, the sides of his lips curling down. He glanced at Mira. "It may not be my place," he said, "but your wife, does she know you keep company with a woman as beautiful as the deepest blue?" He nodded slightly towards Mira.

"I am no woman," snapped Mira. Even so, she nodded her head as she added, "Though I am quite beautiful."

Edmond muttered, "And I'm the one with an ego?"

"No woman? What do you mean? Are you—you underage?" Calder glanced at Edmond, speculatively.

Edmond quickly shook his head. "That's not what she meant." He continued smoothly, cutting Mira off as she attempted to open her mouth. "Don't worry about her. It isn't what you might think. I'd much rather *not* be saddled with her if truth be told."

"She seems a boon. And not only on the eyes." Calder watched as Mira corked the two potion bottles with deft hands, her gaze still fixed on Edmond.

"Save your praise, Signerde," said Mira. "The goddess you serve finds no ally in me."

"And what quarrel do you have with the Betrayed Mother?"

"She once tried to kill me." Mirastious set the bottles down with a threatening clatter.

Calder looked like he'd been about to say something else, but at this declaration he stopped, mouth gaping. He glanced at Mira sharply now, examining her face.

"Ignore her," Edmond said quickly, interjecting with a nervous chuckle. "Thank you, Calder. You've been nothing but helpful. I have one final request."

Still watching Mira, Calder tilted his head.

"Is there a side exit we might use? One that could take us to an alley? I think it best our friends upstairs don't see me like this."

GRAVEYARD GODS

Mira inclined one of the potions to him. "Your appearance," she said. "Do you wish to change?"

"Not yet. I'd like to distance myself from witnesses of the fight. They saw this face with you, and you're, well, kinda memorable. If they see a different face walk out of here with you, that's a link I can't risk. "

Mira nodded and watched as Edmond took both bottles from her and pocketed them.

"There is an exit," Calder said. "It'll take us behind the Kindly Roost. I do have some mangled root of nightbreath you might be interested in—"

Edmond shook his head. "Not yet. Once I have some coin, then perhaps. We'll remember you, of course. I'll do my best to stop by before I leave again. This time with more coin in pocket."

"I'll call in for extra stock in anticipation. Well, if that will be it—I'll show you the exit. Follow me, *deniz dostu*."

Calder stepped past Edmond back into the dingy hall, beckoning over his shoulder. Together, double-checking their newly acquired supplies and satchel were in order, Edmond and Mira fell into step.

Chapter 23

THE MOON HUNG HIGH over Carabas and looked down on Augustin like the half-mad stare of some cyclopean god. Cold and mirthless, it seemed to him that Vicente's path ran through darker streets of the sprawling city; the very darkness spoke of the corruption that seeped deep within the criss-crossing roads; burrowing pathways little more than the inky, congealed veins of a bloated corpse drifting South. Around them, the weak trickling of gutter sewage churned over the sound of wet, wracking coughs from alleyways and unlit windows.

"Are we nearly there?" Cristobal asked, his rumbling voice seeming out of place in the still quiet of the city.

Vicente cocked his head back, tapping a booted toe against the cobbles. "What? Don't care for the wharf-walks?" he croaked, taking a quick sip from the bottle of senza.

That made Vicente's third pull from the bottle since they had left the Stone Priest and come down Verian Hill. The bottle's honeyed liquid turned the moonlight golden as the light fell through, and Augustin noted the bottle's contents had indisputably diminished. Twinging with guilt, Augustin eyed his friend's unsteady gait as Vicente turned to face Cristobal.

"Don't you worry, my friend. Vicente sees the way," the old knight said, stowing the senza bottle. He smiled, and his amber eye nestled into the kindly creases of his cracked face, but the yellow eye did not look out to his friends. Instead, it peered hungrily to the edges of his periphery, moving with its own unalterable determination. Yet another sign of the insatiable demon bound within that yellow band.

Cristobal nodded solemnly, but his heavy-lidded eyes gave the quiet, plastered buildings around them a suspicious look.

After a few steps, Vicente said, "Trust me, my noble friends. We have been to far worse places than Crawler's Way."

The moon had slipped another two fingers along its skyward arc when the alleyway they followed met the North-West corner of the Maiden's Doubt. Augustin looked up at the ramshackle assemblage of wood and plaster and wondered how it could stand under the strain of its own weight, let alone that of the riotous patrons that shook the building with every shout.

Cristobal shook his head. "It's like everyone in the city is here."

"Gambling, drinking, whoring, what's not to love?" Vicente chuckled. "Besides, it's the only thing to do between West Wharf and the South jetty. Di'ladrion made sure of that."

Augustin's dark brow beetled in irritated concern. "This place is a Kindly Roost?"

Vicente murmured a confirmation as he leaned against the alleyway. Augustin clutched the grip of his rapier as he stared up to the second and third floor windows. Red lantern light filtered through the glass and stained long curtains as they draped from the open windows, caught in the sea breeze off the nearby bay. To Augustin's eyes, the rippling fabric flowed down the stucco walls like blood pulsing from a wound, and the vision sent a prickle of nervous energy through his spine. He didn't like the idea of trying to track the man through the crowded corridors of a Kindly Roost. Too many things could go wrong, and the likelihood that their quarry had met up with friends was a possibility that Augustin could not afford to ignore.

That and the fact that Commodore Severelle's aunt owns the Roosts. No, if only for his mother's sake Augustin couldn't afford to make trouble in one of the Kindly Roosts. He turned to face Vicente in time to see the man pull one of his fingers from his teeth, spitting out a thin, reflective sliver of nail.

"Our tomb raider is inside?" Augustin asked.

Vicente rolled his eye while the yellow band of his demon eye locked on the Maiden's Doubt with a vibrating intensity. "Yeah. He's in there. Our man—he is a man, just in case you had any doubts— he's coming up from the basement."

Augustin considered their options for a moment, his left hand slowly smoothing his mustache in unconscious thought. "Is he alone?"

Vicente shrugged. "You know it doesn't work like that. I can see him and only him. Though-" The craggy wrinkles of Vicente's face bunched up in puzzlement. "I can't quite make him. It's like he's—blurry. Like his face is candle wax after a long burn, or like he's got the sun behind him."

Vicente held up the bloody knife and stared at the rust red stain. Cristobal and Augustin watched him patiently. Despite his puzzled look, Vicente lounged back against the stucco wall. "I don't know," he finally said, tucking the diver's knife into his belt. "It's hard to explain."

"Could it be the senza?" Augustin asked. He tried to keep the caution out of his voice. He didn't want to provoke Vicente more, and the best way he knew was to be assertive.

At first, Vicente only sneered and threw up his hands in disgust, but when Augustin did not react, he folded his arms and muttered, "It's not the senza."

Unsure whether or not he believed him, Augustin nonetheless looked back to the Maiden's Doubt. It had no towers or roundels, but under the invisible shield of Sofia Di'ladrion, the ramshackle goliath felt like a fortress.

How are we going to find him here? Augustin thought. His side twinged, and Augustin's lips curled in the faintest hint of a grimace. *Damn it.* He knew it would be days before the wound would start to relax. *'Longer if you don't stop aggravating it.'* Catali's voice reprimanded him in his mind.

"Where are you going?" Vicente muttered.

Augustin looked back at Vicente.

The old knight's yellow eye wandered, drifting over the cracked plaster wall as he said, "He's moving." Vicente perked up. With a sloppy grin, he pointed up the alleyway behind the Kindly Roost. "There. The stage is swept. The curtain is rising. And now—" Vicente's yellow eye slid into focus, matching the other as he looked up the dark back-alley. "—our actor appears."

***

"Hello." The heavy voice calling up the alleyway drew Edmond's attention away from the Signerde. The narrow walls of the alleyway shadowed the figure, but even in the gloom he could tell that the approaching man was enormous, with broad shoulders that rolled with muscle. Edmond glanced to Calder.

"Friend of yours?" he asked.

Calder's eyes narrowed as he slowly shook his head. Edmond frowned. It was passing curious to be hailed in a dark alley at midnight. Especially in a place like this. Most people knew better than to try and cause trouble at one of the Kindly Roosts.

The giant stepped closer. He walked with a confident gait, squared with his shoulders.

"Pissoff!" Calder spat, throwing his hand up in a rude gesture.

The man's eyes glinted as he turned his head, revealing a slough of scarred skin where an ear should have gone. He looked from Calder to Mira, and finally to Edmond.

Blue fire and black fish! One of the men from the frigate. Edmond's arms and legs tensed as the shock of recognition sank in. *What is he doing here?* He remembered the trio he had spied from the docks in Sile and blinked a few times, trying to adjust to the alleyway's darkness. The big man stopped a few steps from the group. Still looking between them all.

"Are you deaf?" Calder shouted. "I said. Piss. Off."

The giant still did not answer, his expression stony and resolute, appraising them like fish in a market. But, something in the big man's gaze unsettled Edmond, almost as if the man was looking through him.

No, Edmond realized. *He's looking past us.* Edmond spun on his heel in time to see two men creeping up behind them. One of the men cursed and started to raise the short barrel of a flintlock. Edmond swatted the gun out of the way, and it flew from the ambusher's grasp. As it clattered to the stone, the pistol wielder flashed an excited grin from a face wrapped in scar-rent stubble, and drew a rapier from under his muddy red coat. This man, he didn't recognize, but the second ambusher, Edmond vaguely acknowledged as the Lord Captain from the docks.

The captain drew his own rapier from his hip in a crisp, efficient arc that fell into a duelists stance with the finality of a nail struck home. Edmond sucked in a quick breath, darting a step back from the sword wielding men.

"Enough," the Lord Captain said in the clear clip of a command. "Surrender."

Edmond froze. His instincts told him he was well and truly surrounded. He raised his hands to his waist, keeping his palms flat. He looked over to Calder who had drawn a slender dagger. The Signerde raised a bony eyebrow, and Edmond shook his head 'no'. He had to be smart. They wanted them alive—for now. Edmond cleared his throat.

"Who are you and what do you want?" The words were mostly a play for time. Edmond's eyes hunted for a gap, any sign of the giant or the raggamuffin with the rapier relaxing their guard. He didn't bother looking at the Lord Captain. Everything from the man's professional stance beneath that ridiculous tricorn hat to the fastidiously kept uniform told Edmond there would be no cracks there. At least not the sort he could run through and keep his head. But, he suspected, the man would talk.

"I am the Lord Captain Augustin Mora," the professional said, keeping his rapier at the ready. "Four nights ago, a God Grave was plundered in forbidden waters."

Edmond didn't hear the rest, distracted by a sudden sinking sensation in his gut. Augustin Mora's eyes held a hard determination beneath the coal black slope of his eyebrows. This gave him a hawkish appearance that his hooked nose only exaggerated. Dark specks of stubble fumbled around the shadow of a neatly kept beard. Putting these together with Mora's appearance in Sile—

He's hunting me. He's been hunting me since the first day. Edmond's mind reeled. He had to get out of here. *How did they find me so fast?*

At that moment, Mira tilted her head, her dark hair flowing down over her shoulder. "Augustin Mora?" she said. "Is that really you?" Her youthful voice held the playful music of a doting relative and seemed to carry an unspoken compliment.

A momentary pause flitted by, dragging with it the sound of the tide rolling against the stone docks. All eyes were on Mira as her dark eyes smirked over the curtain of her veil.

"I'm sorry, my lady, but I'm not sure that I've had the pleasure," he said. Mira laughed, a light sound that seemed to disarm the circle of men.

"No," she said. Lightly resting her fingertips on her veiled cheek, she shook her head. "You would not. You would have been too little."

Edmond looked around. She had their attention. Even the Lord Captain seemed to barely mind his sword. Slowly, Edmond lowered his hand, reaching for the new component pouch at his belt.

"Your mother," Mira continued. "Tell me, is Dominga well?"

Augustin's eyes narrowed. Unspoken calculation passed behind his flitting iris'. "How do you know my mother? Who are you?"

His voice held the firm tone of command, but something rode beneath it, Edmond noted with distracted curiosity, as his fingers pushed through the little, wax-wrapped components in the pouch.

Red phosphorous.

Mira spoke. "It looks like she was right. You've grown into quite the strong and handsome man, but—" here Mira drew her hand over her mouth. "What are you doing in Carabas? Your father was going to take you all to live on Godshaven."

Edmond's fingers snared another wax wrap, probing the contents quickly with deft, practiced motions.

Dragonfly wings.

Another pause passed as Augustin lowered his sabre. This time his voice coasted on a broken exhalation, scarcely a whisper as apprehension and uncertainty rose in his face. "Who are you?" Mira took a half-step towards the Lord Captain.

"Who do you think I am?" she said.

Edmond only vaguely heard her as he licked his lips, focusing his will like water turning to ice.

Gibberish.

Snatching his closed fist up from the component pouch to his mouth, Edmond yelled, "Ham-nam giva-ring-ding-wocky, clam!"

He had a very brief moment to appreciate the look of utter confusion from the Lord Captain as Edmond flared his clenched fingers out into a trumpet shape. At once, a swarm of bright, crackling lights flew from his closed palm and filled the air like a blizzard. As the sparks rushed around the alleyway, they flashed like miniature sunrises, and with each effulgent burst, they let out a staccato of sharp pops.

"Alchemist!" Augustin shouted, but most of the word was swallowed by the noise.

Holding his eyes closed, Edmond grasped blindly through the air, catching hold of Mira's hand and giving a forceful pull. His shout of "Run!" dashed itself apart in the cacophony, but, to his immediate relief, she followed.

They did not have to go far, before Edmond heard the popping of his alchemical fireflies at his back and opened his eyes. He didn't see Calder, and he spared the Signerde a momentary hope of good fortune, before devoting his attention to his own retreat. Under the watchful eye of the noonday sun, the streets of Carabas were a tangled net, but in the middle of the night, with only the baleful moon to witness—they were truly a labyrinth. The thought encouraged Edmond as he hurtled along with little care for where his path carried him. He had learned long ago that cities protected thieves. If he just ran, the knot of streets, gutters, and alleys would conceal him. *I just have to get a few corners ahead.*

Mira ran beside him like a ghost, and when he looked her way, she would look back to him, her eyes curious, but unconcerned.

"Tell me," she said as they sprinted, her voice steady and unaffected while they made their third sharp turn. "Why did you not try and speak with those men?" She tilted her head, her voice giving her question the tone of some great philosophical inquiry.

"Wh-what?" Edmond fought to say even that much as his lungs heaved. He glanced over his shoulder. Only the empty street and the endless washing of the tides met him. Deciding he had run far enough, Edmond slowed to a walk, heaving in air as the sweat beading on his forehead immediately chilled in the cool breeze. He propped a hand against one of the squat buildings beside him as Mira folded her hands across her waist.

This should be far enough, he thought, still fighting to catch his breath. While she waited on him, Mira turned and examined a deep crack in the wall. Edmond watched her, his eyes trailing the soft black of her hair down the slope of her back, settling on the graceful curve of her hips. He closed his eyes and rubbed at his neck, letting the darkness behind his eyelids soothe him. When he opened his eyes, she had not moved. Edmond wondered if the former goddess could even see anything in the crack, and he thought about her luminous, black eyes. Were they like cat's eyes, maybe? Or maybe, she doesn't see like we do? In that moment, he saw once again the preternatural stillness of her figure. No breath filling her lungs. No blood coursing through her veins. *No heart either, I'll bet,* he thought.

A smile crept over Mira's cheeks, blossoming in the corners of her eyes. Even under the veil, Edmond could see it as plainly as the rising bloom of morning. "What are you smiling about?" he said with a note of rebuke.

"There is a hole in the daub here. A mouse has dug it out to make her home. Her bed is in order. She has even decorated it with a coin. A coin someone made and someone else spent. I wonder if anyone is missing it?" A wisp of sadness drifted up from the question.

'The night would whisper and tell me things. Now I cannot hear its voice.' Edmond tried to dismiss the remembered words. *She's a goddess*, he reminded himself spitefully. If there were any creature less deserving of sympathy—Edmond clenched his jaw. He couldn't lie to himself. When alchemy demands your truth, you can't afford to lie to yourself. He closed his eyes again and knew the feeling in his chest was the meek candle-flame of sympathy. No, he couldn't lie to

himself, but that didn't mean he had to listen. With a sharp intake of breath, Edmond reached within himself, feeling for that small light of sympathy and smothered it.

"Come on," he said gruffly, grabbing hold of Mira's elbow. "We need to keep moving."

She nodded in silent acquiescence and turned from the mouse hole, her eyes moving from the stucco to the sparkling starlight shining down over the city. Edmond could not tell if her dark eyes were wet with tears or simply catching the light from above. He let go of her elbow, turning to lead the way up the street. In front of them, the cobblestones gave way to broad flat stairs, worn down to rounded edges with generations of use, and as Edmond looked to the top of the stairs, he froze. The Lord Captain Augustin Mora looked down at him, sword in hand. The giant and the pistol wielding ragamuffin stepped to his side. The oldest one raised the two pistols, one in each hand, and leveled them at Edmond.

Tilting his chin in a look of irritated condescension, Augustin spoke. "As I said before, tomb thief. Surrender."

Chapter 24

Edmond's mind reeled as he looked between the three men at the top of the stairs. He opened his mouth, then closed it again, his words lost somewhere in the churning of his stomach. It didn't make any sense. He had lost them. He was sure of it, so how had they tracked him down again? And so quickly, too.

The ragamuffin and the giant began to walk down the steps, and a chill breeze sent the tails of the ragamuffin's red coat snapping behind him. The man's heavy black dreadlocks slid back behind his shoulders and the pale moonlight highlighted the ruinous scars that ran from his chin up to his eye.

His eye! Shocked he had not seen it before, Edmond saw the coiling yellow band sparkling in the ragamuffin's left eye. *Oculomancy,* he thought as dread threatened to rise up in his chest. *That's how they found me. They have an alchemist.* Edmond rolled his fingers, forcing himself not to freeze up. *They have something of mine.* In the space between their approaching footfalls, Edmond's mind flashed images of his escape from the forbidden waters in the dogger, his arrival in Carabas, the fight in the sinking boat on Sile. *Sile!* His side twinged at the memory. A flesh wound, it had been nothing. *But now they have my blood.* He knew then, he could run and run and run, but he would never be free of them. Not while they had his blood.

The ragamuffin pushed aside his coat and stowed one of his pistols. "Alright, you lot. Fun is fun, but this will go easier for you if we all stay nice and polite. Sound fair?"

To Edmond's ear, the man seemed to be slurring his words. *Is he drunk?* Edmond thought, desperately analyzing the predicament and looking for any possible advantage.

The ragamuffin stood close and as he pushed aside his coat, a sour smell of pickled eggs and stale beer wafted from him. Mira's nose scrunched in distaste, but Edmond's nostrils flared as he picked up a third smell. The corner of his mouth curled as a small seed of a plan sprouted in his mind.

The giant stood behind Mira, placing one enormous paw gently on her shoulder. "Please be easy, m'lady." His voice rolled down heavily, thick with his Dumasian accent, but the undertone of reassurance was difficult to miss.

Mira did not reply, but neither did she recoil from his touch. As the big Dumasian settled behind Mira, he turned to the ragamuffin, "Hurry up, Vicente. It will go better if we get them to the Stone Priest before sunup."

Stone Priest? Wait. That's an inn on the hill, Edmond silently noted.

The ragamuffin, Vicente, stepped forward. With one hand he held the pistol towards Edmond's chest, with the other he reached out for the component pouch at the tomb raider's hip.

"Sorry, friend-o, but we can't be havin' any more nasty surprises."

The words carried the smell to Edmond's nose once more. Now, he was sure. He had a chance.

With a sudden twist of his hips, Edmond pulled his body away from the pistol, grabbing the barrel of the flintlock and shoving it skyward. A sluggish shot reported from the gun, and Edmond felt the small flush of heat as the flintlock shuddered in his hand. With a jerk, he pulled the pistol free and shoved Vicente back.

"Alright, you drownin' piece-of-shark-shite-sonnova-bastard!" Vicente cried out. He patted at the flapping lapels of his frock coat. "You want to play with Vicente? Then we're gonna-we-re gonna-" His voice trailed off and Vicente blinked a few times as he realized his second pistol no longer rested in his bandolier.

Edmond leveled the pilfered weapon at Vicente, stepping towards him with a cock-sure grin. "You should be careful with senza," said Edmond, his rough voice dropping into mock concern as he threw the spent pistol clattering onto a nearby roof. "It's hell on your reflexes."

Flushed, Vicente reached for the rapier at his side. Edmond lunged forward, bringing the second pistol around like a hammer against Vicente's head. A stomach turning crack clipped though the stone street, and Vicente fell into a heap. With the senza coursing through his body, Edmond would be surprised if the man woke up before sunrise. However, as the sound of Augustin's booted feet racing down the stone stair reminded him, he had other problems at the moment.

* * *

Augustin already had his sabre drawn when Vicente fell to the cobblestone. His heart raced. It was all slipping through his fingers again. This grave-robber had eluded him twice already. Once as he faked the sinking of his ship, and again as he blinded them outside the Maiden's Doubt. As Augustin hit the bottom step of the street's stone stairway, he did not see a man. He saw a two legged viper; a pitiless and venomous predator. This tomb-thief's tanned skin and strong arms, his plain appearance that would match a thousand dockworkers from Gamor to Trabson, all of it hung over him like a cloak; a camouflage concealing the poison within. He could not let him escape again. He would *not* let him escape again.

The tomb raider held up the last remaining pistol. He held it, strangely, in his left hand. "Come no closer. I won't hesitate." He pulled back the flintlock's hammer.

Augustin stopped. Holding the keen point of his rapier in front of him, he said in a low voice, "You have one shot. There are two of us."

The tomb-thief edged back, giving himself space while he glanced over towards the woman. He let the man's deep brown eyes confirm that Cristobal still securely held his lady. "Surrender. This is the last time I will ask."

The man hesitated. Augustin watched as his eyes flitted with apparent indecision. *Or plotting,* Augustin reminded himself. He took a slow breath. He had to remain calm. Any hint of desperation or fear would be all the encouragement a man like this would need to try something stupid. Keeping his head high and his back straight, Augustin fought back the concern that urged him to look at Vicente's crumpled body. *Surrender,* he willed towards the grave-robber. *Gods dammit! Surrender, you viper!*

The man raised a hand. He touched something hanging around his throat. *A potion?* Augustin tensed. An alchemist with a ready potion was a variable he did not savor. As the man fingered the simple, dark bottle he let out a grim chuckle and turned a gallows grin on Augustin.

"I can't surrender. I still have miles to go before I can rest." At once, the tomb-robber surged forward, raising the pistol and firing.

Augustin flinched as the eruption of fire and smoke shrouded the space between them. The shot went wide, and Augustin plunged forward. He saw the shadowy form of the tomb raider in the swiftly dissipating smoke and slashed out at him. His blade parted the smoke like rippling water, and at the last moment, the tomb raider fell into a roll as the rapier whistled through the air above him.

Augustin spun on his heel as the tomb viper crouched sharply over Vicente's prone body, and with a rapid tug, yanked the rapier from the unconscious man's belt. Augustin cursed and approached; the tomb raider fell into a guarded stance, presenting the point of his blade. Augustin paused. *That's an Academy stance. He's been trained.* Cautious, Augustin raised his own sword. His expectations of the man, he realized, continued to betray him. *Very well,* thought Augustin, taking a steadying breath. *If he wants to make a duel of it—*

"On guard," Augustin said. With a solemn tilt of his head, Augustin turned the flat of the blade to the grave-robber in a salute.

The tomb raider moved his own blade, as if he were going to return the salute, but then, at the last moment, he used the casual movement of his blade to surge forward, striking at Augustin's half tilted head.

The lord captain quickly ducked out of the way, but the flicking steel caught his hat, hooking on the end. The tomb raider cackled in delight and pulled sharply back, catching the tricorn captain's hat before it hit the ground.

The man made a big show of dusting the hat off on his leg before placing it on his head. From beneath the brim, he winked at Augustin. Then, he struck again.

This time, Augustin parried the blade easily, and brought back the point of his rapier in a vicious riposte. Edmond fell back, scrambling out of reach as Augustin held his guard. "You sir," he spat, struggling to quell his outrage at the dishonorable strike, "have no honor!"

"I must have dropped it back in that God Grave."

Augustin suppressed his anger at the impudent response, slowly adjusting his stance. Then, like a leaf caught in an autumn gust, his rapier swept forward.

***

Shit.Shit.Shit. Edmond fell back from the onslaught of thrusts, desperately trying to keep his blade between him and the lord captain's hungry rapier. *It's ok. You're ok. Just like the academy,* he told himself while guards and parries, rusted and awkward from disuse, came back to him. Augustin let out a quick succession of angled cuts. Edmond leapt back, holding the rapier at arm's length as he tried to buy time. *Yeah, but you failed out of the academy.* He managed to block another probing slice, and the rapier shivered in his hand, sending a vibration all the way to his shoulder. *Blue fire and black fish, but he's strong!* Edmond fell back again. *I can't stay like this. He's just testing me. I need to get out of this duel before he takes my head off.*

Edmond's gambit had paid off. He figured a clean pressed officer like Augustin Mora would be an academy trained swordsman. He was right. That meant Augustin would recognize the basic academy stances Edmond could remember. Right again. And, because he'd never met one of these Imperial peacocks that didn't believe all the self-aggrandizing shark-shit about how *superior* an academy swordsman was-well, that meant he'd want to test Edmond and get the measure of his skill before going in for the kill. This brought him precious, precious *time.* Edmond made a mental note to congratulate himself if he lived.

***

Augustin watched the grave-robber. The man had a vigilant eye for defense, he could say that much for him. He also held the rapier with his left-hand. Unusual, and the sort of thing that would confound a novice, but Augustin had years of experience under his belt. With exaggerated, almost playful, sweeps, Augustin attempted to draw the man into attacking, but time and time again the tomb raider declined, raising his guard and retreating. *Is he mocking me?* Augustin thought. He had known duelists in his tournament days that made it part of their strategy to annoy and anger an opponent into fighting more aggressively, leaving them open for a cleaner counter-attack, but this—*He says nothing. He leaves his guard, inviting the attack, but when we join, he retreats.* If any other man stood before him, he would have assumed, and rightly so, that they only had a cursory knowledge of dueling. *But this is no ordinary man*, he reminded himself. *This is the Viper.* The moonlight glinted off the potion that hung from his neck, and Augustin once again found himself wondering what nasty surprises it might hold.

Dropping back momentarily, Augustin changed hands, now holding the sabre in his left to match the grave-robber, the Viper in his mind now. Still there was no change from his opponent's strategy of total defense. Another fencer would see the insult in an opponent fighting with their off-hand. The Viper seemed not to even notice. A ruse? Perhaps. Augustin had one more test. He launched a swift attack, that predictably sent the Viper scurrying back.

Augustin did not pursue, instead tilting his rapier to invite a counter-attack as he called after him, "I see that you are a lover of the 'ninth parry'. Understandable. It is good for the legs, is it not?" He'd seen duelists fly into a rage at such a taunt, for it was well understood by trained swordsmen that the 'ninth parry' was no more than a euphemism for turning tail and running away. The Viper, did not respond. *Interesting.* Augustin lunged forward.

***

The glimmering steel of Augustin Mora's rapier caught the moonlight and flashed against the gloom of the darkened streets. The blade's cold serenity seemed a perfect consummation to the stony calculation on Augustin's face. As a slash leapt for Edmond's right shoulder, Edmond brought the body of his rapier across to meet the attack, but instead of the bone-shuddering impact he was expecting, the rapier made only the slightest tap as Augustin twisted his wrist, bringing the back edge of his blade hooking around towards Edmond's throat. In a moment of inspiration, Edmond threw himself forward. He narrowly avoided the hungry edge by throwing his shoulder into the steel guard of the sword. He hissed in pain as he felt a welt break across the skin of his right arm, and while Augustin recovered his blade, Edmond scurried back out of reach.

*I can't keep this up. If only I could create some fog, or another flare. Anything! But, I can't use my alchemy without some time. If I'm not careful—*The image of the writhing black djinn rampaging through the boat on Sile flashed behind his eyes. *Think, dammit. Think!* He looked around.

The giant Dumasian still held Mira by the shoulder. Her hands were folded at her chest. Was she praying? It didn't matter. Edmond looked at the exhausted pistol he had dropped. He looked at the unconscious body of Vicente. He felt the cold glass of the vial as it bounced against his chest. The sweat on his face and hands. The sting in his shoulder from where the rapier's swept guard struck him. Finally, he met the Lord Captain's eyes as Augustin raised the blade of his rapier in a hanging guard over his shoulder, like the culling blade of a scythe. Those dark eyes were no longer calculating. A hard certainty had settled into them, like words etched in iron, and they said 'you have been weighed, and you have been found wanting'.

At that moment, a voice rose in Edmond's mind. *Careful doesn't matter if you're dead. And, you have to live, River's Gift.* In an instant, Edmond knew what he had to do.

With a decisive twist, he threw his rapier at Augustin. With practiced speed, Augustin Mora ducked behind his guard as the blade sheared through the air past him. The throw had missed, but Edmond hadn't really expected it to hurt the master duelist; only distract him for a moment. Edmond stuffed his hand into the component pouch, grasping wildly, and came out with a stick of cinnamon. Edmond's mind clawed for some alchemical combination as realization shot wide in Augustin's eyes. Without pausing to think, Edmond grasped the first thought to cross his mind and swiped the cinnamon stick across his forehead, soaking the sweat into the fragrant bark. Augustin surged forward as Edmond screwed his eyebrows into a storm cloud of menacing focus. Raising up the sweat soaked cinnamon bark, Edmond shouted, "Stop!"

Augustin halted, the rapier still poised to strike. He had been too far to close the gap in time, and as Edmond watched Augustin's hawk eyes darting between the alchemical ingredients in his hand and him, he knew that he only had a moment.

"Do you know what this is?" Edmond said, pointing to the damp cinnamon in his hand. Augustin did not reply, so Edmond continued. "It's cinnamon, sweat, and a threat." Edmond took a step backward, edging his way towards the stair, and Augustin followed with a matching step of his own. "Lord Captain Mora, if you set one foot on this stair, your friend down there will die." Edmond nodded towards Vicente's unconscious body.

Augustin's eyes narrowed in response. "You think your hollow threats mean anything to me, grave-robber?" Augustin continued to follow as Edmond backed up onto the lowest step of the stair.

"The threat is real, lord captain. The alchemy would reject it if it weren't."

That gave Augustin pause, and Edmond took another retreating step.

"I'm leaving, and you are not following. Mira." The dark haired goddess nodded her head. She made as if to follow him, but the Dumasian held her firm by the shoulders. She looked from the big man's hands to Edmond, a look of mild frustration on her face. Edmond frowned. "Mira," he said again. "Would you tell the Lord Captain and his associate what sort of alchemy you can create with cinnamon bark, sweat, and an honest threat?" Mira cocked her head, her dark eyes narrowed as she gave Edmond a searching look.

"Nothing. You can't-"

"That's right," Edmond interrupted. "Not a gods-damned thing. But-" Edmond's retreating steps brought him half way up the small stairway.

Augustin now stood just below the bottom step, a venomous glare on his face as he listened. Swallowing, Edmond continued, "Sweat is sorta like salt water, and salt water is sorta like sea water." Mira's black eyes began to widen. Edmond could see, but not hear as she vaguely mouthed 'oh, no'. His heart raced. His stomach twisted itself in his knots as he continued to climb the steps, increasing the gap between him and Augustin. He swallowed to keep his voice level. "And cinnamon's a tree bark. That means it's kinda like pine bark. At least, that's my guess. Now, Mira. What sort of alchemy could someone make with sea water, pine bark, and an honest threat?"

The goddess pale face twisted in anger. "You don't have sea water or pine bark, you lead-brained maniac. You have sweat and cinnamon. If you try and-"

"Mira!" Edmond snapped. The goddess huffed, raising her voice as she replied.

"A Cloud of Nightmare. That's what you'll try to do, but you'd need the will of Death himself to make that work with your-your—" She fumbled for the words as exasperation overran her tongue. "—your shit ingredients!"

Near the top of the stairs now, Edmond grinned down with what he hoped was an insane smile. He really had to sell this part. "That's the great thing. It doesn't have to work." He let that settle. At the bottom of the steps Augustin lowered his sword, shock written large on his face.

His voice hoarse with disbelief the Lord Captain said, "You'd summon a demon in the streets, just to make your escape?"

Before Edmond could even reply, Mira answered, she seemed calmer now. Resignation hung heavy in her voice. "He would.

I've traveled with him." Augustin turned to look her in the eyes, and she looked back into his. "Augustin, if he said he would sink Carabas into the ocean, I would believe him."

A fearful pause passed between them all before Edmond broke the silence from the top of the steps. "You heard her. Now let her go."

The giant Dumasian holding Mira shook his head. "No," came his booming reply. Augustin spun around to face the big man.

"Cristobal?" he said, seemingly as surprised as Edmond to hear the big man speak.

Glowering up at Edmond, Cristobal took one massive hand off of Mira's shoulders, holding her in place with the other.

"No," he said again. "You would not leave her. You would not see her hurt." Cristobal took his free hand, wrapping his thick, calloused fingers around her throat. Mira opened her mouth in surprise, but no sound escaped except a hollow choke. "Drop your alchemy. Come down. Or, I will break her neck."

Edmond looked down at the grim giant. Peering through the dim light, the man was unreadable. Would he really do it? Mira now struggled in Cristobal's grasp, but her small frame could do no more to break the big Dumasian's grip than it could a stone statue. Edmond took a deep breath, letting it out slowly. He watched as Augustin suddenly seemed torn between daring the stairs and rushing to Cristobal. Would he really break her neck? He knew that Mira didn't need to breathe, not really. She didn't bleed either. *She's not mortal. Not human.*

Neither was I, River's Gift. Edmond blinked back the small flush of shame he felt in his neck. *She's not Signerde, either.*

Making his decision, Edmond called down. "Break her neck then. Or not. I don't care."

Turning on his heel, Edmond sprinted up the street, away from them all. Their bloodhound would be out for hours, and he knew where they would be. As he ran, his hand squeezed into a fist, until the sweat-damp cinnamon broke apart and fell in wasted clumps, adding to the sludgy waste that ran through the city's gutters.

CHAPTER 25

Gasping, back pressed against the rough grooves in the stack of pallets serving as shelter, Edmond peered in the direction of the lord captain, his giant and the unconscious bloodseeker. The tatter-eared giant had Mira's forearm gripped in an enormous paw. He held her firmly, but with no small amount of gentleness. He delicately guided her over a puddle and then seemed to double check to make sure she was alright.

Edmond knew the type. He wrinkled his nose in disgust. The only knights he'd ever known particularly well had been the sort of bullies and louts who espoused virtue and honor while simultaneously rummaging through a victim's pockets in search of 'godly tithe.' As Edmond eyed his attackers, he frowned slightly. Lord Captain Augustin Mora looked familiar. And not just from the time in Sile. It was obvious they were hunting him. But no, something else about the man's pulled back hair and moustache beneath his hooked nose was familiar.

Edmond's gaze darted to the man's rapier, which he was gripping like a mother holding the arm of a beloved infant. Then it struck him—the tournament in the Crook from a couple of years ago. He recognized the Lord Captain as a competitor. Not only that, but if Edmond's memory served him, the Lord Captain had *won* the entire occasion.

He wet his lips nervously. He really had been playing with fire by trying to duel the man... He inhaled shakily through his nose, the residue of adrenaline tilting through his veins. At least he lived. At least he'd made it out.

Edmond, of course, had little interest in tournaments, jousting, fencing or any of the knightly wastes of time that self-important minor nobles committed themselves too. At the time, he'd been looking to barter a map off one of the tournament coordinators though, and he'd caught the final half of the final bout.

This, Edmond surmised, while a pleasing feat of memory, only brought with it the revelation of trouble. The giant was a knight, the Lord Captain was a renowned fencer, and the bloodseeker was... well, a bloodseeker.

Clearly, by robbing Mira's grave, Edmond had pissed off more than the usual sorts.

Edmond hissed sharply and ducked behind his pallets as the lord captain scanned the area, still stooped over his bloodseeker's fallen form. Inhaling through his nose, the two potions pressed firmly against his pockets, Edmond strained to listen.

He heard soft murmuring, followed by a grumbled reply, but he couldn't determine the content of the exchange.

Edmond had, perhaps, a few hours before the bloodseeker woke. In that time, he had to rescue Mira and recover every ounce of his blood they had. Either they'd recovered some from the demon in Sile—the creature had partly been made of Edmond's blood, amidst the rust. Or, they had recovered some from the room where he'd been stabbed in the pearl diver's tavern.

One way or the other, reclaiming the blood was paramount.

Rescuing a goddess and stealing blood... It, perhaps, wasn't the simplest of assignments. And, he had to accomplish it all before the bloodseeker woke and warned his allies of Edmond's movements. He'd popped the yellow-eyed man a good one, but there was no certainty in such matters. An hour, perhaps more, then the man would wake.

An hour was no large amount of time.

Edmond swallowed, then eased back around the pallets, watching the men once more. The giant now had the bloodseeker draped over one shoulder, and the lord captain gripped Mira. She tried to pull away, but he held tight and muttered something sharp beneath his breath, and the goddess of secrets stopped struggling.

Then, together, the unlikely group moved off through the streets, disappearing from sight.

As they left, Edmond broke out of his hiding spot, and began to follow. One hand moved to the potion at his chest. In his mind's eye, he focused on the lord captain's appearance, doing his best to recollect the exact proportions of the man's face. Then, he reached to his head and removed the tricorn hat he'd stolen from the lord captain.

Turning it over, he spotted a good number of dark hairs laced inside the brim. Smiling, Edmond picked up the pace, following his attackers into the heart of Carabas.

CHAPTER 26

"Quick bastard, wasn't he?" Cristobal said as they stepped through the door of the Stone Priest. The shattered glass from before had been cleaned and there was no sign of the bravos from earlier. A few quiet customers nursed drinks in corner booths, keeping to themselves, their forms illuminated by the pink and orange of the dimming sky spilling through the shattered front window and open door.

Augustin nodded, running his fingers through the dark matte of his hair with a frown. "The tomb robber will answer to justice, one way or another."

Cristobal readjusted Vicente across his shoulder and tightened his grip on the female accomplice's arm. As Augustin led the others towards the counter, a hunched man with crooked teeth and skin tags quickly began shaking his head, tapping a long, spindly finger against the lacquered counter. "No! No! You three, I want no more trouble. Begone with you!" The man behind the counter gave a justificatory nod to the shattered window before turning a kindly smile to the woman. "Apologies miss, but the company you keep embitters the heart towards hospitality." Then, just as quickly, his expression soured once more. He fixed Vicente's unconscious form, and Augustin and Cristobal's conscious forms with an equally severe look.

Cristobal growled, tugging the woman closer to the proprietor and hefting Vicente on his shoulder. He raised an eyebrow, which, like many of the large Dumasian's gestures, could communicate an undercurrent of threat regardless of how he inclined it.

But before Cristobal could say anything, Augustin stepped forward, clearing his throat. "Do you know who I am?" he said. "Do you know what this insignia represents?" he pointed towards the Lord Captain symbol of three golden loops pinned to his cloak.

The proprietor glanced at Augustin, his withering gaze flicking to the insignia. "Indeed," he said. "But station or not, you broke my window. Your golden-eyed friend is drunk—no surprise there, given his carousing over the last month. And," he raised his voice significantly, "You've kidnapped a woman by the looks of it. I don't want any more trouble. Emperor's servant though you may be, there are other establishments to house you."

Augustin bristled at this. Cristobal knew they had little time. Dragging their newfound hostage and an unconscious Vicente to a new inn or taking the hour long trek back to the ship would not do. Every moment that passed, the tomb raider slipped further from their grasp. Augustin straightened his back. "How much?"

"It's not a question of money. I'm asking you to leave, politely," said the proprietor, licking his lips nervously. He had the air of a man backpedaling from a tentative position, but having nowhere left to retreat. He swallowed a couple of times and wiped a bead of sweat from the corner of his brow. "I'm just suggesting, there are other establishments, with intact windows, that you can patron. You wouldn't want to stay here anyway, would you? If those bravos come back, and find you..."

"Or," said Augustin, resting his hand on the hilt of his rapier. "Perhaps, I should just issue an order to my men to take up residence in the Stone Priest for the next week. I'm an imperial officer. Under the Emperor's decree, you are required to provide food and shelter to me and my men, if I deem it necessary. Of course," Augustin's tired eyes honed in on the innkeeper with the threatening darkness of a midnight storm, "You could just let me pay for the window and get out of my gods-damned way."

The proprietor licked his lips. Then, with a low grumble, he said, "You know where the room is. Here's the key you returned earlier." He emphasized the word, 'returned'. "Don't break anything else." He grumbled a few more times as he procured a brass key from a keychain, and handed it to Augustin. Augustin dropped a small handful of d'oro onto the counter, then turned and headed up the stairs with Cristobal and his cargo in close tow.

As they ascended, the woman turned to Augustin, and said, "Would you really have? Taken the man's livelihood for a few weeks just to prove a point?"

GRAVEYARD GODS

Cristobal saw Augustin's jaw clench as he tried to ignore her, but after a moment the lord captain let out a relenting sigh and said, "No. By rights I could, but no." He looked back to the unconscious body of Vicente, still speaking to the dark haired woman, "Does it really offend you? The prospect of ruining someone's life?" Augustin shook his head with a derisive snort, "I apologize if we couldn't live up to the exacting moral standards of a tomb raider and his accomplice. Thanks to you and your companion, that damned viper, we can't exactly afford to be polite."

Cristobal cleared his throat, and Augustin trailed off. He puffed his cheeks, exhaling deeply. "My apologies," he said, a note of sincerity rising in his tone. "I should not have spoken to a lady in such a way. Who is he? Who is your companion?"

The woman fell silent at this. She frowned for a moment, contemplating something birthed by a ridged brow and pursed lips, but then didn't volunteer further information. Instead, she seemed to eye the key in Augustin's hand with strange curiosity.

"I wonder what sorts of things go on behind locked doors in a place like this. I bet you these rooms hold many a secret." Her voice sounded nearly wistful, longing even, like the voice of the lover mentioning an absent sailor, wondering when they would return from the sea.

Augustin shivered and remembered the words the woman had uttered to him earlier in the alley. It almost seemed like she'd once been a friend of his family. Or had heard of him. It was a strange thing. The tomb raider kept odd companions, that much was clear.

Mira continued to gaze at the key in Augustin's hand, but at the same time, it almost seemed as if she were looking through it, past it, around it, someplace else. To someplace no one else could see. She let out a soft, quavering sigh which almost sounded like a sob. Cristobal loosened his grip slightly on the woman's arm. He gently put his large hand in the small of her back, ushering her up the last remaining steps and down the hall. The key in Augustin's hand unlocked the third door on the left, and they found themselves entering Vicente's old room.

Cristobal grunted as he heaved Vicente off his shoulder and lowered the man onto the bed. He slapped Vicente's face a couple of times with the back of his hand, but Augustin called him off, saying, "He'll be out for a while. Not just from the blow and the senza; He hasn't used the sight in a while, remember the last time, on the Crook?"

"Yeah. We pushed him a bit too far that time, didn't we? Took him nearly a week to recover." Cristobal glanced down at their old friend, frowning slightly. He then looked up again, glancing across at his Lord Captain; he held Augustin's gaze for a moment, but didn't say anything. The large Dumasian had been told he spoke with a thick accent, but Augustin understood him better than anyone. And he didn't need to speak to communicate his thoughts.

Augustin sighed. "He'll be fine. In these times you can never have too many friends."

Cristobal still said nothing, but the look in his eyes prompted Augustin to continue, as if trying to explain himself.

"We have to catch that tomb raider. And I need the backup on the ship. You know how Agreo is. You know how things are. If I don't have more men that I can trust, and not just you Cris—I know you have my back. I know you'd do anything for me. But even you, a stone brick wall against any force—even you have your limits. I don't want to put you in harm's way any more than you want Vicente to be. The only way I see forward is if we share the burden."

Cristobal gave a slow nod. "Speak it once, my ears will hear. But... this tomb raider, how do you plan to snare him? He's a slippery fella. An alchemist."

"I didn't count on that. But we do have his friend."

The woman glanced between the two of them with an uncomfortable level of fascination. She seemed to have rekindled a similar interest that she had directed towards the key. She looked directly in Cristobal's eyes, studying him, stripping him down raw and naked with a glance of her inky gaze. "You love Augustin," she said of Cristobal, her eyes wide. "You'd die for him."

Cristobal cleared his throat, frowning. "As a brother, yes."

Augustin smiled and winked. "Had always wondered why you haven't had as much luck with the ladies as me."

The large knight rolled his eyes, "Perhaps not as much quantity, but twice the quality."

Augustin lifted a finger, "Careful."

Cristobal held up his palms apologetically, "I'm sorry. I spoke without thinking."

Mira frowned for a second, then opened her mouth in realization. "Oh, there is something there. Did I say something to make you uncomfortable? I always forget with mortals. You don't like discussing your emotions. You feel uncomfortable, don't you?"

"Mortals?" said Cristobal, frowning. "You speak as if you aren't one of us."

The woman smiled softly, and then glanced to Augustin. "Your mother always knew you'd make something of yourself. She has things she never told you, you know. About your father, about the sacrifices your family had to make. She will one day, I'm sure. She was actually seeking my guidance not long before... Well, that's a long time from now I suppose. You mortals are strange folk. I have half a mind to think perhaps my quest would be better suited in the hands of beings more stable... Perhaps a couple of doves or a cat."

Cristobal and Augustin were now both sharing a strange look behind the woman's back. Vicente grumbled in his sleep, turning slightly one-way then the other, his eyelids flickering, glinting flashes of gold.

"This tomb raider," said Augustin. "Do you even know his name?"

"I know a good many things. But I don't share them; the things I hold in my mind are mine to savor, collected for my own delight and shared only if needed."

"This tomb raider?" Augustin pressed on, resiliently. "You share your knowledge with him?"

"He's godless, and so I owe him little allegiance. But I don't think he'd take kindly to you knowing his name. At least, not if you heard it from me."

"You're going to speak eventually," said Augustin, his voice a growl. "Or Cristobal will—"

"What?" the tomb raider's accomplice chuckled softly. "He won't hurt me; we both know it. Look in his eyes. He wouldn't hurt those he calls women. I think he's above torturing a man, even. I've known a good few torturers, though," she said, nodding quickly. "The dreadful prayers they whispered above bloodied hands..." The woman shivered, whether in disgust or delight Augustin could not tell. "But no," she turned an imperious eye on Augustin, then shifted it to Cristobal. The big man lowered his eyes, admitting the truth of her words. "You have no threat over me. I don't feel pain, for one—torture holds no place of fear in this soul of mine."

Augustin gaped at her, then exhaled softly through his nose. "These claims you make... They're ludicrous, but the spirit in which you make them; I have half a mind to believe you."

"That's half a mind more than I anticipated. I've enjoyed our chat, but we won't be for much longer, I warrant. Just a guess—I'm good at guessing, you know."

"What do you mean?" Cristobal said, fixing the woman with a firm look. Augustin could tell the giant was growing uneasy around her. She didn't have the bearing of someone afraid, in the hands of official men of the Emperor. The threat of torture might as well have not been issued. But she had the read of it right, Cristobal wouldn't have harmed her, neither would Augustin.

The woman replied. "The man you call tomb raider. He's not going to leave me with you."

"He loves you then?" said Cristobal, returning the jibe.

"No. What a stupid notion."

The knight blinked at the severity of the woman's words.

"He doesn't love me. He needs me. I'm a tool to him but, equally so, he is a tool to me. And, I find the words reluctant to flee my lips, but he has proved himself resourceful. It hasn't been the most comfortable of ventures alongside him, but he has reliably gotten us where we need to go, and so he will come. I'm interested who wins this chess match between the two of you." Her eyes were fixed on Augustin again.

"There is no chess match! This is no game. I will hunt this criminal down and bring him to Mercusi's justice."

"Mercusi is a boor," said the woman with a huff.

"Respect the gods in my presence, if you will," said Cristobal, raising a heavy hand in a warding gesture.

Augustin continued as if he hadn't been interrupted, "He'll stand trial with the reeve's court; the Commodore himself will likely sign his death warrant. And, he'll swing from the yardarm; we'll cut him loose, and he'll float South—just like the rest of them. Robbing and looting the graves of the gods is desecration in and of itself, not to mention assaulting his Imperial Majesty's men. Imagine what the hellcatchers would say if they discovered this tomb raider threatening to loose a *demon* in the middle of Carabas."

GRAVEYARD GODS

The woman smiled, she shrugged. "I can't speak for the hellcatchers, but I don't think the occupant of the God Grave would have minded so much."

"And why's that?"

"Well... It's a grave, isn't it. Anything found inside is dead."

"And what would you know of it," said Cristobal, jutting out his chin. "Show some respect to the gods. They've been faithful to us. It's the least we can do."

Instead of looking offended at the rebuke, the woman looked downright pleased. She reached across and patted Cristobal on his large chest, smiling softly as she did. "You know, I think I quite like you. I might share a secret or two with you yet."

At just that moment, there came a sharp knock on the door. A creaking sound rolled out as the rusted hinges acclimated to their motion, and a head popped in. It was the face of the wizened proprietor, instead of scowling now, though, he had a slight look of unease about him. "Lord Captain Augustin Mora," he said, his voice shaky.

"Yes?"

"You are wanted outside for questioning. City guard in the employ of the Kindly Roost. They say that you kidnapped a woman." The proprietor gave a significant glance towards the tomb raider's accomplice.

"I did not kidnap her," Augustin snapped. "She's in my custody; she was the accomplice to a known and wanted fugitive."

"Even so," said the proprietor. He gave a half shrug. "You're wanted outside for questioning."

Augustin frowned, scowling, his mustache bristling on his upper lip. "Damnation. I've never..."

"You want me to go with you?" said Cristobal.

"And leave her with Vicente? I'll handle it. You stay here and do not let her out of your sight. On second thought, don't let *him* out of your sight either."

The large knight nodded once. "Shout if you need me. Make it loud."

Augustin smiled at his old friend, then, hand on the hilt of his rapier, he followed the proprietor out the door. The door slammed shut. And through the wood, Cristobal heard Augustin shout, "Lock it please!" Then, the sound of footsteps receded, dwindling with the creak of a stair. Cristobal grumbled as he approached the door, and reached for the key, preparing to lock it shut. But, just then, as he gripped the doorknob, the door opened.

Cristobal frowned and looked through the cracked door. Augustin stared back at him, eyes wide.

Cristobal relaxed slightly, easing his grip on the door handle. "Did you forget something?"

Augustin nodded fervently, but Cristobal pointed to the man's head. "You found your hat, I see. Was that what the guards wanted to talk about?"

Augustin once again wore his tricorn Lord captain's hat, however, something in his appearance puzzled Cristobal. Instead of the official blue-grey uniform with golden cuffs, upturned cowl and rank insignia, the lord captain now wore loose fighting, black pants and a plain shirt. Cristobal wasn't the most attentive sort when it came to fashion, but even the big Dumasian knight could tell when a man had changed his garb completely in a matter of seconds.

Cristobal frowned slightly. "Augustin, what's the matter? You don't look yourself."

Augustin hesitated for a moment, then dropped his earnest expression. He grinned a slightly crooked smile like a fox who has spotted entrance into a hen house, and then his foot lashed out, kicking the door.

Cristobal was a large man, and if he'd kept his hand bracing the door, Augustin would have broken his foot. But as it was, the door slammed into him, sending him reeling back into the wall with a thud. Augustin followed quickly into the room, a pistol coming out from behind his back, clutched tightly in his left hand. With a steady grip, the pistol pointed directly between Cristobal's eyes, just out of punching distance.

"Turn around, sit down, and put your hands on your head."

Cristobal didn't move.

"You're a tough brute, I give you that. You're large too. But my accomplices have your friend outside. Their daggers are pressed to his throat as we speak. If I have to fire, I'll hurt you. You might even survive. But he won't. And in that time, William, Jerel and my nephew Fernar will cut his face up, and you'll lose this Lord Captain of yours. So I'll ask you once more, sit down, turn around, and put your hands on your head. Please.

Cristobal glared at this man pretending to be Augustin. "Grave Thief," he said with a growl.

"You can call me by name—surely, Mira told you."

The woman in the corner threw up her hands. "I didn't tell them your name. Though I see you have no such reservation."

The man frowned. "Oh, I honestly thought you would have."

"I'm a keeper of secrets. Do you think I can betray trust for the sake of whimsy or grudge? What sort of incompetent lummox do you take me for? And what's with all this." She waved her hand up and down, indicating his face and his ensemble.

"I didn't have time to get his whole wardrobe," said the grave robber with a note of reproach.

"Yes, but the complexion is wrong too. Did you toast the hair fibers before placing them in the potion?" Then, scandalized, she added, "Surely you didn't drink it cold."

The grave robber, wearing Augustin's face, glanced sheepishly to the side. He cleared his throat a couple of times, then shrugged with one shoulder. The self-proclaimed keeper of secrets rolled her eyes. "Well, are we leaving?"

The Viper glanced over his pistol, his hand still steady. "Depending on this brute. I don't want to have to shoot him, but I will."

The woman glanced at Cristobal. "I like him; I'd rather you didn't hurt him." But, then, addressing Cristobal, she said, "He will shoot you if you don't sit down and turn around."

Cristobal was a man caught in indecision. Half of him thought for sure the Viper was lying about Augustin being ensnared. Augustin could be a slippery eel too. He rarely found himself on the wrong side of an ambush. But, if he wasn't lying, if Augustin was really in jeopardy, Cristobal couldn't risk it. It was the giant Dumasian's lasting weakness. His friendship with Augustin had cost them in the past before. He wasn't willing to give up the only family he had left. Not even if it was a slight risk, suggested by the lips of a liar. If it had only been the pistol in his face, Cristobal would have tried something. He wasn't as intimidated as most by bullets. It was hard to maintain the same fear of pistol shot when he'd been subject to eight of them. But, a bullet to the head? That was a different thing. Cristobal was fast for his size, but not that fast. And, if Augustin's life was on the line...

Slowly, growling, and fixing a hateful gaze on the man wearing Augustin's face, Cristobal dropped to his knees, turned and facing the wall, placing his hands in the air.

A sharp blow struck him across the back of the skull.

He roared, rubbing at his head, but stayed kneeling.

Another blow hit him.

"Blue fire and black fish!" he screamed, "What are you doing you daft bastard. Shoot me if you want to kill me!"

The raider muttered, "Your head is as thick as the waist of a Trabson jetty clerk."

"Hit me again," said Cristobal, hands up defensively as he glowered at the wall. "And forget my friend or your pistol, I'm coming straight at you."

Quiet murmurs ensued for a moment where the Viper whispered quietly to his companion, "Can't believe it didn't knock him out. Hit with all I had."

"Not surprising at all you had failed to knock out a man. Even after a second try."

"It worked on him, didn't it?" Cristobal couldn't tell where the thief was looking, but he surmised that he'd indicated Vicente. "Hang on one moment," said the man's voice. There was the sound of cloth moving, quiet muttering. A couple of thumps. Cristobal turned slightly, peering out the corner of his eye, he noticed the man wearing Augustin's face fishing something out of Vicente's jacket. It was the blood-stained dagger.

"There we go," said Edmond, a note of relief in his voice. Then, there was more rustling and something clinked as what sounded like a purse exchanged pockets.

"A common pickpocket too?" called Cristobal, his back still turned. "You lack all manner of honor."

"Call it recompense for emotional damage on account of him waving a pistol in my face."

"Vicente should have fired. Next time, we will."

"Are you volunteering your own purse, hmm?"

Cristobal scowled, still staring frustratingly at the wall. "We keep our coin on the ship. And, if you try to frisk me I'll break your fingers."

"I don't think you quite understand how this whole pistol holding business works. I will shoot you if you do anything.

But, you strike me as the sort that might be telling the truth. Fine, the coin is on your ship—I believe you."

Cristobal muttered, "If you want to go steal it, you can try to make your way past one hundred armed men on the dock outside of Trekker's Wharf. Ask for Agreo—insult his mother. I'm sure he'll love to show you around—might even introduce you to the keel."

"I'll take it under advisement."

There was another pause, no footsteps, indicating they weren't moving towards the door. On instinct, Cristobal jerked his head down slightly. "Don't hit me again!" he roared.

"I wasn't going to hit you!"

The woman said, "He was going to hit you."

"Just shut up," said the raider.

Now there was the creak of footsteps against wood, the door swung open with a creak. Then, the patter against the floorboards faded down the hall. Cristobal whirled around, surging to his feet and raced to the edge of the banister. He watched as the man wearing Augustin's face and the woman at his side hurried down a side hall, likely heading towards a back door. There was no sign of Augustin, or any accomplices with knives in their hands.

Cristobal growled and took two giant steps towards the top of the stairs. In his rage, he didn't watch where he was going; his ankle caught on a line of rope that had been tied across the top of the stairs from banister to the lower door hinge of the second room. With a shout and a tremendous cry, Cristobal tripped head over heels, stumbling down the stairs. He didn't stop until he slammed at the bottom with a painful grunt.

It took him a bit longer to get to his feet this time, testing his bones, and blinking back the black dots across his vision. More hurried footsteps. Then, Augustin's voice echoed out over him, "Cris, what are you doing?"

With a roar, Cristobal sat up fully on the stairs, his giant fist grabbing Augustin around the neck. He blinked a couple of times, before he realized this Augustin wasn't wearing his hat, and was back in his proper uniform. Immediately, he loosened his grip with a disgusted yell.

Coughing slightly, and glaring with a wide-eyed look of reproach, Augustin said, "What in the blue hells was that for?"

Cristobal choked out, "Did you see them? Yourself. The woman."

"Did I see who?" said Augustin, frowning in confusion. "I was just outside. There were no guards or Roosters. No one wanted to speak with me."

"The proprietor," Cristobal said, gasping. "Bribed. He came in wearing your face!"

"What are—who did?"

"The alchemist!"

Augustin stiffened, staring at his friend. "The Viper?" He dropped down to a knee where Cristobal was still massaging his head on the bottom step. "They were here?"

"He got the woman!"

"How? He took my face, you say? Did Serenia use to be able to do that? Where is he? Where is the woman?"

Cristobal heaved a massive sigh, lifted his hand in a half-effort to point to the side door, but then lowered it again in disgust. "They're gone. They escaped."

Chapter 27

From his seat by the window, Augustin watched the sun rise over Carabas. The white plaster glittered with morning dew and the light songs of small birds played over the discordant keening of gulls off the bay. A breeze carried the salt smell of the harbor across his nose and cooled the dark rings under his tired eyes. Behind him, Vicente lay sprawled on one of the beds, while Cristobal wrung out a clean rag, trickling water back into a waiting basin. The big man had a fatherly gentleness to him as he handed the cool cloth to Vicente, who murmured his thanks and lay it over his pained eyes.

For a stretch of time, no words passed between them. Augustin glanced to the corner of the room again. Empty. Only a couple hours before, the mysterious woman had stood there in her simple dress and veil.

Who are you? The thought had plagued Augustin since her first words to him in the back alley of the Maiden's Doubt. She spoke like a woman well beyond her years. *She knew me. She knew my mother.* It did not surprise Augustin to consid-

GRAVEYARD GODS

er Dominga had connections to the Kindly Roosts. It made sense as well that she may know Sofia Di'ladrion, or at least have some contact, as the ancient crone was her lover's aunt. Describing his mother and Commodore Severelle as 'lovers' would be putting it generously at best, but somehow thinking of them in this way turned his stomach less than the truth. Dominga had played a dangerous game. She had stolen the lustful rat's heart, if only for a moment, and teased from it a promotion for her only son. A tournament knight, upjumped to Lord Captain of an Imperial Frigate. What she must have endured to make it happen-

Augustin looked up into the rising sun, squinting his tired eyes. Three more days. Three days to bring Severelle the tomb raider. *The Viper.* The hollow feeling in his chest settled lower. The Viper had stolen back his accomplice, he had stolen back the bloody dagger, and moreover, he did it all while wearing Augustin's own face. Augustin felt the muscles of his shoulders coiling as his anger threatened to boil over. *No, there has to be a way. We can't lose him here.*

Folding his arms behind his back. Augustin let the soldier in him take over. He let out a long hot breath through his nose, and relaxed his shoulders. He raised his chin. *Think, Augustin.*

"Vicente." Augustin turned to face his companions. His voice sounded harsh and Augustin swallowed to try and clear the dryness from his throat. Vicente did not stir from his place on the bed. "Vicente, you're sure that you still need the tomb raider's blood to follow him?"

It was a longshot, and he knew it. Vicente tilted his chin in the barest approximation of a nod. Then with a sound like the croaking ghost of his usual rasping voice, Vicente replied, "I need something. Blood is best, but hair, skin, even spit will do."

Cristobal raised a hand towards Augustin, an idea brightening his expression. "You dueled him, Augustin. Did you check your sword? Did you cut him?"

Augustin sighed and shook his head. He had thought of that already. The Viper had played him.

"When we started the duel," Augustin said, "he gave just enough of an impression of skill that I fought overcautiously. I did not cut him. If I had pressed the attack, I could have disarmed him in a moment." The bitterness in Augustin's voice dripped.

Cristobal crossed his arms, looking uncomfortably to the wooden floor, and Augustin swallowed the rest of his words, however, a small doubt continued to niggle at him. The Viper had flounted his expectations at every turn. *Was he as hopeless as all that, or was it a deeper game? A hidden blade or spring-trap pistol?* Augustin stopped himself. Speculation of this sort did nothing, but fuel his own doubts, and he was through with them. *No. I can't anticipate him. That's his game. I have to play to my own strengths.* Augustin stretched his calloused fingers. *The next time we cross blades, I will give him the full measure of my skill.*

"Wait." This time it was Vicente who spoke. "I have a feeling—No, a thought. Wait, yes, yes. An idea." From his place on the bed, Vicente raised an arm, pointing blindly to the roof in pain-dulled excitement. He pulled the damp rag from his eyes and pushed himself up. "Gus, w-whoa—"

As Vicente's eyes unfocused, he swayed on the bed's edge, and Cristobal made a quick dash to catch him before he could fall to the floor. Still jabbing one finger skyward, Vicente closed his eyes and did his best to hold still. From the small movement of his lips, Augustin guessed his friend was fighting a losing battle with nausea.

"Pan." Vicente's half-belched request was answered by Augustin snatching up an empty bedpan from the floor and holding it out for his friend. Vicente took it with both hands and retched into the brass bowl. Augustin took a half-step back while Cristobal took hold of Vicente's black dreadlocks, holding them behind his ears.

"Oof. That felt good. Not good. A bad kind of good, but good," Vicente muttered as he finished and spat the taste from his mouth.

Augustin replied, "I'm surprised you're even conscious. After that blow you took to the skull, the ale, the senza-"

"Aye," Cristobal added. "How are you not dead?"

Vicente cackled, pushing himself on unsteady feet, he slumped against the wall by the window and dumped the bedpan out into the street. After briefly considering his own reflection in the smeared brass, Vicente tossed the bowl under the bed again and leaned against the wall.

"Can't die yet," he murmured. He seemed on the point of saying something else, when he waved his hand in front of his face. "Wait. Stop distracting me. I had an idea."

Augustin and Cristobal waited patiently, while Vicente focused himself. Augustin thought his friend may have fallen asleep while leaning against the wall when Vicente spoke again. "What about the other one?"

Cristobal and Augustin looked to each other in confusion. Augustin asked, "The woman? We lost her, remember. I don't know how we'd track her either."

Vicente squeezed his eyes closed, swaying slightly in frustration. "No, no, no. The other-other one. The skinny drowner out back of the Roost."

Augustin thought back. They had been so focused on capturing the Viper that he had forgotten the other person. A variable Augustin had not considered.

"Go on," he urged Vicente.

"So, it's like this. Our grave-robber. He comes to Carabas. He needs to find his friend. He goes to the Kindly Roost. That tells Vicente that our man knows his friend will be there reliably. If he counts on him to be there, maybe we can count on him to be there too." Vicente grinned and held up his hands like a street performer calling for applause.

Augustin felt a small flicker of excitement in his chest. His tired mind focusing on the thought with renewed clarity. *It could work. If the Viper knew to go to that particular Kindly Roost, the* Maiden's Doubt, *then maybe we can find his friend again. At the least, someone who saw him. Someone who knew him.* It was a lead, and like a drowning man thrown a lifeline, Augustin took hold of it.

***

GRAVEYARD GODS

In the scrutinizing light of the morning sun, the Maiden's Doubt slumped down into the streets around it like the aching essence of a hangover made physical. The cracked plaster showed dark stains of mold, and the flowing curtains from the upper floors displayed every patch and stain. The dilapidated building seemed one wrenching cough away from death.

Cristobal made a warning gesture with his hand. "It looks so different. Sort of dead."

Vicente blew through his lips derisively, patting Cristobal on the shoulder. A pint of ale and the walk down from Verian Hill had done much to recover his spirit, though he still halted and staggered at odd intervals. "Of course it's dead. It *should* be dead. Have you ever gone to a gambling den in the morning?"

His words flowed easier, the slurring had nearly dropped off completely. Though he had energetically refused Augustin's recommendation to stay at the Stone Priest and recover, Augustin had eased their pace down to the wharf-walks. He still didn't trust that Vicente hadn't cracked his skull and wouldn't keel over into the gutter at any moment. Augustin's worry spiked momentarily as Vicente slapped Cristobal's stomach and made a line for the front door of the Maiden's Doubt.

"Eh, I'd be surprised if the door wasn't—" Vicente paused, having reached for the handle.

As Augustin and Cristobal caught up, it became clear the reason for the old knight's hesitation.

The door hung slightly ajar. The dark strip of void between the frame and the door seemed alive with malignant intent.

The three companions looked to one another. Augustin pushed open the door with one leather gloved hand, and a squeal of decrepit hinges sounded back at them. The sunlight seemed reluctant to enter the gloom and Augustin could see no further than ten feet before shadow swallowed up the room before him. He stepped inside and felt the crunch of broken glass under his boot as it tinkled in minute snaps against the wood. Somewhere beyond the edge of his sight something dripped onto the wood floor with a determined splut, splut, splut.

"This is not right," Vicente said in a whisper.

Augustin had to agree. One hand reflexively curled to grip his rapier's hilt as he stepped further in, peering into the darkness to let his eyes adjust. Cristobal stepped up beside Augustin and drew a small pack of waterproof matches from his belt pouch. He struck one against the rough wood of the door frame and held it up. The dim illumination coaxed the outline of the bar and nearby tables from the darkness, and Cristobal crept forward to light one of the thick-bottomed candles that clung to the bar's edge. As he lifted the candle, he turned and held one thick finger to his lips.

Augustin stepped toward him, careful not to move through any more of the broken glass. Cristobal pointed over the bar, and as Augustin leaned over to look, he saw the candle light dancing in a reflective pool of blood. A lanky man in a stained hemp smock slumped against the back of the bar. One arm was raised and pinned in place by a thin stiletto dagger that punched through his wrist, and blood dripped from the wound into the puddle beneath him.

Augustin eased back from the bar as Vicente leaned in and whispered, "Can't be dead more than two hours. Probably, fresher than that."

Nodding, Augustin drew his rapier with a metallic whisper. "Cristobal, lead with the light. Vicente, you still have one pistol. Keep it ready, but do not fire unless I order."

Without another word they formed into a compact triangle, with Cristobal leading while Augustin and Vicente eyed the surrounding darkness with renewed suspicion.

Discarded piles of colored shells lay chipped and scattered between upturned tables. Here and there the greying plaster walls were marred by trailing sprays of blood. They found the next body, a large, well-muscled man, at the top of a staircase. It looked like the stairway had at one point been sealed away behind a door that now hung open on one bent hinge. Cristobal bent down beside the dead man and pointed to the rooster tattoo on his neck. *Whoever did this had no fear or respect for the Kindly Roosts.* Augustin shuddered to think what sort of person would intentionally cross Sofia Di'ladrion. *The Viper?* Augustin remembered the wild look in the tomb-robber's eyes as he threatened to intentionally summon a demon into the streets. A cold feeling of steel settled into his heart.

"Eyes sharp," Augustin whispered. "He might have come back here."

Cristobal nodded grimly, and Vicente's lips curled into the eager lines of a vengeful grin. From the darkness at the bottom of the stairway, a wailing cry of pain sounded. The trio froze.

It sounded like a man, and just as suddenly as it appeared, the sound vanished.

He's here, Augustin thought. Sliding past Cristobal, Augustin took up the lead.

Now in single file, the trio descended the steps. They were nearly to the bottom. The meager candlelight showed one red splotch against the corner of a step. A large man, who could have been the twin of the one at the top of the stairs lay sprawled at the bottom of the stairwell. His neck had broken and reflective blood pooled from behind his head where it had struck the floor. Further in the wide room, the red gold of a few scattered coins winked from the edge of a sandy circle where an overturned table seemed to lay in indignant silence. The wood beams and lime-washed walls yellowed in the mixed light of the candle and lanterns. Augustin stepped into the room.

In the center of the sandy pit stood a hunched figure under a black hood and cowl. At the figure's feet lay the crumpled form of a man, shorter, with strong limbs wrapped in coiling ridges of shimmering bone. No, not a man.

The Signerde from the alleyway. Augustin's muscled forearms strained in his sleeves as he glowered at the scene. Beneath the Signerde's unmoving body, the pit's sand dutifully drank up his blood into a red mud. The hunched figure glanced over its shoulder.

"If you were looking to join our little party, you're a bit late, Mora." The voice had the rolling quality of the East. A Trabson voice that fell and rose, so that the statement seemed nearly a question, and yet it seemed to linger in a flinty grey tone, like slate. Neither malicious nor welcoming. Neither caring nor spiteful. Augustin had heard that voice before. His mind flashed back to Borgo Tortrugha and that day of carnage, and for a moment the smell of sweat and blood from the fighting pit fell away before the memory of gunsmoke and oiled steel.

"Muergo," Augustin said.

The candlelight flickered as Cristobal flinched, and Vicente's rapier point rose into a guard.

The figure gave a throaty, mirthless chuckle and lowered his hood. Underneath, dark stringy hair fell over pale strands from a nearly bald head. He turned to face the trio, and Augustin saw him wiping the blood from the serrated edge of a thick knife. Muergo held up the freshly cleaned steel and then tucked the blade into an empty sheath at his hip, nestling the blade among a cluster of other handles. *His collection has grown,* Augustin noted grimly as he saw there must have been at least a dozen daggers and knives of various sizes and shapes at the hunched man's waist.

Cristobal spoke next, stepping defensively beside Augustin. "What did you do to him? What are you doing here, mongrel?"

Muergo adjusted the cowl around his shoulders, and tugged at a hidden knot. From under the cowl fell a thin black cape that wrapped around his body, turning his silhouette into a black pillar holding his pale and ugly head aloft.

"He didn't tell you. Interesting." Muergo's pallid, fish-like eyes flicked between the three companions in some cold calculation.

Augustin's tired mind was in no mood for games and he barked in response, "We needed that man for an investigation. We're here under orders from Commodore Severelle, and you've killed him."

"Drowner," Muergo said flatly. When Augustin only narrowed his eyes in confusion. Muergo said, "Not a man. A drowner."

Augustin pointed with his rapier to the corpse. "A person. A person important to my mission, and the Commodore's orders." Part of Augustin wondered if he would be justified in putting down Muergo right now like the mad dog he was; part of him didn't care. Only the smallest remainder of reason remembered that it didn't matter. His real objective was the Viper, and he slipped further and further away.

"Not as important as you might think," Muergo said. "He didn't know where the grave robber went. He would have told me." He spoke with absolute certainty and the statement fell with the finality of a stone hammer. Vicente let out a growl of frustration.

"What are you blathering about you dog-fish?"

Muergo stepped forward, uncaring of the swords that hung ready in the air. He did not sigh. He did not laugh. It seemed he did not even breathe, but stepped forward like a walking corpse. "Commodore Severelle sent me to capture this tomb raider. If he did not tell you, then we are not meant to cooperate." It seemed for a moment as if Muergo might walk straight into Augustin's upraised rapier, but at the last moment Augustin turned his blade, lowering the point to the sandy floor. Muergo did not react, but walked between the companions like a wraith, and ascended the stairs. No farewell called back to them, and after a few moments, Muergo disappeared into the dark above them.

Silence fell in the fighting pit as Augustin looked down at the dead body of the Signerde, his last lead, broken, brutally dashed and thrown into the sand.

"This is it," Augustin murmured. "He's won."

If he had more time, he knew that he could search port to port, city to city, to find the Viper. *If I only had more time.* The sentiment felt hollow, almost petulant. His hand trembled as it gripped his sword.

"No," Vicente said. He sheathed his rapier, and put a hand on Augustin's shoulder. He shook him until Augustin looked him in the eyes. "No," he said again. "There may be only three of us now," he pointed from himself to Cristobal, landing the jabbing finger squarely in Augustin's chest. "—but we are still the Order. The Order of the Honorable Lily does not retreat." Vicente's harsh voice slid through the air like brewing thunder. "The Order does not give up. We do not surrender. We do not despair."

Cristobal put his large hand on Augustin's other shoulder, "We protect," the big man added, his heavy voice dropping near a whisper. Augustin shook his head. His neck flushed hot with shame. He remembered now why he wanted to reform the Order. Separate, they could be broken, but together—Augustin raised his chin, taking a deep breath.

"I am sorry, my friends." He patted Vicente's hand, and his companions released his shoulders. "You are right. We are not beaten. We have three days yet." *Three days, and no trail.* Augustin looked once more to the fallen Signerde. "We should check the man for some clue. He met with the tomb raider, perhaps they exchanged a note or something that may tell us his intentions."

Cristobal nodded and stepped forward. He rolled the Signerde over onto his back. Sand stuck to his body where the blood had spread, and the stab wound pulsed a fresh flow of blood.

Cristobal's eyes went wide. "Ververiona! His heart is still beating."

At once Vicente and Augustin rushed to kneel at the Signerde's side. As Cristobal propped up the Signerde, the bleeding man shivered, and his eyes fluttered.

"*D-deniz dos-dos-*" He did not seem to be fully aware. His eyes rolled blindly as his body trembled with the pain of his wounds. Augustin reached to his satchel and withdrew a spare bandage, pressing it to the pulsing stab wound. Now that he could see the fellow clearly, his stomach tightened at the assembled horrors Muergo had wrought on his body. Each hand missed several fingers. Bloody gashes oozed across his arms where ridges of bone had been slashed and pried from his flesh. Innumerable minor cuts stood across the flesh between, in some places so closely overlapped that they made his skin look like a plowed field.

"Vicente, the senza," barked Augustin, hurriedly.

Vicente reached into his coat and withdrew the bottle, gingerly pouring some of the honeyed liquid into the Signerde's mouth. Some dribbled from the corners of his lips, but Augustin watched as his throat began to bob, swallowing the thick draught. After a moment, the Signerde's eyes began to focus. His chest still rose and fell only weakly with shuddering breaths, but now he saw Augustin.

"H-he'll kill him," he said.

Augustin's brow beetled in confusion. "Who?" he asked. "Who is killing who?"

"The *den-deniz dostu*; friend—sea friend. He—cave-fish will kill him. He'll kill him—like he-he's—" The Signerde gasped, biting his lip as blood trickled out from behind his teeth. "He'll kill him, like he's killed me."

Sea friend? Augustin did not know much about the Signerde or their ways, but he understood comradery. This Signerde dying in Cristobal's arms wanted him to save the sea friend; the *deniz dostu*. The bandage in Augustin's hand had nearly soaked through. He had seen enough injuries to know when the matter was settled. Even if Catali was in the room with them this very moment, there would be no saving him. He only had moments.

"Who is the sea friend? Is it the tomb raider you spoke with?" Augustin asked, the urgency in his heart driving his words out rapidly. There would be no guarantee they were the same person, but it was a chance, a slender chance.

The Signerde, gave a puzzled look, recognition coming slowly to his face. "I know you." Augustin pushed on insistently. "Who is the man you spoke with last night?"

The Signerde's face screwed up in a troubled look of pain, tears beginning to run from his eyes as he made some hasty debate within his mind. Grabbing Augustin's coat he tearfully cried, "Swear to me, the cave-fish will not kill him. The pale man with dead eyes will not have him."

Augustin took one bloody hand from the bandage and laid it over the dying man's knuckles. "I swear. I will not allow Muergo to kill him."

At this the Signerde seemed to relax. His hand dropped and for one moment Augustin feared the man had died. Then, with the ghostly remains of his voice, the Signerde said, "He is a brother to the Eldest. Husband to an heiress. His way is revenge. He travels with a woman who is no woman. He came to me for supplies, but where he goes—" Here the Signerde lolled his head in a tired of approximation of 'no'.

"What is his name?" Augustin asked desperately. The description so far made no sense to him, and he saw the light leaving the Signerde's weak eyes.

"*Deniz dostu.* Protect him. I go to my Mother's house." One last rasping breath shook from the Signerde's chest, then all shuddering stopped. Augustin stood as Cristobal gently laid the man into the sands.

Chapter 28

EDMOND STROLLED UP TREKKER'S Wharf, still wearing the face of the lord captain. His boots thudded against the sturdy jetty as he approached the second frigate they'd spotted. The men accompanying him were muttering in their harsh, grating language and shooting distrustful glances in his direction when they thought he wasn't looking.

"You haven't the foggiest what you're doing, do you?" said Mira. She walked alongside him, putting distance between herself and the twenty bravos at their back.

"We have a crew, don't we," said Edmond with a shrug.

Mira glanced over her shoulder towards the bravos. Their bangles and banded rings shifted and clattered as they followed along. Their hair, cut short on one side, but braided through with polished stones and glass bobbles on the other, dangled over half their faces, casting their eyes in shadow. The bravos' silk bandanas and scarves had moved from places around their arms or shoulders, and now were being used to wipe the sweat from their brows as they watched Edmond carefully.

Granted, a crew was only as useful as the pay they received. And, for the moment, there was no pay. The last of Edmond's earnings from his fight with his new Signerde friend and what he'd purloined from the bloodseeker had been spent bribing the old, wrinkled owner of the Stone Priest. The first bribe had been to lure Augustin Mora away. The second had secured information. When Edmond had asked if the proprietor knew of anyone looking to join a crew, he'd immediately recommended a man by the name of Kurga.

The bravo leader had been easy enough to find. After being kicked out of the Stone Priest for disorderly conduct, and sustaining injuries to a couple of his men, the sometime-pirate, sometime-sellsword had spent his time roaming the many wharfs of Carabas with his brethren looking for 'honest work,' he'd said when questioned on it. Though, Edmond was near certain, he'd caught the men eyeing seemingly abandoned vessels when the jetty guard weren't looking.

"Hat-man," said Kurga, his rasping voice bringing to mind lock files and pestles. "Where is this ship you say—uh? Where she be?"

"Just up ahead!" Edmond called over his shoulder. He glanced back, flashing a would-be appeasing smile.

Kurga, the shortest man in the group, also carried the most pistols. A criss-crossing bandolier of the firearms dangled across the diminutive bravo's chest, many of them inlaid with pearl or silver. Clearly, this man was a collector. Though, judging by the rank smell and state of his trousers, Edmond felt the impressive accumulation of powder weapons had much taken the place of basic hygiene.

Kurga rubbed a yellow-stained silk scarf across his forehead, then blew his nose into it. Then, he wrapped the scarf back around his throat. "My family," he said, "they grow restless. You mentioned coin."

"That I did," said Edmond. He turned around now so that he was walking backwards, but facing the bravos. "And remember when you agreed not to stab me?"

"I remember how you are with that blade, uh?" said the short man, nodding towards the sword at Edmond's hip. "I touch fire once, thus life teaches. I touch fire twice? Thus life mocks. I am not a man to mock, uh?"

Edmond shook his head quickly. "Of course not." He still hadn't quite figured out what Kurga kept going on about, but as much as he could gather, Augustin Mora had run-ins with the bravos before. At the very least, they had near recognized him when he'd approached them on the Dena Jetty—three wharfs down.

A couple of the bravos had tried to strike him. Another had aimed a pistol at him, but the promise of coin, Mira's presence—which had entranced the men—and Edmond's way with words had reached a bargain. Fair wages for fair labor; at least, that had been the promise.

Now, it was up to Edmond to secure those wages. And judging by the restless nature of his new quarter crew, he was running out of time in which to do it.

Edmond turned back around, picking up the pace once more. He'd spotted three imperial ships in Trekker's Wharf. The long jetty, supported by large, white-stone slabs broke off into smaller wharfs, cutting through miles of shore.

Already, he'd been sent scramming from one of the ships. They had neither recognized him, nor been interested in his offer. This left two options left: His Imperial Majesty's Ship *Devout*. And HIMS *Intrepid*. When the giant Dumasian had let slip their ship was on Trekker's Wharf, Augustin hadn't thought it would be so difficult to find out *which* ship. He'd desperately tried to recall the name on the ship back at Sile, but amidst the adrenaline and injury it had eluded him.

Now, as he led his small band of men up the jetty, around a crook and towards *Devout*, he moved with a bit more urgency, adjusting his captain's hat and clearing his throat.

He reached the edge of the gangplank where four sailors were lounging on upright barrels, and dozing off in the evening sunlight.

Edmond cleared his throat as he reached them.

Two of the men looked up, rubbing the sleep from their eyes to examine him.

"Do you know who I am?" Edmond demanded in as bold and brash a voice he could muster.

The four men were now all looking at him, curiously, and a few faces had also appeared over the railing on the deck, peering towards the jetty.

"No," said one of the men, hesitantly. He glanced at the hat, then at Edmond's loose-fitting cloak and form-fitting black clothing. "Should we? You, Petar? Do you know this man?"

Another one of the crew hesitated, scratching his chin, then shrugged.

"Perfect," Edmond said. "In that case, I have a deal for you."

The sailors glanced dumbly at him.

"A deal," Edmond repeated. "For—you know what, can I speak to your captain, please?"

There was the thud of boots against wood and someone stepped off the ship onto the top of the gangplank. "I'm the captain," said a voice. "What is it you want? We have no room for bravos aboard my ship—we're at full capacity."

Edmond looked up, eyeing the captain. She wore the uniform like a living portrait—hat and insignia orderly, pants neatly pressed. She wore a sabre low on her hip, and kept her hands well clear of it. As Edmond moved towards the gangplank though, all four sailors immediately reacted, stepped in front of them, their hands moving to their weapons.

The bravos behind Edmond shuffled, their bangles and rings rattling on their own sabres.

"Don't do anything," Edmond said quickly, holding out a hand to his tentative crew. He looked up at the captain of the *Devout*. "I'm not looking for trouble." He glanced down at one of the sailor's hands which was still pressed against his chest. Daintily, he pulled at the man's pinky, removing the offending appendage and stepping slightly to the side with a grimace.

"I—ah, I couldn't help but notice you're floating a bit light, aren't you? In need of more cargo, perhaps?"

At this, the weaponless captain eyed him with interest. "Aye," she said. "We're running light. Just unloaded this afternoon in fact—not that it's any of yours what we were carrying."

"And I wasn't asking," Edmond said quickly. "But—how do you like the idea of making a real pretty penny. And you wouldn't even have to leave this wharf."

The captain eyed him up and down, pursing her lips. "And how's that? Offering your services in turning straw into gold are you?"

The sailors all laughed at the joke, nodding in appreciation.

Edmond resisted the urge to roll his eyes. Clearly this was a captain who had earned the respect and affection of her crew. An impressive feat, no doubt, but it did little to help Edmond reach his goals. And still his twenty would-be sailors were watching him like a colony of bats waiting to break ranks and charge. And as with fables of vampires, he knew to calm them he would have to procure silver and gold. But he didn't have much time to do it in. The lord captain, his giant, and his bloodseeker could be returning to the wharf any minute now. And this plan would take a certain amount of time.

"Cannons," Edmond said, quickly. "I'm selling my guns."

The captain frowned, eyeing him. "You're a captain?"

"Lord Captain Augustin Mora," Edmond said, bowing.

"Script Captain Katrina Renor," said the no-nonsense captain.

Edmond flashed a would-be charming smile. "Might I add just how dazzling I find your presence?"

Mirastious groaned next to him.

"Stow it," Katrina Renor said, brusquely. "I'll ask you to conduct yourself professionally or our conversation ends."

Edmond sniffed, but nodded acquiescence. "So, cannons?"

"How many? What shot?" she asked, frowning. "It is true we're light. But, we're not normally in the trade of armaments. And *Devout* isn't a merchant vessel. We're in the pay of Baron Wamler from Godshavens's..."

As she continued, Edmond nodded, acting as if he were listening, but at the same time, he leaned back, glancing up the jetty towards the third and final imperial ship he'd scouted: the *Intrepid*.

He squinted, counting quickly beneath his breath. *Twenty canons? No. Two decks of guns. Forty, then? Wait—no, he'd miscounted... Blast. From the start then. One... Two...*

Kurga cleared his throat from behind Edmond, stepped forward and tilted the braided side of his head towards Katrina. Edmond knew, from what little he'd heard of the bravos, that a nod on one side was a greeting of honor, a nod on the other was a challenge to a duel. Kurga glanced up at Edmond, and smiled, flashing a gap-toothed grin displaying rotting teeth and senza damaged gums.

"Forty-four cannon," he said, nodding towards the *Intrepid*. "Eighteen pounders."

Edmond shared a look with Kurga who grinned again, then, almost imperceptibly, with the eye beneath his braided strands of hair, he winked.

Edmond stifled a smile of his own and returned his gaze to Katrina.

"Forty-four eight pounders?" she said, whistling softly. "I'm afraid that may be too rich for us."

"Ah, excusi," said Kurga. He held up a small finger which seemed to be permanently scorched on either side from gunpowder. "It is, no eight, but *eighteen*. Uh?"

At this Katrina started shaking her head sadly. "I wish that I could," she said. "We have the space, but not the coin. "Forty four guns like that..."

"I'll give them to you discounted," Edmond said quickly. "It's my ship, after all." He glanced out of the corner of his eye at Kurga who didn't react in the least to this declaration. The small man stared stonily ahead, his expression impassive. Now that their leader had joined the conversation, the rest of the bravos seemed to have calmed somewhat. He couldn't help but notice, either, that where earlier their postures had been neutral, or the shaved sides of their heads had been inclined slightly towards him, now, the braided parts of their hair, glinting baubles and beads were on display as they listened quietly.

"Even then," Katrina said, shaking her head sadly. "A single eighteen-pounder is what? Two-hundred d'oro?"

A couple of her sailors nodded.

GRAVEYARD GODS

Kurga raised a finger again, once again displaying its blackened, gunpowder stained skin. "It is, I think, two hundred fifty, in fact."

Edmond frowned. Katrina frowned. The sailors frowned, as did most of the bravos. Each of them, Edmond supposed, trying to do some quick math.

Again, though, it was Kurga who interjected. "Two hundred fifty per cannon. Forty four cannon. This is, uh, *eleven* thousand d'oro. Flat."

The bravos were now listening. Intently. Kurga's expression was of a kindly old man, presenting his wares behind a seaside booth. Edmond knew this was only half of it. But he was starting to suspect that bravos weren't given their reputation as reliable sellswords, and sometimes pirates, for nothing. They had a strange notion of honor from what he knew of them. Bravos were loyal only to each other and to coin. But once they had been paid and a contract negotiated, they were loyal until the death. Or, until the expiration of said contract. Then, nothing prevented a quick knife in the dark and a quiet mutiny. But, until the expiration, until the d'oro ran out, it was a pride to them to follow through with their given word. A strange notion of honor, but one Edmond quite understood.

"We don't have eleven thousand," Katrina began to say, but Edmond quickly said, "Four thousand! Four thousand for the lot, and me and my men will help move the cannons to the jetty. From there, you trundle them to your ship—there are carters in town, even in the evening looking for work I warrant."

Katrina stared at him, mouth agape. "Four thousand? For all your cannons. Are you sure your commodore will—"

Edmond waved his hand. "My commodore is an ass. You can tell him I, Lord Captain Augustin Mora, said so. But yes, I *can*. They're my cannons, and it is my contract."

Katrina hesitated. She'd frowned when he'd called his superior officer an 'ass'. But the thought of getting her hands on that many cannons for such a ridiculously low price was clearly alluring her beyond her usual scope of acceptable unprofessionalism.

"Three thousand," Edmond said, his voice taut, like a line attached to a lure, pulling a landed catch the last few feet to the edge of the boat.

And like that landed catch, Katrina Renor took a step towards Edmond, down the gangplank. As if certain he might change his mind, lest she refrain from speaking, Katrina nearly shouted, "Deal! Three thousand d'oro for forty-four eighteen-pounders. You remove them from the ship, we load them onto ours. Fair is fair."

The captain of the *Devout* pulled her powdered glove from her hand, revealing a weathered palm that was no stranger to the rigging and ropes of her vessel. Then, she spat into her hand, extending it towards him.

All four of her sailors, and many still on the ship, watched Edmond with wide eyed looks of anticipation, licking their lips as if they found their mouths suddenly dry. Three thousand d'oro was no small amount. Most sailors took home four d'oro per week. The sum Katrina had agreed to was worth more than fourteen years of most the sailor's salaries. But even more than the three thousand was the eight thousand d'oro worth of profit they stood to make from the deal. Judging by the way the sailors glanced at their captain and watched Edmond, he supposed she was the sort to share, at least in part, good fortune with those in her service.

And for Edmond, he'd agreed to pay the bravos slightly elevated wages—it had spared him being stabbed. But even with the five d'oro a week he'd promised to each of them, and the ten he'd promised Kurga, he could retain the entire crew in his employ for more than seven months, purely on this one deal. Of course, that didn't account for ship repairs, food, water, unforeseen health circumstances... But, Edmond wasn't worried about that. Three thousand d'oro was enough to set things in motion. It was enough to begin to plan.

And so, Edmond spat in his own hand and gripped Katrina's extended palm. Laughter and applause broke out on both the *Devout* and among the bravos. With a skip in his step, tilting his tricorn hat, Edmond turned and led his quarter crew towards the *Intrepid*, while the captain of the *Devout* began organizing her men for the transfer.

The imperial frigate was certainly a magnificent vessel. The gleaming white-oak hull glistened above the water-line, pockmarked by red gun ports, which, on the lower level had been sealed shut, but, on the upper deck remained open, revealing the polished metal of the cannons.

Turning to face Kurga, Edmond said, "You had best wait down here. Act casual."

Kurga rolled his eyes. Turning to the group, he let out a rattling command in Chelleck, and the group of bravos spread out.

They settled into small circles that leaned on the nearby walls and crouched at the mouths of alleyways as dice and cards came out.

Satisfied, Edmond drew up his shoulders into straight-backed posture. Turning to Mira, he muttered, "Time to see what sort of captain Augustin Mora is."

As he approached the ship, sailors spotted him and saluted in greeting. Edmond repressed his smile. The gambit was paying off. This *was* the Lord Captain's ship then, after all. An equal number stared past him with slack jaws at Mirastious, eyeing her up and down with a wolfish hunger.

"Look professional, men," Edmond snapped, clapping his hands. Immediately, the sailors leading the way to the *Intrepid* tried to look busy, moving about the jetty, or back up the gangplank.

Edmond put his fingers to his lips and took three leaping strides up the gangplank until he reached the rail. Then, with one hand still in his mouth, and the other gripping the rigging, he whistled sharply past his fingers.

"All of you in my charge," he called, "I need you to immediately stop what you're doing and unload the canons. *After* that, you are asked to remove yourselves and your possessions from the ship. Anything that can't be tied down, you're welcome to take. Cargo, armaments—everything heavy, it has to go! Understand? Well? What are you waiting for—"

Before Edmond could finish, a croaking voice that reminded him of a slimy toad emitted from a man who physically supplied similar recollection. The man glared from hooded eyes, waddling towards Edmond.

"Augustin," said the man, his voice barely a sneer. "And where's the giant?"

"Cristobal?" said Edmond, remembering the name he'd overhead. "Ah, yes... He's with Vicente."

The snidely man frowned. "Who?"

Edmond glanced about the crew quickly, but noted similar looks of confusion. He cleared his throat and shook his head quickly. "Never mind," he said. "He's not here. Regardless, I need you to follow my orders. We've found the disgusting, nasty, no-good tomb raider. The nameless bastard is holed up inland, so we're making an expedition."

At this, the toad-like man gaped at Edmond as if a fly might buzz into his gaping mouth. "An expa-what?! No! If he's gone inland, he's someone else's problem. The Commodore would never allow-"

"He did," Edmond said. "That's where Cristobal is. With the Commodore. You know how these things go. Orders is orders."

"Show me a written order!" the man snapped.

Edmond frowned, glaring down at the man. The other sailors on the ship were all glancing between the two of them. Clearly, Augustin Mora hadn't commanded the same loyalty from his sailors that Captain Katrina did on the *Devout*.

Edmond quickly looked around, then pointed at one of the *Intrepid's* rig monkeys. "You," he said. "Do you know who this man is?" he pointed towards the toad, his tone filled with strange inflection in an effort to disguise his own ignorance.

"Er, you mean Crewmaster Agreo, sir?"

"Exactly," said Edmond. "You and I both know Agreo is a good sailor, and a great Crewmaster."

The rig monkey hesitated, then gave a half shrug-nod. "Aye, sir?" He'd inflected it as a question.

Edmond couldn't help but chuckle. "Ah, they don't like you much, do they, Agreo?" he winked. "Is it because you're keeping all the grog to yourself?" He wiggled his eyebrows at Agreo's ample belly. "I've always admired contented men. But those who hoard the grog?" Edmond tutted, shaking his head. "Hard to make friends that way."

A few of the sailors were snickering into their hands. The others were outright grinning at the crewmaster. Agreo, for his part, looked shellshocked. He stared at the man he assumed was his captain, mouth agape. "I—I," he said, his face the color of sunburn.

"Catch your words," said Edmond, "Then, catch your breath. You'll need it to unload the cannons." At this last part, he'd raised his voice again.

Agreo, much deflated, stared venomously at Edmond as if nursing his wounds on sheer hatred. Edmond didn't mind. He'd be long gone, and his face would change before Agreo could make good on the silent promises he was likely mulling over at that very moment. The good Lord Captain on the other hand... Well, Augustin Mora might have a problem or two to deal with whenever he decided to return from the Stone Priest. Of course, Edmond had seen a determination in Augustin's eyes that had impressed him.

GRAVEYARD GODS

This was not a man to give up lightly. Tournament fencers were often competitive by nature. It was the reason Edmond had come to the wharf. The one place he knew Augustin wouldn't look for him was back on an imperial ship, which was why Edmond suspected he would have enough time to carry out this audacious plan.

Mira hadn't been a fan of it when he'd outlined it to her, but he hoped to show her wrong.

Already, as if Agreo's spell on them had been broken for the moment, through the power of sheer mockery, the crew of the *Intrepid* were hurrying about, rushing to the lower decks and approaching the swivel crane, readying the first cannon to be lowered to the jetty.

It would take hours to unload all the cannons crew, but for the moment, for perhaps the first time in a long time, Edmond found himself with time to spare.

Chapter 29

NIGHT HAD LONG SINCE fallen, dropping to the wharf and the surrounding ships like shattered shards of ebony on a beach of moonlight sand and reflective ocean. The aroma of salt and wood and rot wafted on the warm breeze, testing the tongues of wind and providing a taste of the seaman's fate. Edmond Mondego was no seaman, not really. His time, his years, among the Signerde, though, had made him a master sailor. Few men or women knew their way around squalls and swells, surface currents or secondary sea gusts as well as Edmond did. He'd never sailed a full-rigged frigate before. In fact, he'd never sailed any sort of frigate. But, Kurga and his men were moving deftly up and down the spider's ropes and quickly along the deck. Twenty cannons remained on the dock, facing each other. The rest of the cannons had been removed from the *Intrepid*, and carted over to Katrina's *Devout*. For it's part, *Intrepid* was completely devoid of armaments and ammunition. For an extra couple hundred d'oro, Augustin had managed to get Katrina to agree to take every other item on board his ship. Already, glancing across the jetty, he could see her own vessel starting to lie low in the water. Whether her eyes were writing a bid her ship couldn't claim wasn't Edmond's concern in the least.

By now, the *Intrepid* was near bare. The promised d'oro were locked in the captain's cabin in a chest beneath the bed. The key for that chest now dangled next to his vial around his throat.

The bravos had promised him five months when they'd made their deal. And, if the stories were true, come god, storm, or titan, the bravos would keep to their word for those five months. The d'oro, it was rumored, would have been equally safe in the middle of the deck in a pile as beneath the bed under lock and key.

But, Edmond was a cautious man, and he trusted man's greed more than he did his honor.

While he tallied his suspicions, Edmond gave one last thought to the crewmaster. The look of utter loathing he had worn throughout the process of stripping the frigate spoke of some simmering hatred, ready to boil over at any provocation. *I wonder what he'll do when he realizes I lied about arranging an inn for him and the men?* When the cannons and cargo had been offloaded, Edmond had told the crew to head into the city.

"We leave at first light. Beds are arranged at the Inn of the Stone Priest, and Agreo if I catch one man out drinking or fornicating tonight, I'll have you from the yardarm." Edmond smirked to remember the way Agreo's round face had burned a bright cherry red at that. He almost wished he could keep him around a little longer, just to see the bravos come out of the alleys and board the ship.

Sails were already unfurling as the bravos shouted to each other in Chellek. They started to pick up speed, sails taut against the burden of wind ushered in from the East. The men hummed cheerily as they went about their work. Continuing on as they left the Bay of Bianchetto and the city of Carabas in their frothing wake.

Edmond stood, his hand gripping the lacquered taffrail of His Imperial Majesty's Ship *Intrepid*. Mirastious stood at his side, her dress fluttering in the breeze, showing more ankle than polite society would have allowed and drawing cheerful looks from the bravos. For her part, Mira seemed unconcerned.

"This," she said. "This is your plan? To steal an imperial ship."

Edmond glanced at her, then shook his head. "To sell it more like. We're now one of the fastest vessels in the imperial fleet. No cannons, no cargo, a fifth of the normal crew. Frigates normally eke out about twelve knots. Like this, though, stripped down, and with me directing our course, we'll like as not make twenty-four. We'll outrun their frigates, and even most of their sloops. That is assuming they even guess where we're headed."

"And, when we reach where we're headed, what then?"

"Then, we sell the ship, or break it down for parts." Edmond shrugged. "Either way, it's more funding for our mission."

"The mission you promised me?"

GRAVEYARD GODS

Edmond glanced at her, but then gave a small shrug. "The mission I promised myself. The mission I promised my love."

All waters meet again, River Gift. Edmond closed his eyes, listening to the words of a fading memory as breeze dusted his face.

"You don't think there will be hell to pay for stealing an imperial frigate? Selling its cannons? Even if we do reach our destination, you think selling the ship won't further risk your safety?"

Edmond chuckled and glanced out across the sea, facing away from Carabas now. "It's a rare man to catch storm wind and keep it near his chest. A doubly rare man to find the heart of a crashing wave."

Mirastious hesitated, but then looked up at him, watching his face, watching as his hair swished against his forehead, her eyes trailing down his cheek to his left hand gripping the railing. "You said that to the Signerde. The fighter."

"Calder, aye. I hope to see him again. I quite liked that Eldest."

"And, you think you're a rare man?"

Edmond turned, meeting and holding Mira's gaze. There was no arrogance in his tone as he said, simply, "Do you disagree?"

This time, the goddess looked away, glancing out to sea. "It was a double torture, you know," she said, shivering. "Being buried beneath the waves. I hate the ocean."

Edmond frowned. "You do? It's quite beautiful."

"No people. No *humans*. The ocean keeps me far from the hidden things and the dark undercurrents of life and love and death. In the ocean there is crushing pressure, creatures of old—interesting as they are—but none of it compares to a city filled to the brim with delectable intrigue and doubt and fear and worship and the taste of..." Mira inhaled shakily through her nose, her tongue tapping the top of her lips.

"The bodies float South in the water," said Edmond. "I'm sure they carry plenty of sordid secrets."

"Perhaps," said Mira. "There were rumors... In fact." She frowned now. "Before I died actually. Right before... I was hearing... hearing things among the pantheon. I discovered something." Now, Mira was frowning, shaking her head slightly. "But, but Edmond..." She stared at him, with wide eyes, a shocked, horrified expression on her face. "I don't remember, Edmond. There was something. Something I learned before I died. Before I was buried. But, I don't *remember*. I don't forget things, Edmond. It was taken from me. Someone pillaged my mind!" As she spoke, her voice increased in volume and her gestures became more wild, more erratic. The sailors glanced over, but continued their duties, carrying them further out into the Western Sea.

Edmond hesitated, then reached out, gripping Mira by her shoulders and holding her steady. "Look," he said. "I'm sorry. No—I'm not just saying it. I mean it. I don't know what it is to be a god. Mother knows—as my wife used to say—I'm no devout. But to lose your powers, to be buried, to have your memories violated... It is no good thing. I will help restore you. I will uphold my end of the deal."

Mira breathed heavily through her nose, her eyes still wide. Her gestures had calmed somewhat, but her voice was still shaking as she murmured, "It was something about the corpses... Something about *why* they float South. I think—I think I knew. I think," she stared at Edmond, then swallowed. "I think that's why I was killed. But, I don't remember."

Edmond moved an arm, wrapping it around Mira's shoulders. He noticed a few of the sailors throw up their hands in disappointment and grumble as they turned back to their work. Regardless of how it looked to his crew, Edmond kept his arm around the goddess, pulling her close. There was no warmth to her body, no heat pressed against him. But, he could feel her, the softness of her. Quickly, he lowered his arm and stepped away, now placing both hands on the railing, leaning on it and staring out.

He felt Mira join him, leaving a slight space between them, but maintaining her gaze on the same horizon.

"To Godshaven we go," said Edmond. "If I am to gain the Emperor's ear, I'll have to rise the ranks of nobles. The Emperor keeps close track of these sort of things; I'll have to keep it as above board as possible."

"This ship, these men... It's a start," said Mira. "The gold."

Edmond nodded, his lips barely touching as he murmured. "Men. Ship. Gold. Yes, it is a start." He smiled softly, staring out at the ocean, watching the waves and the water speed by beneath them. It almost felt, as the sea reached up to meet his newly acquired ship, that the cresting waves touched by moonlight and frothing white were reaching to ensnare his vessel in an unyielding grip. The sort of grip that accompanied a handshake, a certainty, an embrace.

Edmond's own grip mirrored it, twisting on the railing, eyes still to the horizon. "I'm coming for you," he said softly. He could feel the vial on his chest shift and move, tapping gently against his collarbone. He inhaled deeply, his eyes fixed out to distant sea.

Chapter 30

AT FIRST, AUGUSTIN FELT his body go numb. As he stared from the stone dockway to the empty berth where the *HIMS Intrepid* should have been, he simply could not comprehend what had transpired. He saw a cluster of a few dozen sailors standing on the dock in front of the empty space looking out into the bay. At their side lay a line of cannons being carted to the adjacent berth. The sailors held rucksacks and small satchels of the sort travelers used for their personal effects, and the moonlight illuminated faces and features that Augustin recognized. His crew milled about with their belongings, but his ship had disappeared. To his side, Vicente let out a low whistle.

"Wonder what that's about," he said before turning to face Augustin. "So where is your ship?"

Cristobal replied, "That's a good question."

At this, Augustin approached the crew. His face flushing with mounting anger, he shouted at the few dozen men assembled,

"What is the meaning of this?" Startled faces looked up at him. A few of the men twisted their heads, looking from the bay back to Augustin. Quiet muttering bubbled amid the cluster, but no one replied. Augustin waited a moment, standing erect as his furious eyes darted from man to man. "Someone tell me, where is the *Intrepid?*"

"That's what I'd like to know."

Augustin felt a curl of disgust as Agreo's spiteful voice croaked out from the group. A few of the sailors shifted, allowing the wide crewmaster to sidle his way towards the front. Despite the dim light, Augustin saw a reflection of his own fury in the crewmaster's red face. Agreo pointed an accusing finger as his raw voice shouted in return. "First you order us off the ship, telling us we're making an inland expedition. You send us trekking into the city only for the innkeeper to turn us back!"

A few of the sailors expressions soured at this reminder and some angry muttering simmered below Agreo's rant. "What's more, we come back here to find the *Intrepid* gone, and some haughty bitch loading *our* blighted cannons into her hold." Agreo gestured behind Augustin to the line of cannons being slowly carted away. "She says to us that you and some black haired whore loaded the *Intrepid* with a crew of bravos and sailed more than an hour ago!" Agreo half-turned, letting his voice carry to the assembled men. Flapping his soft arms like some flightless bird, his squawking drew more angry muttering from the crew. "So I'd say, *cap'n*," he said, spitting the the words out like rotten meat. "You have some nerve showing up here. Because, I'm just a humble sailor, but even I know treason when I sees it."

The few dozen crewmen were standing now as the tension between the crewmaster and the Lord Captain reached a boiling point. They were angry, confused, tired, and here Agreo stood, whipping them to frenzy like a shark hunter dropping bits of blood and gore into the water.

Augustin stared back at Agreo, his mind racing. *The Viper. Damn him! I should have known he would try to use my face while he had it. Of course, he knew I'd have a ship here. I should have come immediately to prepare my men.* For the faintest moment, he sniffed, his nostrils flaring as he marveled at the sheer nerve of the tomb raider. Someone like that was a threat—someone like that flouted every law of the Empire... His promise to the Signerde though had been hastily made. How in seven hells could he spare the tomb raider's life when he insisted on acting like an ass of magnificent proportions?

Augustin's eyes were hard, and he had to fight to keep his voice crisp. The crewmen—though only a quarter of the ship's regular crew were present—would be more than enough to see him off if things got ugly. The tone of command rang from his throat as he held back the black ire roiling in his chest. "You were deceived by an alchemist. The tomb-robber we are hunting is a face-changer. He took my appearance and—"

"Shark shite!" Agreo called out in a mocking tone. "Really, Augustin? Yer expectin' us to believe t'was some sort of doppelganger? No, no." He shook his head disdainfully. "You're not going to talk your way out of this one. I don't know why you've snuck back, but this ship has gone from bad to worse under your so-called command."

Cristobal's foot slammed the stone dockway with a crack as he stomped forward. "You are addressing your Lord Captain, cur.

Hold your tongue before I cut it out." His booming voice rolled over the group of men, but Agreo did not so much as flinch. Augustin's ears picked up a vitriolic growl from the sailors around the crewmaster.

He's not afraid anymore.

"Of course," Agreo said with overwrought disdain. "Your guard-dog is here to bark at me. Well, bark all you like, pup. We are done with your abuse." A chorus of agreement rippled out from the clustered sailors as the group edged forward. "It's treason I calls it. Treason."

The cry echoed out from the approaching sailors. Treason. Treason. Agreo's toad like mouth widened into a worming smile as his eyes glinted in malevolent delight. "We don't have a yardarm to hang you from anymore, but I think we'll make do. Seize him! Traitor!"

The sailors let out a roar and surged forward as daggers came loose from their sheathes. Augustin drew his sword.

The angry sailors around him quickly outpaced Agreo as they dashed for Augustin. He had a bare couple of seconds where he thought about the men who had been under his command these last few weeks, and he prayed that Mercusi would see the blood he was about to take as just. Then, as the first of the incensed crew reached him, he let the soldier within him take over. Augustin's rapier flashed with the cold moonlight as he drove back the first wave of men, leaving bright wounds wherever his blade leapt. Beside him Cristobal crashed forward like a tidal wave, sweeping men aside with his powerful arms while he bellowed like a bull. Within moments, the press of men formed a semi-circle as they spread around the sides of the melee, pressing Augustin and Cristobal back to back. The Order of the Lily stepped back into pace as if they'd never left it. Sailors in the second and third wave stumbled over the fallen bodies of their allies as they closed in. Nearly ten men fell to Augustin alone before they reached him, but still... Two men against forty. A futile effort.

A hand grabbed hold of Augustin's arm while another pried the sword from his fingers. No less than four men piled onto Cristobal while a dagger punched into his calf, dropping the big man to his knees. The press of men dragged Augustin to the ground, but he kicked at them all the same. If this would be his end, he would not go quietly. From above the shroud of silhouetted bodies holding him down, a muted voice shouted and a space opened. For a moment, Augustin had a reprieve and he took a deep breath as he glimpsed the sky above.

Then, against the night, Agreo's smiling face appeared, and said, "Hang the traitors."

With a cheer, a knotted rope fell into the gap, and the press of hands forced the noose around Augustin's neck. The crowd of sailors shifted back, leaving two men holding Augustin by the shoulders while a third held his fallen sword. The lord captain choked as the noose abruptly tightened, and his free hands clutched for the rope at his throat.

He saw Cristobal lying prone on the stone dock as seven men fought to hold him down. The giant's mouth moved as though he were shouting, but Augustin could hear nothing over the pounding of blood in his ears.

This is it, Augustin thought. *I'm going to die. They won. Agreo. Severelle. The Viper. They all beat me.* Spittle fell from his lips and Augustin felt an immense pressure surge in his head. Out of sight, the rope had been looped and with an excruciating jerk, Augustin felt himself pulled up onto his toes. With a second pull, he now dangled in the air. His legs tensed as his fingernails dragged bloody lines in the skin of his neck where the noose held his throat closed, and he gasped for air that would not come. He would never capture the tomb raider, nor would he earn the honor to marry Isobella de Morecraft. He would die in disgrace at the hands of his own mutinous crew.

At that moment, a deafening roar clapped across the dock like a thunderbolt as a burst of hot flame and black smoke shot through the crowd. Sweet air flooded into Augustin's lungs as he fell to the stone ground, coughing and gasping like a fish.

A moment of stunned silence fell and several of the sailors also dropped to the ground and covered their heads. Augustin blinked his eyes, trying to clear the wet and blurred vision, following the direction the gout of smoke had come from. There, Vicente stood beside the line of cannons. Three of the eighteen-pounders were twisted to face the crowd of sailors. Smoke trailed from the barrel of the first, wreathing Vicente's yellow eye in an infernal shroud. He held a burning fuse in his pinched fingers as he propped his booted foot on the back of the second cannon. "Next two are both loaded," he called out conversationally as if he were telling the men to mind a low door. Though stopped already, the men seemed to grow pale and froze in place. Even Agreo blanched as he slunk back to put some of the sailors between him and the cannons. "I'll tell you what, you mutinous-clay-brained-sacks-of-shark-shite, if you hell-hated-dog-hearts can send the good cap'n and my mate Cris over my way without doin' anything stupid, well, maybe you and the lilly-livered-sway-bellied-toad can walk away. I know. Generous I am. But, unfortunate-ly this offer is only good until ol' Vicente finishes the verse." Vicente lowered the fuse towards the cannon as he began to sing out.

Mir-i-am is the girl we all know,

Weigh-ho! And roll them bones!

She drinks spiced rum and chews to-ba-cco,

Weigh-ho! And roll them bones!"

As the first call of "roll them bones!" cracked out in Vicente's harsh voice, the sailors nearest the cannons spun on their heels. Their hands shook as they grabbed hold of Augustin's torn and slashed coat, pulling him to his feet. They made no move to stop him as he threw the noose off his head, only giving him small pushes from behind as he stumbled towards Vicente. Cristobal joined his Lord Captain and offered a shoulder that Augustin gratefully took. Blood ran from the big man's arms, but he did not seem to mind. Augustin felt hoarse and coughed as he tried to talk. Keeping his silence instead, they moved together to stand behind the cannons with Vicente.

"Quick as whips! Look at that!" He pointed to the group of sailors, shaking his head in mock amazement. Then, taking the fuse in his mouth like a cigar, he enthusiastically clapped. The sailors glowered back, and Augustin felt a small twinge of concern that Vicente might overplay his hand. Even with two cannons they couldn't hope to overcome the dozens of men that remained.

"Vicente," Augustin croaked. His throat felt raw and he had to force out the words, feeling as though he swallowed shards of glass with each one. "We should go. Now."

Nodding in response, Vicente took the fuse back in his hand. "Alright lads, fun is fun. Your exit is that way, though." Pointing behind the crewmen, he made a shooing gesture with his free hand. "Now, let's see if'n you can be out of range by the time I finish the chorus."

The sailors did not hesitate. Turning to run, Augustin watched the swaying form of Agreo as he and the rest of the mutinous men scattered into the streets, leaving the empty berth with only a dropped length of rope and a few scattered packs between the bodies of men too injured to retreat.

***

In silence, Vicente led the way. They did not have far to go until they found themselves in a dockside pub. Cristobal dropped a few coins, and soon all three of them nursed tall glasses of ale. When these were near empty, Vicente waved over more. Augustin's hand drifted to his side, feeling the empty scabbard where his rapier should have been. Half-dead, Augustin accepted this loss with a resigned sigh. He had used a dozen different blades in his life. He could find another. Augustin stretched his neck, feeling the early formation of a scabbing line across the torn flesh of his throat, and a fresh surge of anger rose in him. The ale soothed his voice somewhat, but as he leaned back, he felt his side ache. Cristobal looked down in concern. Sure enough, the bright wet of blood mingled with the deep rust of what had already dried.

"Don't tell me, it's opened again."

The three companions turned in their seats. Behind them stood a woman with a shaved head in the simple white smock of a surgeon. A sympathetic smile played across her lips, but her eyes tilted with concern.

"Catali," Augustin said in a hoarse whisper. Dropping her rucksack beside the table, she stepped forward to examine his wounds.

"Doesn't look too bad. You're lucky, m'lord captain," she said as she drew out a roll of the gauzy bandages from her bag. Augustin took another sip of ale.

Lord Captain. Even if it wasn't official yet, he knew there would be no coming back from this. He had no ship. He had nearly been murdered by his crew. "I'm not a Lord Captain anymore," he rasped.

"Sir Mora, then." Catali said without hesitation. "I saw. I came back only a moment before you drew your sword." She shook her head, cinching the fresh bandage. Then, turning to Cristobal she grabbed his glass and took a long pull of ale. Setting down the half-empty glass, she said, "You going to let that stop you?" Augustin cocked his head in confusion. Catali simply looked back at him, her eyes implacable with the question.

"I was just hanged by my own crew," he said at length.

"Almost hanged," Catali replied, nodding towards Vicente. "This one of the people you told me about? The Order of the Honorable Lily?"

Augustin turned to Vicente. "Yes," he said. Vicente flashed a wide grin, and his mismatched eyes beamed. She was right.

He'd only been able to come this far because of Cristobal and Vicente's help.

Catali grunted and put a hand on Augustin's shoulder. "Lucky you decided to come find them. Looks like you're going to need the help after all."

"Help with what?" Augustin asked.

Catali smiled a disbelieving smile. "Getting your title back, of course. Making Agreo pay." Augustin scoffed, taking another drink, but Catali's smile stayed. "Today's villains are tomorrow's heroes, Sir Mora. You know how their game is played. You just need the right opportunity."

Augustin tilted an ear. It was absurd, of course. *And yet*—A plan began to form in his mind, the shadow of an idea. Maybe there was a way? It would require the other knights. The Order of the Lily would have to be reassembled—in full this time.

Looking back to Catali, he glanced over at the young surgeon. As she leaned forward on the table, her eyes were set on his, daring him. Her expression had a certain hunger to it that he had not seen in her before. "What do you get out of this? Why are you here?"

At this, Catali winked, pushing herself up and stepping around to sit at the table. "I just want to see a good man get the revenge he deserves."

The End

Except it isn't. In fact, we are just getting started.

Scroll or turn the page to see the next title in this enthralling series.

GRAVEYARD GODS

READY FOR THE NEXT ADVENTURE?

TITAN'S FOLLY

A HUNDRED-YEAR-OLD FEUD SPARKED **by gunpowder and gold may have met its match in an alchemist tomb raider and a disgraced Lord Captain.** Edmond is scheming again, and this time his plans take him to Titan's Folly—a small, divided town in the heart of Godshaven. In order to achieve his ends, he takes the face and place of a serial killer newly appointed to reeve. His goal: win the annual peacekeeping tournament, avoid igniting the feuding families to war, and claim a prize glinting like gold, hidden in plain sight.Mean while, the Order of the Lily has reassembled. Augustin Mora and his knights have been taking the odd job, but recently they've been hired to track a suspected serial killer. It just so happens, he was recently appointed as reeve in a distant town in Godshaven. As if cursed by fate itself, Edmond and Augustin's paths are on collision course once more; this time,

GRAVEYARD GODS

they find themselves atop a town full of gunpowder and greed, which only a spark could ignite into all-out catastrophe.

WANT TO KNOW MORE?

GREENFIELD PRESS IS THE brainchild of bestselling author Steve Higgs. He specializes in writing fast paced adventurous mystery and urban fantasy with a humorous lilt. Having made his money publishing his own work, Steve went looking for a few 'special' authors whose work he believed in.

Printed in Great Britain
by Amazon